THE

EXTINCTION

TRIALS

REBEL

Storm wanted to run. She did. But already she could see that the powerful legs of the spinosaurus were more than a match for the three small men. The dinosaurs were catching up fast.

"Run!" Reban's face was directly in hers, spit coming from his lips.

"I won't leave Dell," she insisted. She couldn't pretend she wasn't terrified. But would she sacrifice her former friend?

ABOUT THE AUTHOR

The Extinction Trials is S. M. Wilson's first teen series.
She lives with her family on the west coast of Scotland.

susan-wilson.com
@susanwilsonbook
#ExtinctionTrials

Books by S. M. Wilson:
The Extinction Trials
The Extinction Trials: Exile
The Extinction Trials: Rebel

THE

EXTINCTION

TRIALS

REBEL

S. M. WILSON

USBORNE

To my three favourite heroes: Kevin, Elliott and Rhys Bain.

To my dad, John Niven Wilson, who has been pestering me
for an early read of this book for forever!

And to my two Sarahs – Sarah Hornsley and Sarah Stewart
– for making this dinosaur journey such fun!

First published in the UK in 2019 by Usborne Publishing Ltd., Usborne House,
83-85 Saffron Hill, London EC1N 8RT, England. www.usborne.com

Text © Susan Wilson, 2019

Cover images: eye © Joe Rimmer / EyeEM / Getty Images;
palm leaves © Malden / Shutterstock

"The needs of the many outweigh the needs of the one," in reference to Spock and
Kirk, *The Wrath of Khan*, 1982, screenplay by Jack B. Sowards.

A CIP catalogue record for this book is available from the British Library.

JFMAMJJASO D/18   ISBN 9781474954860   05152/1

Printed in the UK.

PART ONE

EARTHASIA

ONE

LINCOLN

The streets were packed, voices were angry, and Lincoln lowered his head as he tried to dodge through the crowds. Bony elbow after bony elbow jabbed into his sides. The faces around him were like his – gaunt. Food provisions were down yet again and the perpetually empty stomachs were making tempers flare.

He turned the corner and stopped dead. The crowd around the parliament building was a hundred deep. In a land where some of the other buildings were crumbling due to overcrowding and neglect, the parliament building still stood proud, like a snub to the entire, hungry nation. Set across huge thousand-year-old tree trunks and built with bricks the same colour as the reddy-brown bark, the round building looked as if it had grown out of the trees. Creeping vines and branches had wound their way around the outside.

On other days, and in other circumstances, people might stop to admire the beauty of the building. But not today.

Lincoln skirted around the edges of the crowd, trying to weave his way towards the back doors of the parliament. It was hard work. The mood in the air was ugly. Starvation would do that to you.

For the briefest of seconds, one of the black-cloaked Stipulators appeared at the main entrance. For as long as Lincoln could remember, the Stipulators had governed Earthasia. Each of the forty zones had a Chief Stipulator who came and sat in parliament making the rules for the entire nation. Their word was law – or it had been. The roar from the crowd started almost immediately, with shouts and jeers of disgust.

"Give us more food!"

"We can't live like this!"

The normally arrogant Stipulator baulked at the size and noise of the crowd, and turned back around. Lincoln stopped walking for a second. Was that fear in the Stipulator's face? Surely not.

Crack. The guards at the parliament door flinched, as something flew from the crowd and hit the back of the Stipulator's head.

He stumbled for a second, before turning around in disgust, clutching the back of his skull. One of the guards bent down and picked up an old worn boot, dangling it between two fingers. The crowd cheered as the Stipulator muttered under his breath to the guards.

It was clear he was telling them to pursue the assailant. But the guards weren't stupid. In the past, they would have obeyed the Stipulator's command without a word. But over the last few months, things had changed. For the first time in Lincoln's lifetime, the stern rule of the parliament and the Stipulators had wavered.

People didn't seem quite so afraid of them as they were before. The blistering plague that had previously meant death for a large part of the population was under control, thanks to the roots and leaves Lincoln and his colleagues had brought back from the neighbouring continent of Piloria six months ago. The plants had finally been encouraged to grow in the colder climate using special greenhouses and had been turned into a wonder treatment for the disease. But more people meant more mouths to feed, and crops were already at an all-time low. Overcrowding meant there was no land to grow food, and the land that was available had been overused and stripped of its nutrients.

After a few angry exchanges, and some awkward shaking of heads by the guards, the Stipulator stormed back inside the parliament building. Momentum was growing. This revolt had been building for days.

"Oof!" There was a sharp elbow to Lincoln's face as he tried to push his way through the crowds.

"Watch it, boy," growled a crooked-toothed man, stepping in front of him.

"Watch it yourself." Lincoln shoved the man, trying to clear a path through the packed bodies.

He ignored the comments behind him and kept going. Piloria – the continent of the dinosaurs – had taught him many things. To not be afraid. To stand up for himself and those he loved. To not trust anyone. He'd grown muscles in places he didn't know they could exist and developed a steely determination. With a final push, he reached the back door of the parliament.

"Lincoln Kreft for Octavius Arange." The guard at the rear entrance blinked at the name of the Captain Regent and shot Lincoln a curious stare. Did he recognize him? Lincoln had brought home the cure for the blistering plague from Piloria. It wasn't unusual for him to be recognized. Some people thanked him – some people cursed him. But the guard merely checked his name on a list, then sent him through the security checkpoint.

Inside the parliament was just as chaotic as outside. A swarm of angry black-cloaked Stipulators stood shouting at each other in the main foyer. Their aides, in pale blue, stood along the edges of the atrium, occasionally responding to an irate shout or gesture.

Lincoln sighed. The first time he'd come in here, he'd been amazed at the beauty of the building and terrified by the sight of so many Stipulators. For all his life these people had ruled unchallenged.

But the world he'd known was unravelling around him. Lies had been exposed, treachery revealed, and his own betrayal weighed heavily on his shoulders.

He moved across the atrium, avoiding the eyes of the

most self-important Stipulator – Silas. The man was bellowing at the Stipulator opposite him – trying to belittle and intimidate him. But the other man's chin was proudly tilted in the air as he fought back. Things were definitely changing around here.

Lincoln reached Octavius's door and resisted the temptation to turn and walk away. This was the fourth time Octavius had summoned him to parliament. What now?

He knocked sharply.

"Enter!" a voice inside boomed.

Lincoln rolled his eyes and pushed the door open, closing it behind him to block out the din outside. Octavius was perched on his strangely shaped chair behind his impossibly high desk, his short legs dangling. From the first second Lincoln had met him, he'd been bewildered that such a loud voice could come from such a diminutive man.

Octavius scowled behind the reading aid perched on the end of his nose. His snow-white hair was pulled back from his face. Storm had mentioned once that when she'd met Octavius she'd been shocked. She'd never seen anyone this old, and neither had Lincoln. People in Earthasia generally didn't live to an old age; they were wiped out by the lack of health care or the blistering plague.

"Where have you been?" snapped Octavius, as he jumped down from the high chair.

Lincoln tried to find some patience. "I've been exactly where I should be – in the lab helping replicate the cure."

Octavius's scowl deepened in his saggy face. He bustled

past Lincoln and climbed a set of steps to his large bookcase.

"This is all your fault," he muttered.

"What's all my fault?"

Octavius waved a gnarled hand in the air. "The people outside. You bring home a cure with no thought to the consequences."

Lincoln's hackles raised. "I brought home a cure for my sister."

Octavius pulled a large book from the shelf and tossed it at Lincoln. It was amazing how spending time on a continent of dinosaurs could heighten your senses. His hands instantly plucked the book from the air before it hit him in the face.

Octavius walked back down the steps and snatched the book from Lincoln's hands as if that behaviour was entirely normal. "You left her," he muttered, shaking his head. "You left her there."

Lincoln pressed his lips together. For the past six months, the last glimpse he'd had of Storm – of her and her father standing on the beach of Piloria – had been imprinted on his brain.

"We've gone over this," he sighed. "I didn't *want* to leave her behind. She *chose* to stay. She chose to stay with her... father."

It still felt odd using that word to describe the man who was the disgraced Chief Stipulator of Ambulus City. No one had known he was Storm's father – not even Storm – until a few months ago.

Octavius turned angrily towards him. "And what will

14

happen to her there? How can she survive, with barely any weapons? Nothing to protect her from the host of monsters who live there?" He held the book up, clutching it between his gnarled hands.

Lincoln stepped forward. Books were uncommon. They were a luxury that had vanished as the wood supplies had been depleted on the continent. Not enough space for people meant that trees had been surplus to requirements.

Lincoln couldn't help himself. He reached out and touched the dark-blue cover with gold lettering. He'd never seen anything quite like it – even though he'd been here before, he'd never really had a chance to look at the books up close. Before Octavius could react, Lincoln had taken it from his hands.

"This is it," he said, realization dawning. "This is the book Storm told me about."

He laid it on the table and gently stroked his fingers over the lettering. *The Continent of Monsters by Chief Stipulator Magnus Don*. Lincoln turned to Octavius.

"This is the book you wanted her to update, isn't it? The one I heard her and Reban talk about."

Octavius's face softened. He reached his thin hand over and flicked open the book. It landed on a page with a hand-drawn sketch of a roaring T-rex.

Lincoln shuddered. He didn't need a reminder of what lived on Piloria. He'd experienced it all too vividly himself.

"She did update it," Octavius said softly, "for the most part." His hand was shaking slightly as he traced his fingers

15

over the drawing. It was the first time Lincoln had seen any sign of vulnerability from the old man.

When Lincoln had first been in this room, Octavius had spent the whole time screaming at him for leaving Storm behind. He'd been so tempted to shout back. To tell Octavius how angry Storm had been when she'd found out that Octavius was her great-uncle and he hadn't bothered to tell her. How hurt she'd been.

But that wouldn't have helped anyone. Things were delicate enough. His sister, Arta, and Rune's and Kronar's brothers and sisters had all been ejected from the care facility. Storm and Lincoln's first trip to the dinosaur continent had been a contest which Storm had won – but two of their friends, Rune and Kronar, had died. As the victor, Storm and her family were entitled to extra rations and health care, so, in an act of kindness, she'd declared their families were her own. But now Storm wasn't here, all that was gone. Arta had been sent back to live with Lincoln and their mother in the caves. As for Rune's and Kronar's brothers and sisters? He had no idea. Lincoln could only hope they'd gone home to their parents in Norden.

The one plus point was that – because he worked at the lab – Lincoln had unlimited access to supplies of the ointment. Before Piloria, Arta had been on the brink of death. Now her skin looked almost completely better, even though she was thinner than before, thanks to the more restricted rations.

There was a loud noise from outside. Octavius's frown

deepened and, despite his slight frame, he moved swiftly to the door and yanked it open.

The bedlam from earlier had increased. Lincoln's eyes widened as he looked across the atrium. The dark ominous doors on the other side were now wide open and the Chief Stipulators were shoving their way through into the large chamber beyond. The bright white of the parliament debating chamber was a startling contrast to the black cloaks of the Stipulators, but Lincoln's eyes were drawn to the blood-red chair at the far end of the room.

Silas, the blond Chief Stipulator of Norden – who'd staged a coup against Storm's father and now governed the capital, Ambulus City, as well as his own region – seemed to be leading the charge.

"Get me my cloak!" ordered Octavius, his voice booming beside Lincoln.

Lincoln jumped and looked around in surprise. "What?"

He still didn't really understand the workings of the parliament, but Storm had told him Octavius was the Captain Regent. If anyone was in charge here, it seemed that it might be him.

"Over there!" bellowed Octavius, pointing him towards a drawer set in the wall. Lincoln walked over and opened it, pulling out a dark-green, heavy cloak. He shook it out and the gold trim reflected the light. Although it was heavy in his arms, it was small; perfectly sized for Octavius.

Octavius appeared in front of him, turning around so Lincoln could drape the cloak over his shoulders.

"Wait here," he hissed, as he took off across the wide atrium.

Lincoln watched. He'd never seen the doors to the debating chamber open before. White seats lined the walls and the Chief Stipulators, each representing all the zones of Earthasia, settled into them. Lincoln frowned. Were all four hundred of them really here?

Octavius strode across the vast room and, using a small box, got up onto the red chair. There was a staff beside his seat, which he banged angrily on the floor.

Lincoln held his breath. The parliament doors were still wide open. Was this normal?

He could see some of the staff dressed in pale blue shaking their heads, sidling closer to the open doorway to watch.

"Who called this session?" shouted Octavius.

"I did," said Silas haughtily. He turned to his right and grabbed hold of the man next to him. Even from here, Lincoln could see the Stipulator's cloak was torn, his face bruised and his knuckles bloodied. "There has been a revolt in Tarribeth. Rufus barely made it out in one piece." There was a collective intake of breath around the parliament. "The people are uncontrollable. It's time to take a stand."

One of the Chief Stipulators snorted. "And do what? We've already cut rations again. Our Stipulators barely have enough nutrition to stand on their own two feet."

"Isn't that what we're trying to do? Starve the population into submission?" asked another Stipulator, who had the dark skin of the Lambora zone.

"And starve ourselves too?" sneered another.

"We need to get the ointment supplies under lock and key. The more people get treated, the more people there are to feed."

One of the Stipulators turned to Silas and pointed his finger. "This is your fault, Silas. This happened on your watch. That lab was supposed to be focusing on dinosaur DNA. Instead, it starts to miraculously produce a cure for the blistering plague. A cure that has been replicated in all the other labs across the continent!"

Lincoln shifted uneasily. They were talking about his lab. The one he worked in. As soon as he'd got off the ship from Piloria, he'd headed straight there to place the samples he'd collected into Lorcan Field's waiting hands. The head scientist had been as desperate for a cure as Lincoln – his own daughter had been dying from the blistering plague.

Lincoln had brought as much ointment as he could from Piloria, along with seedlings, plant samples and even dirt. In a matter of hours, the temperatures in the greenhouses had been turned up as high as possible to try to replicate the conditions on Piloria, and thanks to that, and the newly imported nutrients in the soil, the plants had started to grow quickly. The recipe for the ointment was simple – it was a combination of two plants from Piloria – and within a few weeks, his lab had produced its own first batch.

He hadn't thought about the implications for the population. He hadn't thought about how the people who previously would have died – and now would live – would be fed on an already starving continent.

He'd only been thinking about his sister, Arta.

His sister, who was now looking better than she had in years.

One of the other Stipulators got to his feet and shook his head. "You should have stopped this, Silas. Things have got out of hand. What happened to Rufus is on your head."

It happened so quickly that Lincoln barely had time to blink. Silas crossed the parliament chamber and punched his colleague square in the jaw, sending him sprawling back onto the white chairs.

"How dare you challenge me? You, from Steroma. When was the last time your zone produced enough food to sustain your population? You've stolen from the rest of us for the last five years. *We've* been feeding your people, and all at a cost to our own populations."

The crowd in the atrium were still moving, slowly but surely, closer to the parliament doors. It seemed that no one was bothered about keeping the business in parliament private this time. They could hear every word – and wanted to hear more.

Octavius banged his staff on the ground. "Order!"

For a few seconds there was silence. "Silas, you called this session. Do you have a solution to our current problems, or do you only wish to apportion blame?"

It didn't matter that Octavius had a small and wizened body. He had the heart and mind of a warrior. And he wasn't afraid to show it.

Silas turned back towards the accusing faces. "This situation is spiralling out of control. It can't be allowed to continue. I suggest guards in the labs. The ointment will have to be rationed, along with food. Without the blistering plague, our population numbers are unsustainable." The frown in his brow was deep. "We all know what happens next. If we don't get things under control – there will be no other option."

Silence in the parliament. There were a number of anxious glances, followed by a few murmurs.

Again, Octavius banged his staff on the ground. "Put plans in place to get your labs under control. We'll reconvene in a few days."

He jumped down from the bright-red chair and swept out of the chamber. As he strode through the atrium, the pale-blue uniforms parted in his wake. They all knew better than to question Octavius's authority.

As he reached the door to his office, his sharp eyes met Lincoln's. He gestured him back inside.

Lincoln followed warily, as Octavius's movements slowed and he walked back over to the table, running his hand over the book of dinosaurs.

Lincoln's insides were churning. Get the labs under control? That couldn't be good for him, or for his sister. Arta was so much better now. But the ointment wasn't a complete cure – even though everyone referred to it that way. It only kept things under control. But he'd brought the ointment here. He should be allowed to use it.

"I need that ointment," he said, through gritted teeth. "Twice I've been on the dinosaur continent. None of the Stipulators have even set foot on it. I have a right to it. Arta has a right to it. She needs it. She won't survive without it."

He expected anger. He expected retribution. Instead, Octavius gave a tired wave of his hand. "None of us will survive," he said quietly, his eyes fixed on the drawing of the T-rex.

There was something in the way he said those words. As if he knew a whole lot more than Lincoln did.

But of course he would.

Octavius's jaw tightened. He spun around, his heavy cloak billowing out behind him as he faced Lincoln again.

He regarded Lincoln carefully for a few seconds – as if he were weighing up things in his mind, making decisions that Lincoln couldn't know or understand. His voice was still low and his grey gaze was steady. "Promise me that when you get word, you won't hesitate. You'll get whoever is important to you, and get to the *Invincible*."

"What?" It was the last thing Lincoln expected to hear. His brain couldn't even begin to consider what the old man might mean.

Octavius raised one long wizened finger. "Not a word. Not a word to a single soul. Just be ready." Then his expression changed back to his usual frown. "Or don't," he added, shrugging as he pushed past Lincoln and swept back out of the room.

Lincoln's feet were rooted to the ground. His brain was spinning with a million possibilities – none of which were good. Was this why Octavius had called him here? "I have a bad feeling about this," he muttered.

PART TWO

PILORIA

TWO

STORMCHASER

"Shh," whispered Reban as they crouched in the undergrowth.

"Don't shush me," Storm replied, her voice barely audible.

Reban shot her the glare she had long since become immune to, as the velociraptor continued to perch on its hind legs with its nose in the air. The red crest on its head stood to attention and the fearsome claws on its hind legs were digging into the earth at its feet.

It was searching for prey, balancing with its strong tail outstretched as it sniffed for a scent in the air that it had clearly locked on to. They could only hope it wasn't theirs. Both of their faces were smeared with a strong paste made from the evergreen leaves that surrounded their dwelling. Blaine had assured them it threw the dinosaurs off the human scent. He'd used it on frequent occasions and managed to stay alive on Piloria for more than nine years.

Storm pressed her lips together and stared at the trampled earth beneath her feet. On more than one occasion in the last six months she'd wished Blaine were still here.

Blaine had been a former Stipulator, abandoned on Piloria as punishment after it was discovered he had a family – something forbidden for all Stipulators. He'd been expected to die, but he'd managed to survive on the continent of dinosaurs. However, Piloria had taken a toll on both his physical and mental health.

Storm's father had been one of the Stipulators who agreed to Blaine's punishment. So it was ironic really that nine years later he'd realized Storm was his daughter and he'd suffered the same fate and been banished to Piloria himself.

Blaine had blamed Reban for his years in exile, and the years he'd missed from his children's lives. They'd hated each other. Even when Blaine had finally been reunited with his daughter, Jesa, things hadn't gone quite to plan, and when Blaine had died, Jesa had been anxious to head back to Earthasia. She hadn't had the option to stay with her father on Piloria like Storm had. But Storm often wondered what decision Jesa would have made, given the same choice.

The raptor tilted its head back and let out a loud caw. The hairs on the back of Storm's neck prickled. Her father turned to her with anxious eyes. "We might need to run," he mouthed to her. "I think they've managed to catch our scent."

She swallowed, her mouth instantly dry, and nodded. The last six months living on Piloria had been a steep learning curve. One of survival. Because, on Piloria, survival was all that mattered.

On her first visit here, they'd suspected the raptors were communicating with each other – something no one had considered before. Dinosaurs were supposed to be mindless monsters, but that wasn't what she'd seen. It wasn't what she'd experienced. At times, she'd seen intelligent behaviour. Behaviour that frightened her. Particularly when it came from beasts that hunted humans for prey.

But in the last few months, things had been more pronounced. Now, she didn't just *think* they might be communicating – she was certain.

There was another sound. A returning caw, followed by a more high-pitched squawk. The raptor's head turned towards the sound. A moment later, it disappeared in the opposite direction from them.

Storm was still holding her breath.

The raptors looked different too. There was still one that was slightly larger than the rest of the pack. But the first time she'd seen them, the difference between the leader and the rest of the pack had been stark. Now, the rest of the pack seemed larger, stronger, like someone had fed them overnight and they had instantly filled out. Before, the smallest raptor's hind leg had been about the same width as Reban's thigh. Now? They looked like they'd all doubled in size.

Reban reached over and grabbed her arm, his eyes scanning the area around them. "They're communicating. It's time to get out of here. Wait for my signal, and then we'll go."

Storm knew he was only looking out for them both, but it grated to be ordered around by him. She still couldn't get used to the idea that in order to survive on Piloria, she had to work in partnership with the man she'd initially hated.

After scanning the trees and bushes for a little while longer, Reban gave her arm a tug. She knew exactly what came next – they'd had to do it more than once.

She started sprinting in the opposite direction to the raptors. It was impossible to be quiet as she thrashed bushes and leaves out of her way, thudding through the jungle terrain. Reban's footsteps were right behind hers. They didn't speak, didn't utter a single sound – they were being noisy enough.

Her heartbeat started hammering in her ears, her chest tight as she continued to run. It didn't matter where they explored on the dinosaur continent, they'd learned they always needed to have a plan.

Trying not to get eaten was always the first priority. Trying not to get injured came a close second.

But things could happen in a split second on Piloria. Dinosaurs could appear in the blink of an eye. On a few occasions they'd had to split up, running in opposite directions, not quite sure if they would ever see each other again.

The first time it had happened, Storm had ended up in an area she was unfamiliar with. One wrong turn had meant she was lost for three days, with no water and only what she could forage in the forest to eat.

When Reban had finally found her, he'd roared at her so much that she'd started to believe he might actually care.

Their arrangement was unorthodox. How did you go from finding out someone was your father and hating them, to deciding to stay with them alone on the dinosaur continent? The truth was, her decision hadn't all been about Reban – Piloria had called to her. This continent was so different. Green, with open spaces and plant life she'd never even seen before. It was so different from the cramped, grey world of Earthasia. From the first second she'd arrived, she'd been fascinated by the dinosaurs, both docile and fierce. She'd never wanted to steal their eggs and try to kill them. This was their continent, not hers, and she was grateful just to be here, learning as much as she could and living with freedom, even if it did mean unavoidable risks and danger.

There was a noise behind them; a caw that made her heart stop.

The raptors. They'd heard them. Or caught their scent.

"Go!" yelled Reban. His hand thumped on her back, urging her forward even though the muscles in her thighs were already burning.

There was a response to the original caw, followed by loud squawking. Oh no. How many were there? And how close?

Reban was almost shoulder to shoulder with her as they powered through the jungle, dodging tree roots and plants, leaping over obstacles in their way.

Storm had been here before. She'd been chased by raptors.

They could move faster than she'd ever expected. Their strong hind legs could outpace any human. Last time around she'd escaped by climbing a tree, but the raptors' skill set seemed to improve every day. She'd already seen some make a few attempts at climbing trees with lower branches – so, in order to be safe, Storm and Reban needed to find trees with higher branches only.

She scanned around frantically, trying to remember what was on the other side of this jungle. If she could work out what direction they were running in, she might have half a chance. But at this point, she had no clue.

Reban grabbed his backpack from his shoulder as they ran, unzipping it and reaching for something inside. Seconds later he pulled out a grappling hook and rope – something they generally used for climbing cliff faces.

Storm frowned. "They can climb," she hissed as she ran. Her muscles were on fire. She wasn't sure how much longer she could keep up this pace.

A squawk behind her spurred her on. It sounded closer. Louder. She could now hear trampling noises in the jungle behind them as well. Another squawk made her start, but this time it was to their right.

Reban's eyes were wide as he shot her a glance. They were being hunted like the prey they were.

It put everything into perspective. The fights she'd had with her father since she got here; arguments about food, clothing, weather and supplies. When there was only one other person to communicate with on an entire continent, it was obvious they would annoy each other. But when that person was her father, and there was a whole load of underlying resentment between them, things came bubbling to the surface much easier.

Reban shouldered Storm, pushing her to the left, towards some taller trees. "Move," he growled.

She stumbled, only just managing to stop herself from falling.

Fury raced through her. To fall right now would mean death. The few seconds it would take to pick herself up would mean the raptors would be on top of her.

Storm opened her mouth to yell, just as Reban threw the grappling hook. He yanked her arm as the hook caught in the high branches of a tree above them.

"Move!" he screamed again, this time in her ear.

There were no low branches on this tree. Nowhere for her to start her climb.

For the briefest moment, her brain didn't function. Reban had the rope in one hand and his other palm bent low, facing upwards. "Now!" he yelled.

She finally clicked, and put her foot on his hand, allowing him to boost her upwards on the rope. Her heart was still racing as she struggled to wrap her legs around it. She climbed often now she was living on Piloria, but usually the rope had another anchor point and was against a cliff face, rather than dangling in mid-air. This time it wasn't even close enough to the tree trunk to give her some purchase.

Reban must have noticed her struggle, as suddenly the

rope snapped taut, allowing her to steady herself and tighten her grip. Quickly, Storm started to pull herself up, arms first then legs.

It should have been easier than this, but the burn in her arms was all-consuming as she pulled up her full body weight time and time again and struggled to keep her legs wrapped around the rope. She stared downwards. Reban was holding the bottom of the rope tightly, giving her the anchor she needed to climb, his head scanning in every direction. There was a deafening caw just as her hand reached for the first high tree branch. Terror gripped her heart. She knew exactly what that meant.

"Climb!" she screamed.

The rope moved beneath her as Reban gripped it, trying to climb. But there was no one to anchor it for him and it swung wildly. She grappled with the tree branch, wrapping her arm around it, and trying to pull her leg up too as she let go of the rope. Her abdominals seemed to object, her legs not quite reaching and floundering in mid-air. The weight on her arms was overwhelming. She took a deep breath as the muscles in her arms screamed at her, and pitched her leg to catch the branch with the side of her foot. This time her boot caught and she hauled herself up, ending up completely horizontal on the branch.

Maybe that wasn't a good idea. Now she had a completely clear view of the forest floor below.

The rope was flailing backwards and forwards, with Reban only part way up as the raptors emerged from the bushes. There were three of them. They barely paused, all crashing towards Reban as he swung on the rope. One of them caught the bottom of his foot with its teeth and Reban let out a roar.

"Move!" yelled Storm.

The only reason he was still down there was because he'd been helping her. It was the second time he'd saved her from the raptors. The first time had been at a watering hole when Leif, Jesa and Lincoln had still been here and they'd been planting the virus – the virus that had been supposed to kill the raptors off. But the raptors had returned unexpectedly and Reban had stayed behind to give Storm a chance to escape.

Neither of them had really acknowledged it at the time. Even now, six months later, they hardly seemed ready to talk about their relatively new relationship. But that vision of Reban glancing over his shoulder to let her run, while he stood there, gripping his weapon to try to fight off the raptors, had been imprinted on her brain.

It had been the first time since he'd arrived on Piloria that she'd witnessed pure and utter fear in his eyes.

Now she could see the muscles of his arms bulging as he tried to climb the rope. The raptors were furious. They crouched on their powerful back legs, leaping wildly in the air to try to catch hold of Reban.

Storm couldn't breathe. She'd been in this position before, with Kronar – a fellow Finalist – on her first trip to Piloria. These creatures were intelligent. Last time around they'd chased her and Kronar up into one of the trees, then they'd actually tried to leap onto the lower branches of the tree. For a terrifying time it seemed like they might manage it. Thankfully, they'd tired of her and Kronar after a few hours, and finally left.

Reban had picked a tree where there were no lower branches, but it didn't stop the raptors continuing to jump, as Reban swung just within their reach. From up here, Storm had a bird's-eye view. She could see the short feathers on their skin and the three claws on each of their forearms. The bright-red crests on their heads were raised as their heads flicked from side to side, their caws and squawks differing in pitch. She could almost swear they were talking right now, trying to decide the best way to capture their prey. But it was the sickle-shaped claw on each foot that held the most danger. The largest of the raptors made another leap, higher than before, and this time its curved claw caught on Reban's back.

Reban was tugged sharply down, one hand jerked from the rope. His head flew backwards, his mouth open as he let out a cry of pain.

"Hold on!" screamed Storm. Her heart was racing in her chest and tears sprang to her eyes. She wasn't ready. She wasn't ready for this.

She wasn't ready to watch her father die before her. She wasn't ready to be alone on the dinosaur continent.

Reban seemed to flounder in the air. She could see blood drip onto the ground. It was almost as if it fired the raptors on.

Their cawing got louder, their movements more frenetic. She'd heard of sharks sensing blood in water. Were dinosaurs the same? Could their senses be heightened by the smell of blood?

Reban's flailing hand came into contact with the rope again and this time it was as if he'd had a huge shot of adrenaline. His face was clenched and his arms and legs powered upwards, heaving him towards her. She reached out, grabbing at the edge of his vest as he came within reach.

Relief was already flooding through her. It didn't matter that she was stuck up a tree. It didn't matter that she had no idea how they would get to safety. All that mattered was that she wasn't alone.

Reban's face was bright red, and the veins on his neck were standing out. He swung one leg up onto the branch next to her and slid himself along, mirroring her position by wrapping his arms around the thick branch as he almost collapsed onto it.

For a few seconds, neither of them spoke.

The yellow rope swung underneath them. It seemed to taunt the raptors, who continued to jump at it, their cawing high-pitched and angry. Storm watched as a few more drops of blood landed on the ground beneath them.

"Let me see," she said, wondering just how bad his wound was.

Reban winced and shook his head. His jaw was tight, as if he were attempting to keep all the pain inside. "Don't move. You're not anchored. You could slip."

She'd already almost slipped, but he'd missed that. She strengthened her grip on the branch and nodded her head. "Okay. Let's give them a minute and see if they get bored."

The biggest raptor started clawing at the ground where the blood had landed. She'd seen raptors on several occasions and been pursued by them a few times, but something felt off.

"What do you think?" she asked Reban.

Reban let out a long, slow breath. "I think they're on the move. The raptors seem to be getting closer and closer to our shack. They're not normally this far from the nest sites." He wrinkled his nose as he winced again. "And there's something different about them too. They seem more…" He kept watching as he tried to find the right words. "It's almost as if their senses have been heightened."

That was it. He'd nailed it. That was exactly what was different.

"Well, the virus doesn't seem to have worked, does it?" Storm kept watching them too. "Apart from that first one we found in the forest, none of the raptors appear to have died. I don't know. They seem almost…stronger. The big one, the leader, it seemed to jump higher than I remember from before." She paused. "I thought it was going to get you."

Reban's violet eyes met hers. "Me too." He pressed his lips together. "Do you think we caused this? Instead of the virus actually killing them, do you think it could be responsible for the changes we're noticing? Have we made them stronger? Made them into killing machines?"

Storm shivered. "Don't. That's too terrifying for words." She took a moment. "They were already killing machines," she said softly, as memories of previous attacks filled her head. "They're predators. They just seem to be getting better at it."

Reban shook his head and winced as he shifted on the thick branch. "I don't like it. We need to face facts. Even though they heard us running at the end, before that? I'm pretty sure they had tracked us. They seemed to be able to smell us, even though we're covered in this green muck." He wiped some from his bare arm in disgust. "The evergreen leaves don't seem to be having the same effect they did before. That's a definite development since we first met them." He gestured below. "And look at their reaction to blood. I've never seen anything like that before."

Storm nodded in agreement. "The first time they chased Kronar and me, we escaped up a tree. They jumped at the lower branches but that was it." She met her father's gaze. "Last time they chased us, they practically scaled up those lower branches. It's like they've learned something new. And they keep on learning."

The three raptors were still scraping around the bottom of the tree. They kept cawing – it felt eerily like a conversation – and looking upwards. It lasted for more than hour, longer than Storm had ever seen a raptor communicate before. She could swear there was pure anger and frustration in their eyes and in their squawks.

Of course it was wrong to try to project human thoughts

and behaviours onto a relatively unknown species, but she couldn't help the way her brain was working. Storm said the words out loud. "Blaine stayed in the shack for nine years with the evergreen smell protecting him from predators."

Reban rested his face back down on the branch. "And we've been here six months and already we're in trouble." He was stating the obvious. It was clear he was having the same kind of thoughts as her. He held up his hand. "The only thing that has changed here is what we've done. We tried to introduce the virus. It might have worked for the T-rex and the pterosaurs, but something's gone wrong with the raptors. I don't think we should hang about here much longer."

Storm let out a wry laugh. "I'm not sure we're ever getting down from this tree."

He nodded. "We might need to pull the rope up and tie ourselves to the tree for the night." He frowned. "Well, it seems we were lucky last time they chased us up a tree – they got distracted by duckbills running past. This time? Who knows? How long were you stuck up the tree with Kronar?"

"From afternoon until early evening. They might not seem patient, but they have tenacity. It took them a long time to finally leave."

He ran one hand through his hair. "It's almost like they were searching for us."

Her heart flipped. She'd noticed things too. Of course she couldn't say whether their brain power had increased, but if the virus had enhanced their bodies, perhaps it had improved their minds and their senses too. Velociraptors had always been skilled predators, had always been a terrifying opponent. But now…

Instead of killing them, had the virus done something to make them worse?

Storm put her head down on the branch again and shifted her hips. Might as well get comfortable. She could be here for a while…

THREE

STORMCHASER

The sun was low in the sky before the lead raptor eventually tired of the prey in the trees. It was apparent that some other type of creature had made its way into this part of the jungle as all three raptors' heads turned sharply at a distant noise.

Two of the raptors – who were obviously bored – made off almost instantaneously, but the last one, the leader, took a few more seconds. It scratched at the ground and looked upwards once more, with something almost like a haughty stare. Its eyes sent a chill down Storm's spine as she read the unspoken message there: *I'll still get you*. Then it turned and sped off through the jungle, following the squawks of the others.

Reban didn't hesitate. "We go, and we go now." He glanced across at her as he threw down the yellow rope again. "And I don't care how sore or stiff you are. You run like they're chasing you. Once we hit that ground, keep your knives in your hands and don't look back."

She wanted to stop and check his injury, but now was their chance to move – it would have to wait a bit longer.

Reban shifted position, swinging his legs so he was sitting on the branch, ready to grab the rope. He waited until she'd done the same. "Ready?"

Storm nodded. He took the rope in his hands, wound his legs around it, then almost slid downwards. She winced, imagining the rope burn on the palms of his hands. She tugged on the nearest leaf, ripping it from a branch, and using it to shield her own hands, before mimicking his moves.

By the time she reached the bottom of the rope, the leaf had disintegrated but her palms were intact. She pulled out her knives from the sheaths at her waist. Reban gave her one glance, then took off through the trees.

Storm followed, letting her legs power through the squelchy undergrowth. She didn't have time to protect herself from leaves and branches, instead tucking her head low against her chest and keeping her eyes on Reban's feet to give her a sense of direction. Reban's strides were long and her legs were struggling to keep up with his. Over the last six months her physical strength and speed had improved. They'd had to – it was the only way to survive on Piloria. But now her chest was tight, her lungs desperately trying to suck in enough air to send oxygen and blood pumping around her body.

The foliage started to thin and they burst out onto a

grassy plain. Finally, she recognized their surroundings.

Ahead of them was another part of the jungle, *their* part of the jungle. Her senses were on high alert, listening for any sounds behind them that might indicate they were being chased – but there were none. Now they were in the open, she lifted her head.

And stumbled immediately. Reban's injury was now in clear view and much worse than she'd imagined. The deep wound, dug out by the large claw of the lead raptor, had torn a huge and angry strip right down the middle of his back. Any part of the cut that had clotted while they were hiding in the tree must have been released again, disturbed by their movement, as the blood was flowing freely. She looked behind her. On the grass, she could see a clear trail of blood leading back to the forest behind them. It was like a guiding light for any predator who might happen upon it.

As they approached their part of jungle, she powered a little more to catch up with Reban and put her hand on his shoulder. The problem with living on a continent packed with different species of dinosaurs was that running from one predator could often land you in the path of another.

They both stopped running, and Storm tried to slow her ragged breathing, listening closely to the sounds all around her. They waited to hear if their noise had alerted any creature that might want them for dinner.

The breeze rustled the leaves around them, swaying branches. Insects sounded from the ground at their feet. Above them, there was a flap of wings.

44

The sensation of life all around them was overwhelming.

Storm looked around, taking a few moments. When she'd first got here, jungle was jungle. But six months here had made her eyes and senses adjust to the smallest of things. Now she could tell just how deep she was inside the jungle by the amount of light streaming through the foliage above. She could tell if she was nearer the beach, or the loch at the other side, by the changes in the plant life around her.

She leaned forward, putting her hands on her thighs as she tried to catch her breath again. Reban touched her back, "We're good. Let's move."

"We're not," she answered promptly. He started at her words. "We have to stop."

"What are you talking about?" he said angrily.

She pointed to the ground. "I'm talking about the trail you're leaving."

His eyes widened as he noticed the patches of blood on the grass. Storm tucked her knives back into her belt and bent down, grabbing a handful of leaves from the first bush she could. "Stop," she said firmly. "Let me put these against it. We have to break the trail."

She could see the conflict on his face. He didn't want to stop running until they were back at the shack, and as far away as possible from the raptors. But she knew she was right – and so did he.

Reban slid his backpack from his shoulder. "Wait a minute." He pulled another tunic from his bag. Storm packed leaves against his back – his current tunic was shredded and proved useless to hold them in place. She kept her hand firmly against them. "Now." She nodded, gesturing to him to pull the other tunic over his head. There was no point taking off the first. No point wasting time. They had to keep moving. The sun was lowering in the sky and night-time brought out even more predators. The safest place for them right now was the shack.

"Done?" Reban asked over his shoulder.

"Done," she agreed, sliding her hand out from under his tunic.

"Then let's keep going." He took off again, at a slow jog. This time it was easier for Storm to keep up. For the hundredth time, she ignored the sweat running down her back. It was a daily occurrence. She was finally getting used to the hot, humid air of Piloria.

Eventually Reban slowed again, and they started walking through the jungle together, instinct sending them back towards Blaine's shack – the place they'd been staying in for the last six months.

Something snuffled on the ground near them, and the pair whipped round, Reban pulling his double-edged weapon from his pack and Storm a knife from her hip.

Instincts on Piloria were honed to extremes.

They froze as the snuffling continued. A few moments later, a small creature emerged from a nearby bush. An aquilops. The smallest horned, frilled dinosaur – it was around the size of Storm's foot.

"Barney." She smiled in relief as she bent to pick him

up and tuck him under her arm. "I wondered where you'd gone."

Reban scowled. "I told you to get rid of that thing. It shouldn't be following us around, it could lead a predator right to us."

"Calm down..." She shook her head as she continued to talk to Barney. "Where did you go last night? Off exploring?"

Reban tutted loudly as they continued on towards the shack. The aquilops had appeared one day when Storm was down at one of the watering holes filling up their containers. It had snuffled around her feet and followed her back up to the shack. When it had continued to hang around, she'd given it a water bowl of its own and nicknamed it Barney. He'd caused more than one fight between her and Reban, but Storm didn't care. Piloria was lonely enough. If Barney was the only other friend she'd find here, she'd take him.

The shack came into view. To describe it as ramshackle would have been kind. Blaine had fashioned it from whatever he'd found in the surrounding jungle. Made mainly of wood and leaves, it kept out the occasional torrents of rain, and gave them somewhere to sleep at night.

At some point, Blaine had also procured a low-slung bunk, like the one Storm had slept on during the Trials, and strung some kind of material across the shack, dividing it into three spaces. They had a place to wash, a place to sleep and a place to sit.

Living with a new-found father wasn't exactly easy. Storm slept in Blaine's old bedroom and Reban slept on a bedroll in the sitting area. After a few months, she'd finally started to think of this place as home. But it wouldn't be for much longer.

It hadn't taken them long to realize they'd need to find somewhere else to stay. The previous water collection system might have worked for Blaine, but it didn't collect enough rainwater for two people, and there was no natural source of clean water near the shack. Storm had been collecting water from the watering holes that the animals used. They still had the supply of sterilizing tablets they and their colleagues had brought to Piloria with them, but these wouldn't last for ever.

They'd trekked for five days north and then south of the shack, trying to get a feel for the land and the opportunities. The land to the north, beyond the pterosaur nests, seemed even more dangerous, fraught with more killer species, difficult terrain and desert. The land to the south had more potential. But today's encounter had just brought everything to a head. They didn't have time to survey the land any longer. They had to get away from the enhanced velociraptors.

Storm glanced up as Reban took his backpack from his shoulder carefully and laid it down on the floor.

"Let me clean that wound and get some ointment on it," she said, automatically heading over to where Blaine kept his clay bowls – one with the ointment, the other with a type of glue. Since they'd moved in, they'd never changed his system, and had taken turns at just replenishing the supplies.

But Reban shook his head. He looked around the shack with his hands on his hips. She could almost read his thoughts. "It's time," he said decisively. "It's time for us to go. That should be our priority."

She wanted to argue. She wanted to tell him to stop acting so tough and let her tend to his wound. But she'd started to get to know her father. Once he got that look on his face, there was no reasoning with him. Storm sighed. It would be easier to have this discussion first, then insist on cleaning the wound properly.

She reached into her backpack and pulled out the map – originally given to her by Octavius – that they'd continued to add to since they'd begun living on Piloria.

"Okay, I agree. We need to make a decision."

Reban winced, the wound on his back obviously hurting. He moved over next to her. "It has to be this way," he said pointing to the area of land beyond where Storm had found the transporters the last time she'd come here. "We can fish, and there seem to be plenty of fruits growing around the area. We'd be able to live off the land for the foreseeable future. And there's a river – at least we'd have a water supply."

She knew he was right. But the thought of packing up parts of this shack and transporting it by hand didn't really appeal to Storm. Three days' walk there, and three days' walk back. This could be a long process. "How much of this do you think we'll be able to move?" she asked, as they looked around the inside of the shack.

Reban pointed to some of the equipment. "It might be more realistic to try to do this over a few trips. We take the most important things on our first move – just in case we can't get back."

"How much do you think we can carry?" she asked, almost afraid of the answer.

He gave a slow nod. "I think we should try to construct a kind of rig to pull behind us, and cram as much as we can onto it. Things we wouldn't be able to make from scratch."

"Once we reach here," she said, pointing to a spot on the map, "we might be able to use one of the transporters. If they're still in one piece." She sighed. "I just wish they were a bit closer. It'll take at least two days to reach them."

Reban nodded, as Storm silently imagined piling just about everything onto the rig, thinking how much easier it would be on a transporter. She gave another deep sigh as she looked around. "So, this is our last night in here."

Reban gave a slow nod. He looked as worried as she did. Everything was new on this continent. Every day taught them something they didn't know before. She could remember how much she'd longed for this place when she'd been back on Earthasia, and even though she'd remembered the dangers in vivid detail, it still hadn't stopped her wanting to come back.

Now? The truth was, since she'd got here, she hadn't slept a single night without having nightmares. Maybe she'd just been mesmerized by the colours and scents of Piloria. Living on Earthasia was like living in a bland dream. But how healthy was it to live with your senses permanently on high alert?

She wondered how Arta was, and if they'd stopped her care the minute Storm hadn't returned. Her stomach gave a little clench as she remembered the look on Lincoln's face as he left. He'd been torn. She'd seen it. And that meant something. The guy who had so much loyalty to his family – who would die for them – hadn't wanted to leave her behind. She wasn't quite sure how she felt about that.

Then there was Blaine's daughter, Jesa, and her family. She'd gone home to tell her mother and brother that she'd found her father, only to see him murdered before her. And Leif. He hadn't wanted to be here at all. But he'd come back to poison the dinosaurs – the dinosaurs that had robbed him of his two best friends. They had no idea if the other two viruses had actually worked. They only knew they hadn't seen any pterosaurs or T-rexes in the last six months. How would Leif feel if he knew that one virus seemed to have worked in almost the opposite way – instead of killing the velociraptors, it had heightened their skills?

But Storm was here. She'd chosen to stay on Piloria instead of going home with her friends. And if she wanted to stay alive, she had to focus.

Barney nuzzled in at her leg. She reached down to rub his skin. Tomorrow was another day. She closed her eyes and let the sounds of Piloria surround her. The gentle rustle of leaves, the chirrup of cicadas and the distant, low groaning call of a brontosaurus.

Piloria's beauty could almost lull her into a false sense of security. *Focus*, she told herself again. Tomorrow they had to find somewhere safe to live. But was there anywhere safe on Piloria?

PART THREE

THE END

FOUR

LINCOLN

The streets were buzzing as Lincoln made his way to the lab. The sweat-inducing greenhouse would still be growing the evergreen leaves and accompanying yellow vines to produce the ointment at a rapid rate – but for how much longer? Lincoln wondered if head scientist Lorcan Field had any idea that the Stipulators were about to crack down on the labs.

From the moment Lincoln had brought him back the samples, Lorcan hadn't even tried to hide what he was doing. His only priority was finding a way to stop the blistering plague killing his daughter and others like her. He'd mass-produced the ointment, sent instructions and cuttings from the new plants to other labs across Earthasia and made an unofficial announcement in the main auditorium, telling people to come to the lab if they wanted the cure. Lincoln had never seen Lorcan in such a good mood. He might even have washed his wild, grey hair.

Silas had been furious. *All* the Stipulators were furious. They'd come to the lab to arrest Lorcan – probably with the intention of banishing him to the mines, where his life expectancy would plummet to two weeks – but it was already too late. The crowd outside the lab was twenty people deep by that point, everyone wanting the potential cure for the blistering plague. Trying to drag Lorcan outside would have incited a riot – and even Silas wasn't so bold, or so stupid to risk it.

"You'll pay for this!" he'd hissed at Lorcan. "Everyone will starve now because of you. We can't support the population we have. How can we support any more?"

Lorcan had waved his hand. "The food is your problem. The blistering plague was mine. I've solved my problem; maybe you should worry about solving your own."

Within two months, the four hundred zones on Earthasia were fighting with one another. Previously they'd appeared to work in harmony – the general population had no idea what happened behind the closed doors of parliament and did as they were told.

But now, the zones that had managed to produce more food and used to support their less fertile neighbours, had literally closed their borders. They needed the food they produced for themselves. Previous agreements were thrown out. Previous promises abandoned. It was every man – or zone – for themselves.

Lincoln's stomach growled loudly as he walked. He was

getting used to the ache of being permanently hungry. But some families were furious. They couldn't watch their children crying with hunger and had taken to the streets.

Lincoln pushed through a packed crowd as he made his way past the main auditorium. There was supposed to be some kind of announcement later today, but people were already shouting their protests. A throng of black-cloaked Stipulators made their way through, pushing citizens harshly out of their paths.

This was normal behaviour from the Stipulators, and no one had ever objected or fought back before – doing so would earn you a one-way trip to the mines. But today the people weren't so scared. Today, the people were angry.

The first punch came out of nowhere. One of the Stipulators ended up on his back. For an instant, everyone seemed momentarily stunned. Lincoln couldn't remember an occasion when this had ever happened before.

The Stipulator tried to stand and make a grab for the man who had punched him, but the crowd were too quick. Another punch flew, then another. Before he had a chance to move away, Lincoln was in the middle of a mass fight.

The woman next to him landed on the ground. The guy on his other side leaped onto the nearest Stipulator's back. Lincoln was pushed from behind as the crowd surged forward. It seemed that more people wanted to vent their anger.

Part of him panicked. This wasn't right. It couldn't end well. A punch sailed past his right ear, missing him by millisectars. He ducked down and tried to push heavily through the crowd. He had to get to the lab. He had to get away from here.

But even as Lincoln moved, he felt the air around him almost vibrate with the crowd's energy. The animosity and frustration that had been building for years was coming to a head around him. The fight didn't stay in one place either. It seemed to expand in all directions, with more people joining in, more black cloaks appearing and being pushed back, more angry shouts surrounding him.

Lincoln finally burst through the lab doors with sweat running down his back and part of his shirtsleeve ripped. The lab was busy. Just about everyone in here knew someone affected by the blistering plague, and there was nothing like some self-interest to motivate people to work harder.

He caught his breath and walked quickly through to Lorcan Field's office. A few months ago he'd been at the lowest point in the food chain in this lab, but since his return with the samples, he didn't need to bow and scrape any more. He'd earned respect. He still turned up for every shift, put in extra hours when required and fulfilled his lowly duties, but his status meant that he could have conversations with Lorcan that no one else could.

"It's wild out there," he said, as he walked through the door of Lorcan's office.

He blinked. Lorcan's office usually resembled a dumping ground. This time Lincoln could actually see the floor – it was normally strewn with strips of paper with calculations from the lab. His suspicions were immediately raised.

"What's going on?"

"Nothing," said Lorcan, far too quickly for the answer to be true. There was a large box sitting on his desk that was packed full. The waste-paper bins were full too.

Lincoln shook his head. "You've tidied up. Why?"

Lorcan frowned. It was apparent he was searching his brain for a suitable lie. Lincoln had worked with this guy for more than a year. Lying didn't come easily to Lorcan Field. He was far too logical and methodical for that. Lorcan held up his hands. "Time for a clear-up," he said simply.

But Lincoln wasn't fooled that easily. He walked over and pulled out one of the journals Lorcan had stuffed in the box, flicking open the pages. "These are the chemical constructs of the blistering plague." He turned a few more pages. "This is the DNA profiling." There was another, red-coloured journal. Lincoln knew exactly what it held. "That's the notes on the dinosaur viruses. Why would you need these? Why would you be packing these up? Going somewhere, Lorcan?"

He could feel his anger rising. He'd just come from a near-riot on the streets. Now, in his place of work, things were clearly being planned without his knowledge.

The bad feeling from his conversation with Octavius intensified.

Lincoln lifted the whole box. "Where are you going that you'd need all this, Lorcan?"

He was angry. He didn't actually need Lorcan to answer the question. But he hated being made a fool of.

The head scientist shuffled his feet. His grey gaze was flitting nervously from side to side, desperately looking for someone to rescue him from Lincoln's questions. He reached out and grabbed the box back towards him. "I'm making pre...parations," he stumbled.

Lincoln folded his arms. "For what – and for when?"

A woman in pale blue appeared at the door. Her hair was falling out of its braid and her cheeks were flushed. "Someone said Lincoln Kreft was in here?"

Lincoln nodded, narrowing his gaze as he placed her uniform. She was one of the aides in parliament. "That's me."

Relief was evident on her face straight away. "Good. I have a message from the Captain Regent."

Lincoln felt his abdomen clench. "What is it?"

She looked a little puzzled. "He just said one thing." She paused for a second. "Now."

A jolt shot through his entire body. There was no time for anything any more. No time to think. No time to plan. Now he knew exactly what Lorcan was doing.

Lincoln walked over and put a hand on her arm. "Thank you." She must have fought her way through angry crowds outside the parliament, then even more in the streets outside to get here. Other people would have given up and just walked away. This aide had been determined to deliver the message – even though she had no idea what it meant. He kept his voice steady. "If you can, pack what you need, get down to the port and head to the *Invincible*."

Confusion shot across her face again. "What?" But Lincoln didn't wait. He couldn't. From this moment onwards, every second was precious.

He didn't even look back at the floundering Lorcan. He had other priorities now.

"Get everything you need. Pack it up now." He strode straight across the damp cave, picked up the backpack he'd used on Piloria and started throwing clothes into it. His mother's eyes widened. Arta was washing dishes. She walked over, wiping her hands on the drying rag.

"Lincoln?"

He glanced around. They were lucky the other family they shared the cave with weren't here right now. Tensions were bad enough between them. Lincoln wasn't sorry to be leaving them behind.

"It's now," he said, trying to ignore the way his heart was racing in his chest. "I have to go and tell some others."

He looked around the cave with its dull flickering lights and damp walls. It had never really felt like home, but leaving this time was different. This time he wouldn't be coming back – none of them would.

"Travel light. Only take what you can carry. We're going to have to try to get some gear for the other side."

His mother looked horrified. "What do we need for the other side?" She gulped. Lincoln's mother had always dreaded this moment. He'd warned her things were changing, and that at some point, they might have to make a decision whether to stay here and starve, or take their chances on Piloria.

He didn't answer her question. Lincoln hadn't really told his mother everything that had happened on Piloria. If he had, she would probably refuse to come, and if his mother refused, Arta might refuse too. He didn't like not being truthful with his family, but once they were on the *Invincible*, he could give them a realistic idea of what to expect, and emphasize how much they needed to pay attention to what he told them.

He turned to Arta. "Quickly. Don't wait. I'll meet you both down at the port. The crowds are bad outside, it might take me some time to warn the others."

Arta's eyes were bright. He knew it was fear. "Who are you going to warn?"

He swallowed. "Jesa and her family. Leif, if he's with them. And there's someone else – someone I think Storm would want me to warn. I have no idea if any of them will come. But I need to tell them."

Arta pressed her lips together and gave a slow nod of her head. "Then hurry," she whispered. "We'll see you at the *Invincible*."

He ran as fast as he could through the thronging streets. Most of the crowds were around the auditorium and the parliament buildings, but some people were starting a kind of parade – or warrior march. Properties along the way were being damaged, with the ration stores coming under the greatest attacks.

But Lincoln was heading to the city outskirts – the places where most people barely had a roof over their heads. Trouble was, most of the buildings looked the same. Grey and bland, with no real distinguishing marks. He struggled to remember exactly where he needed to go.

The first street he ran down had some doors ajar – as if people had walked out of their homes and left them, without a second thought. The next street was similar. Some people had sacks piled outside their doors. A kid was sitting in one doorway crying. Lincoln's footsteps slowed. Should he stop?

There was a loud bang behind him. An explosion. What on earth was that? The kid darted away, running down the street. Before Lincoln had time to think any further, grey smoke funnelled into the sky. Panic gripped him. The housing was so densely packed that fire could spread very quickly here.

He looked around. Instinct told him this still wasn't the right street. He double-backed across a few entrances. He was getting closer and closer to the smoke. People were piling from their homes, choking as the smoke descended from above. He started banging on doors. "Get out! Get out!"

Lincoln kept going, pulling his shirt over his mouth and nose. His eyes were streaming. Maybe he should head straight down to the docks? Maybe this was a waste of time.

There was a flicker in his vision. A mass of brown curls. His heart leaped as he tugged down his shirt, not caring about the thick smoke. "Jesa! Jesa! Is that you?"

She was bending over, coughing and choking. Jesa had her black backpack over her shoulder – the one she'd used in Piloria.

"Lincoln," she spluttered. "What are you doing here?"

He tugged at her sleeve. "We need to go, Jesa. We need to go now. Where are your family?"

Her streaming eyes narrowed. "Go where? What are you talking about?"

He moved closer, trying to get away from the smoke clouding around them. "We need to get to the *Invincible*. Do you know where Leif is? The riots are only going to get worse. There's no food left. We need to get back to Piloria."

She straightened up and, despite the thick smoke, looked him square in the face. "Are you for real?"

He didn't have time for this. He didn't have time at all. He still had someplace else to go. Lincoln tightened his grip on Jesa's arm. "It's simple," he said. "Do you want to live, or do you want to die?"

Even through the smoke, he recognized the hard glint in her eye. She knew what lay ahead on the dinosaur continent. But from the thinness of her face and the way her clothes hung on her body, it was clear she was as near starvation as the rest of the population.

"Mum, Caleb!" she shouted. She stuck her head back inside the door of her home. "We need to go, now!"

Lincoln grabbed her arm. "Do you know where Leif is?" he asked again.

She nodded. "I'll grab him on the way. He won't be happy."

"None of us are happy," said Lincoln swiftly, "but this is about survival." He squeezed her hand. "I have one other place to go. Get on the *Invincible*. I'll meet you there."

Her brow creased. "What? Where are you going?" Her head flicked from side to side.

But he'd started running through the smoke again. "*Invincible!*" he shouted over his shoulder.

The smoke was blinding now. Fires seemed to have sprung up everywhere. Explosions kept sounding around him. The whole city was in chaos. Lincoln tried to remember scraps of things that Storm had told him. He was heading to the area where the forests used to be, before they'd been felled so more living accommodation could be built. People were stumbling and falling, trying to find their way along the crammed streets. The buildings were so close together that on a normal day the sun couldn't penetrate between them, so today, with the smoke as well, the way ahead seemed almost impassable.

But Lincoln's legs powered him on. By the time he finally reached the doorway he thought he should be at, it seemed the thick smoke had infiltrated his lungs. No matter how hard he sucked, he couldn't get enough air into them. He choked as he banged on the door with his fist.

"Hello?" he croaked.

There was no reply. He felt in his pockets. Nothing – *darn it*. He should have picked up some of the paper strips from the lab floor. He couldn't even leave a message. He took a few more seconds, banging the door again, but it was firmly closed. Lincoln tried a few doors around him, banging and thumping, with no reply.

He couldn't wait. He couldn't wait any longer, there just wasn't time, so he took off back through the streets. Everywhere he went, the roads were packed with people. Most were trying to move away from the blinding smoke. As it started to thin around him, he could see other crowds gathering – angry crowds.

Every body he saw was as thin as his own. No meat on them, just skin covering bones. Pure and utter hunger was driving people to extremes. Before, everyone had been kept under control by the Stipulators and the threat of the mines. Everyone had been hungry, but the rations had been just enough to keep starvation at bay. Now? Things had changed, and Lincoln felt a distinct shadow of responsibility hanging over him.

Maybe this was all his fault. He'd been so desperate to bring the cure home for Arta, he hadn't considered what it might mean for the rest of the population. His attempt at saving lives had caused more repercussions than he could possibly have imagined.

The clamour increased as he made his way to the port.

Fights were breaking out, as citizens surged towards the few Stipulators who'd braved the streets and tried to reinstate some order.

Lincoln's legs were burning as well as his lungs by the time he finally reached the packed docks. The smoke was lighter here, but the sun was in his eyes now.

He stopped running. No. That couldn't be right. The *Invincible* was in dock. But right next to it was another ship – one he'd never seen or heard of before. *Endeavour* was written on the hull.

The area around both ships was chaos. People were crowded around the boarding planks. Stipulators were trying to keep some kind of order and only allowing a few citizens to board. But the black cloaks weren't as prolific as they normally were; in fact, they seemed few and far between. A crane was lifting huge supply crates onto the *Endeavour*. There were a number of burly men pulling chains around pallets and shouting instructions.

Lincoln's heart sunk. How on earth would he find his mother and sister in all this?

"Mum? Arta?"

He pushed his way between people, scanning the crowd for any sign of them. Was it possible they were already on board? The crowd around the boarding plank for the *Invincible* was twenty people deep. How on earth had they all heard about this? His stomach clenched. For some reason he'd thought most people wouldn't want to go to Piloria, that they would be terrified by the thought of it. He knew he was. But it seemed that hunger was a huge motivator, especially when they hadn't experienced the horrors of Piloria themselves.

He raised his hand and shouted, trying to be heard above the crowd: "Let me through. Let me through!"

The few people around him flinched, scowling at him.

It took a few seconds before a flicker of recognition appeared in their eyes. He kept pushing himself forward.

"Lincoln Kreft," he said to the Stipulator who appeared to be acting as some kind of gatekeeper. "You'll be expecting me – and a few others. Have they arrived yet?"

He was using every bit of bravado that he had. But the Stipulator wasn't that easily fooled. "Who?"

Lincoln put his hand on his chest, praying he wasn't about to ruin everything. "Lincoln Kreft – you know, the guy that's been to Piloria twice, and survived. Believe me, you don't want to go back without me. I'm the only one who can keep the dinosaurs at bay." This wasn't strictly true at all, but the Stipulator didn't know that and Lincoln was willing to try any trick he had.

The Stipulator scowled, but Lincoln could almost see his brain ticking. Lincoln pointed to whatever was in the Stipulator's hand. "Is that the list? Octavius will have added my name to it – along with my friends and family."

Something flickered across the Stipulator's face at Lincoln's informal use of the Captain Regent's name. He squared his shoulders and didn't even look at the list. "This ship is full." He waved over to the Stipulator standing on the boarding plank of the *Endeavour*. "Go over there. Tell him Octavius sent you."

Lincoln turned back and pointed to the list. "You're sure none of my family are here yet?"

The Stipulator wrinkled his nose in distaste. "How would I know?" he started, then drew himself up, realizing he was supposed to keep track of everyone on board. "Your family aren't here. If you're lucky, and if you do know the Captain Regent, they might have found a spot on the *Endeavour*. But hurry. We'll be leaving soon."

FIVE

LINCOLN

Lincoln fought his way back through the people, towards the *Endeavour*. The crowd was a little thinner here, the people not familiar with this ship. Truth be told, it was identical to the *Invincible* in every way, except for the black name on the side. Lincoln couldn't help but be curious about the many lean, muscled men working here, who were loading a massive amount of supplies onto the ship.

Someone caught his eye. He pushed forward again. "Dell? Dell? Is that you?"

It was the person he'd gone to warn – Storm's friend. Dell looked up, and automatically frowned. He'd never liked Lincoln.

Lincoln kept shoving through the crowd, grabbing Dell by the shoulders. "I came to your house, but no one was there."

"You came to my house? Why?" Dell looked genuinely confused and a little bit angry.

Lincoln shook his head and held out his arms. "Because of this. Because someone told me it was time...and to let anyone I cared about know to get to the docks."

Dell scowled at him. "You don't care about me."

Someone jolted Lincoln from behind. He was tired, he was stressed and he still hadn't found his family. These ships were due to leave soon, and if his family weren't here, he couldn't get on one. He nodded his head. "You're right, I don't. But Storm does."

Dell froze. "You came to warn me because of Storm?"

Lincoln sighed. "I was told to get everyone down here." He looked from side to side. "I warned my mother and sister, and Jesa and her family. I came to find you too."

"Who is Jesa? And who warned you?"

Lincoln shook his head. He was done answering questions. He didn't have time for this. He frowned as the light was blocked from his face by a large pallet swinging from the crane. "Do you know what's being loaded?"

Dell looked uncomfortably over his shoulder. "Building supplies." He didn't quite meet Lincoln's gaze. "That's why we're here. My dad was 'summoned'. Apparently people who used to work in the forests are a necessity."

Lincoln's eyes scanned the people around him. Now he understood why most of them looked strong and muscular. They were used to manual labour but were also skilled workers. Piloria didn't need people who had worked in factories – it needed people who could farm, who could build shelter and find food. Of course, it made perfect sense.

He should have expected this.

"So, you're going? You're going to Piloria?"

When he'd met Dell at the Trials last year, Dell had made it crystal clear he was only there for the food. He had no wish to go Piloria, or to meet any dinosaurs. This was a complete turnaround. But it seemed his hand had been forced.

Dell rolled his eyes. "You say that like there's a choice. Look around you, Lincoln. You're one of the few people who actually want to get on that ship. The Stipulators need a workforce, and apparently there's food on Piloria, when there's none here."

It was true. As Lincoln looked around he could see many disgruntled faces, and people muttering in low voices to each other. He could only see a few people who looked vaguely excited about getting on the ship. How would this work, if all the people who landed on Piloria didn't actually want to be there?

Dark brown curls filled his vision as someone squashed themselves squarely between him and Dell.

"There you are." Jesa wrapped her hands around his neck, giving him a brief hug. She glanced about, looking curiously at Dell. One sleeve of her shirt was a little torn. It was obvious she'd had just as much trouble getting through the crowds as Lincoln had. He looked behind her. Kayna and Caleb were standing there, their eyes wide. Kayna looked as if she might be sick.

"We're going on that?" she asked.

Jesa seemed in a surprisingly bright mood. "Yes," she said confidently, then turned and raised her eyebrows at Lincoln. "You *are* getting us on, aren't you?"

Panic was starting to grip him. "I need to find my mum and sister. I haven't seen them yet. They must be here somewhere."

Someone nudged him roughly from behind.

"Over here," came a deep voice. He spun around to see the bright blond hair of Leif. He looked far from happy. Leif gestured towards a pile of pallets abandoned behind them, the only thing with a bit of height anywhere nearby. He bent over, clasping his hands together, ready to give Lincoln a punt up.

Lincoln couldn't help the swell of relief in his chest at the sight of Leif. "It's good to see you," he said immediately.

Leif looked him square in the eye. "Honestly, Lincoln? You think I want to go anywhere near that place again?" After they'd come back from Piloria the second time, and the health care and rations had been removed from Rune's and Kronar's brothers and sisters, Leif had been furious and he'd vanished without warning. Lincoln suspected Leif had taken the children back to their parents in Norden, but he hadn't seen or heard anything from him until now – he hadn't even been sure he was back in Ambulus City.

Lincoln knew how much Leif hated Piloria. Two of Leif's best friends had died there. He'd only gone the last time to search for a cure for Rune's and Kronar's brothers and sisters, who were suffering from the blistering plague – that and the chance to plant the viruses to kill the dinosaurs.

Of all the people Lincoln had seen today, Leif was the thinnest. He looked ill, as if a sharp gust of wind could blow him over. The sight made Lincoln's insides twist around. The journey to and from Norden had obviously been hard. Lincoln knew that Leif would sacrifice his meagre rations for someone else in an instant – that was just the kind of person he was.

Lincoln put his foot in Leif's hands and allowed his friend to thrust him up on top of the pallets. He scanned the crowds around him from his higher viewpoint. There was some angry scuffling at the foot of the boarding plank of the *Endeavour*; another fight breaking out.

Lincoln shook his head. He had to concentrate. He had to find his mother and sister. After a few moments, he saw a flash of red. *There.* Arta was waving a scarf to attract his attention. A wave of relief washed over him. He jumped down from the pallet and wasted no time pushing through the crowd to his family. Lincoln wrapped his arms around them both. "I thought I wasn't going to be able to find you." He glanced around again. "It's mad here. I never expected it to be so crowded."

Lincoln's mother blinked. "They wouldn't let us on the ship," she said. "They told us there was no room." She was scared and shaking. Arta was trying her best to look brave, obviously for the benefit of their mother. Lincoln gulped. He hadn't thought this through – he hadn't really had time. He'd just followed Octavius's instructions and got those he cared about to the docks.

What if both ships sailed, leaving them all behind?

He was torn. He looked back over towards Ambulus City. Parts of it were burning, thick smoke rising into the sky. The place was in meltdown. Staying here would be deadly. Either they would starve to death because of a lack of food or end up a victim of the riots. But what about Piloria? Was it really a safer option?

People were panicking all around him. Punches were being thrown, voices raised. It seemed that now they'd glimpsed the destruction taking place in the city, people *did* want to board the ships.

But Lincoln knew that while there might be the chance of fertile land, more space and more food on Piloria, it all came at a cost. A cost he'd witnessed. Could humans and dinosaurs really inhabit the same continent?

He clenched his fists. Potentially, he could be taking his mother and Arta to their deaths.

Lincoln took a deep breath. He'd never missed his father so much in his life. He had spent the last six years being the man of the house. Working hard to try to provide for his family. The blistering plague had claimed his father, and had looked like it would claim Arta too. He'd risked everything to bring the potential cure home. But now, as he stood staring at the ships, he'd never been so scared.

Scared that he might not get his friends and family away from here.

And scared that they all might actually end up on Piloria.

Each outcome could be the wrong one.

There was a flash of black to his right. A group of Stipulators was heading towards the *Endeavour*. Lincoln's stomach clenched. He could almost smell the trouble in the air.

The crowds noticed them immediately. A few catcalls quickly turned into much worse. The mass of people seemed to envelop the Stipulators, impeding their way forward. A smaller figure darted underneath all the broad shoulders, a green cloak trimmed with gold flapping behind it.

Lincoln held his breath. Octavius's nimble frame rushed forward, his short legs speeding up the boarding plank of the *Endeavour*. The Stipulator stationed there leaped back in surprise. It was a few seconds before Lincoln realized his mistake.

"Octavius!" he shouted, waving frantically. "Octavius!"

For a moment, he thought Octavius hadn't heard him above the rest of the noise at the docks. But the small, grey head turned to the side, and then the man halted.

Lincoln tried again. "Octavius!"

This time, Octavius spun right round, scowling as he scanned the crowd. The rest of his Stipulators were still trying to fight their way through the masses. Lincoln grabbed the red scarf that Arta had waved at him.

"Octavius," he shouted again.

This time the old man spotted him. He took a few steps back down the plank and muttered something to the Stipulator blocking the way, gesturing Lincoln forward.

"Come on," said Lincoln swiftly to the rest of them.

"Let's go before anything else happens." He grabbed onto his mother's and sister's arms, keeping a close eye on Jesa, her family and Leif to make sure they followed. Getting through the crowd was tougher now. All of them were carrying bags full of their worldly goods. The last two times Lincoln had gone to Piloria, he'd always hoped to be coming home. This time, he knew that was highly unlikely. He hadn't had a chance to think long and hard about what to take. There had been no time to consider keepsakes or memories. As he'd stuffed his backpack, his mind had been focused on survival and extra clothing. He hadn't even had a chance to ask his mother or Arta what they'd packed.

When they reached the Stipulator, the man shot Lincoln a look of curiosity before standing aside and raising his eyebrows as six other people streamed past him.

Octavius barely blinked.

Lincoln stepped forward. "Why didn't you tell me there was another ship?"

Octavius looked him square in the eye. "You never asked," he replied simply, before turning around, his cloak sweeping out as he moved swiftly up the rest of the boarding plank.

Lincoln wasn't so easily put off. "So, this is it? We're leaving? Just like that? What about everyone else? What about the burning city? We can't just leave people behind. There are women and children out there!" He reached out and gripped Octavius's elbow, angry that the man couldn't even turn around to acknowledge he was speaking.

Octavius did turn around, his grey eyes pointedly staring

at where Lincoln's fingers were in contact with his arm. "Don't touch me," he hissed.

Lincoln pulled his hand back as if he'd been struck. Octavius was clutching something to his chest. The dinosaur book. *The Continent of Monsters*.

"Do you want to sink the ships?" Octavius hissed. "How many people do you actually think we can fit on these boats?"

"So we just abandon them?" All Lincoln's pent-up frustration came rushing out. "And what about us 'lucky' ones? We've had hardly any time to prepare! No time to discuss what we might actually need to survive on Piloria! What chance have we really got?"

He held out his hands as more explosions sounded from the city behind him. Lincoln turned. It was the factories. The fires had spread and now the factories were exploding like volcanoes.

"This is crazy. Is this a temporary move or a permanent one? Do we have the supplies we need?" He ran his fingers through his hair, his jaw tight. "No one has even asked me. No one has even asked me about what we should take to try to survive on Piloria." He threw his arms back out. "Look around, Octavius. How many people on this boat know what I do? Three? Tops. You told me to be ready. But I never thought it would be like this."

He couldn't help himself. All of a sudden he was so conscious of the fact that most people on this ship had no idea what lay ahead. He did, and it made him feel sick to his stomach.

And there was one final thing he didn't even want to say out loud.

What if Storm and Reban hadn't survived?

He couldn't help but think about it – even when things were so desperate. The last thing he wanted was to get back to Piloria and discover that Storm had met the same fate as so many others on the continent.

How would he cope if she was gone? And how could the rest of them stand a hope of surviving, if she couldn't?

Octavius's face stayed surprisingly neutral, but his voice betrayed his true feelings. It cracked as he spoke. "We should have most of what we need on Piloria. Lots of natural resources – we just need to learn how to use them. And there should be others there who can help."

He was thinking about Storm too, though neither of them were saying her name right now.

A few bedraggled Stipulators fought their way through the surging crowds towards the neighbouring *Invincible*. As they ran on board, a horn blasted. Lincoln watched the gangplank being hauled back on board. It was about to set off.

Octavius hurried along the deck, shouting orders at people on the *Endeavour*. It was clear he wanted both ships to leave at the same time. Lincoln watched his brisk manner, but he'd seen the briefest of glimpses of something else from Octavius: a man who'd learned about his family. It was obvious that Octavius felt a protective pull towards Storm. He didn't even seem particularly bothered by the fact the whole city was in meltdown or that the Stipulators – and a government he'd been at the heart of – looked as if it were about to be overthrown.

Lincoln made his way back to the rest of the group, who were standing on the deck, hands on the rail, staring at the smoking Ambulus City. The place they'd always called home.

As the *Invincible* started to pull out of the dock, there was a last surge of the crowds. Heads were flicking back and forth between the burning city and the leaving ship. Which was the lesser of the two evils?

Lincoln stared at the thick smoke billowing from the roofs in the city. This was his fault. He'd started this process. He'd brought home the cure and slowed the natural selection process of the population. The more mouths to feed were *his* fault. The starvation rations were *his* fault. Not Octavius's. Lincoln was responsible for the fact his city was now going up in flames. He felt himself sway, his hands keeping a tight hold of the rail.

"Lincoln?" Arta's hand slid over his. "Are you okay?"

She had no idea. No idea what he was about to expose her to.

A shout came from above. "Get ready!"

The crew of the *Endeavour* all seemed to jump into action. The final load was swung onto the main deck, with the men beneath hurrying to the boarding plank.

There was one more shout, from the dock this time. A bright-blond head was stumbling through the crowd below.

The last crewman had reached the top of the boarding plank, and turned around to help haul it in.

Silas burst from the crowd, pushing a man out of his way and causing him to splash down into the water between the ship and the dock. His cloak was torn, and even from up on the deck, Lincoln could see an angry bruise on Silas's face and blood on his knuckles.

The boarding plank was already pulling away from the dock as the men heaved it back towards the ship.

Lincoln watched the scene play out as if it was in slow motion.

Silas powered forward, leaping from the dock and launching himself at the boarding plank. He caught the edge of it with his hands, his legs hanging precariously in mid-air. Lincoln sucked in his breath, and heard everyone else on the rail do the same.

"Is he crazy?" Leif's voice floated towards him.

The men at the other end of the plank looked at each other in panic – none of them knowing what to do – as the unexpected weight made it tip down towards the sea. Silas's feet brushed against the water, before another man surged forward, shouting for people to help counterbalance the weight.

The men wrestled to stop the plank rising at their end, throwing their weight onto it as Silas continued to struggle, heaving his body onto the plank as it straightened in mid-air. He paused there, catching his breath as he dangled in the precarious position above the water, before he crawled the last few sectars up, tumbling onto the floor of the deck beneath them.

Leif shook his head and walked away from the railing. "Guess Silas is coming to Piloria then," he sighed.

Lincoln didn't move. His eyes were fixed on the burning city, as coiling dark smoke climbed into the purple sky.

The weight of responsibility continued to eat away at him. How many people were dying now? How many people would die in the next few days, or weeks?

Was this the last time he would ever see Earthasia?

PART FOUR

THE ARRIVAL

SIX

LINCOLN

It was Lincoln's third approach to Piloria, and the third time facing an unfamiliar coastline. "Are we ever going to land in the same place twice?" he asked Leif, who was standing next to him, watching the emerging scene.

It was early morning. The *Invincible* had already stopped ahead of them, dropping anchor in what appeared to be a natural harbour – deep enough for the ship's hull, but surrounded on two sides by cliffs and a flat beach on the other.

Leif frowned and leaned over the ship's rail, peering down into the blue ocean. "How on earth is this possible? How can this be deep enough for the ship, but right next to the land?"

Lincoln shrugged. "Must be a natural harbour." He smiled. "A quirk of nature. There are quite a few of them on Piloria."

They watched as part of the hull of the *Invincible* lowered with a huge, long ramp reaching down to the edge of the ridge around the natural harbour. A few minutes later, three large transporters rolled down the ramp, followed by a few large pieces of machinery that Lincoln didn't recognize.

It was a slow process. The transporters were bulky, each with a load behind them. They were bigger and in much better condition than the few old, rickety transporters that had been left behind before. These were as big as the ones that had been used to move people between the Trials back on Earthasia. But these transporters weren't loaded with people. No. It seemed the people were to walk alongside them. These transporters were loaded with supplies.

Leif was still watching the hull. "We've never had a ramp like that before." He sighed in obvious relief. "But thank goodness we don't need to cross the water in boats. Not after last time."

Lincoln shuddered. Last time around, they'd lost more than ten people to the creatures in the initially peaceful-looking Blue Bay. He wasn't in a hurry to repeat the experience.

Thankfully, the journey across the ocean had been uneventful. Both his and Jesa's mothers had suffered from motion sickness and stayed in their bunks for a number of days though. The sight of land would be a relief to them both.

Jesa and her family appeared next to Leif and Lincoln.

"This is really happening, isn't it?" she breathed. "We're all going to live on Piloria."

Even from here, Lincoln could feel the heat from Piloria reaching out towards him, like a giant vine wrapping around him and pulling him in. They were too far away to hear the noises on land, but the scents were drifting across the sea to them. Rich, dark-green scents, mixed with flowers and fruit essences.

He watched as Jesa's mother's and brother's eyes widened and their senses went into overload – the way he was sure his had when he'd first landed on Piloria.

Lincoln turned to Jesa. "Well, we're going to try, anyway." They'd been having these kind of conversations for days, all wondering if this would really be feasible or not. The *Endeavour* was loaded with supplies. Machinery. Clothing. Scientific equipment. Seeds, food, water sterilization supplies. They could only imagine that the *Invincible* was as well.

Much of the equipment was like the supplies they'd used for their last two journeys: camp beds, weapons, climbing equipment. But it seemed that someone had been thinking ahead for quite a while. There were items on this boat that they'd never had before – utensils, crockery, clay, the widest variety of sneakers they'd ever seen, paper, graphite. This time they had a whole host of everyday objects that they would struggle to make from scratch on Piloria. But even with masses of boxes loaded on the ship, Lincoln's stomach clenched. What happened when the supplies ran dry?

"Where do you think we are?" asked Leif, as he scanned the unfamiliar coastline. "I don't have a clue."

They'd never landed at this point before. The first time

had been next to a beach bordered by jungle. The second had been at Blue Bay, where the boats had been attacked by tylosauruses.

"They must have known about this harbour from previous landings," murmured Leif. "There's no way we've just stopped here by chance." He bit his bottom lip as he continued to scan the landscape – just the same as Lincoln was – searching for anything that was remotely familiar and would give them an indication of where they were.

There was something in Leif's face that Lincoln recognized. An element of discomfort. He decided to voice their fear. "What if we're on the opposite side of the continent to Storm?"

Leif shook his head. "It crossed my mind, but we can't be. Surely they'd want to set us down near to familiar territory?"

There was a movement to the side, then a small figure elbowed between them. Over the last week, Octavius had shed his cloak and barely been seen. There were around two hundred people on this boat – many of them tradesmen with old-style skills that they hadn't used in a long time. Apparently, most of them had been made promises about what would await them on Piloria if they agreed to come. There were some Stipulators too – around twenty – plus a handful of scientists and a few people Lincoln recognized from the lab, but Octavius had avoided everyone.

Lincoln looked down. "Are you going to tell us where we are?" he asked Octavius, whose grey hair was fluttering in the wind.

"Piloria," said Octavius simply, giving Lincoln a haughty stare. "I thought you would know that." He looked back out at the surrounding area and the unloading of the *Invincible*. After a few seconds, a smile appeared on his face. "It's so… green," he whispered, then wrinkled his nose. "Strange smell though."

Leif watched Octavius hurry away along the deck. "Do we ever get a straight answer out of that guy?"

Lincoln shook his head. "Not since I've known him."

Leif's hands gripped the rail. "No one has asked us a thing. You, me and Jesa are the only people who've set foot on this soil before and I'm still waiting for someone to ask us something – *anything* – about what lies ahead."

Lincoln nodded in agreement as he looked at the Stipulators ordering people around. "Conceited. That's what they are. And if they keep going like this, it will be their downfall."

"You two. Hurry up. We have work to do!" One of the Stipulators waved them both over. He had a typical sneer on his face. "Through there. Help load the equipment onto the transporters."

Leif turned to Lincoln and raised his eyebrows. "You were saying?"

Lincoln and Leif followed directions down a dark, winding staircase on the ship. It led them to the central hold, where three transporters were positioned, identical to the three they'd just seen unloading from the *Invincible*.

They joined a row of men who were throwing sacks,

boxes and barrels into the back of one of them.

"What even is this stuff?" asked Leif. "There's too much for it to fit into the transporters."

"I have no idea," said Lincoln. "There are more provisions here than I've ever seen before." Something made him instantly uncomfortable. "What if all this is food? What if this is the remaining food supplies from Earthasia?"

Leif was clearly horrified, and Lincoln regretted his words as soon as they'd left his mouth. Leif's family was back in Norden. He'd had no time to speak to them or give them word to join him.

Lincoln put his hand on his friend's arm. "Remember, Ambulus City was one of the worst places for rations. I'm sure Norden is much better. There was a bit more land there – and some rivers for fishing."

Leif's face was tight. During the time they'd spent on the ship together, Lincoln had learned a little more about his friend's struggles since they last returned from Piloria.

By the time the health care had been withdrawn from Rune's and Kronar's families, Leif had at least accessed some of the ointment for the sickest children, Cornelius and Livia – enough to treat their blistering plague, and enough to keep them alive. But what was the point in treating the plague if now they would starve? In desperation, he'd taken them all back home to their parents in Norden, hoping the rations there might be a little more sufficient. Lincoln was almost sure that the only reason Leif had returned to Ambulus City himself was to be with Jesa. Their relationship, which had started on Piloria, seemed to have blossomed. Lincoln had noticed that they were constantly at each other's side.

A few more Stipulators appeared. Lincoln had tried to work out exactly how many people had managed to scramble onto the ships. Silas had kept a low profile on board. He'd barely been spotted – probably to let his cuts and bruises heal. But now they were about to disembark, there was nowhere to hide. As Lincoln and Leif made their way back up to the deck, they could hear Silas's angry voice.

"Call a meeting! We'll give everyone their instructions before they leave the ship."

But another voice was even louder. It was Octavius.

"There's no time for that. The tide will not wait for us. If it comes back in, we'll be unable to unload the transporters, and it could flood part of the hull if we don't get the bow doors back up. You there. Tell everyone to gather their belongings, and let's go."

The message spread across the ship quickly. Lincoln ducked back to the bunks and grabbed his backpack, along with another bag of gear. They'd all been told to carry some of the ship's supplies to wherever they were going to go – though that part still wasn't clear.

Everyone filed off the ship. Absolutely everyone. The bow doors were closed as the transporters exited, with the final members of the crew climbing down a long rope ladder and splashing down into the shallows. There were still supplies on board, but it seemed that on Piloria, no one needed to guard them.

"Can you see anything?" Leif was right at Lincoln's shoulder, his eyes scanning the water as they stepped onto the shore. On their previous trips to Piloria, they hadn't been lucky with water – but this part of the coastline remained calm and the last crew members were helped up the short rock face to where everyone else stood.

Silas was already ordering people around.

"This way, follow the transporters. We'll take it slow, but make sure you don't fall behind." He narrowed his eyes, then gave a wicked kind of smile. "Piloria is not a good place to fall behind."

"How would he know?" Lincoln couldn't help but say it out loud. As usual, even though they knew nothing about this place, the Stipulators were acting as if they ruled all they surveyed.

Octavius seemed to be ignoring everyone, his head immersed in *The Continent of Monsters*. He ducked into one of the transporters without a word.

Lincoln's mother appeared at his side.

"What do we do? Do we follow them?" She knew that Lincoln wanted to find Storm. He hadn't tried to disguise the fact. He'd told them that at some point he would break away from the rest of the group if necessary, to try to find her.

He glanced over at Leif, who was now standing with Jesa and her family, and to Dell, who, along with his father, had joined a large party of workmen. He had to put safety first. "I guess we do. I still can't figure out where we are.

Until we do, I don't know what direction to go in. We might as well see what the plans are. Let's just hope they've got some."

"Didn't you see all that stuff on board?" asked Arta. "There's no way those provisions have been gathered and loaded up in the last few days. They've been planning this for a while. You didn't even know they had a second ship."

Lincoln smiled down at his sister. She'd always been wise beyond her years. She was right – he knew she was. His mind went back to all the supplies that had been stored in the hold. Something flickered in his brain.

He lifted his head as he noticed Silas disappearing into the transporter Octavius was already in.

"Wait!"

Silas halted and looked out, glowering, to see who dared to demand his attention.

Lincoln strode through the crowd. It parted easily as most people recognized him as the guy who'd actually been here twice before. There were a few murmurs.

"Where are the weapons?" he asked Silas.

Colour started to rise in Silas's cheeks. "What?"

Lincoln turned his voice up a notch. He wanted everyone to hear exactly what he was saying. "I don't know quite how far you expect us to travel" – he smacked his hand off the side of the metal transporter – "but it's quite clear that you'll be safe. These transporters are different from the ones you left here. They were all open-topped. Open to the elements – and open to the dinosaurs."

Lincoln spoke slowly as he ran his hand down the side of the transporter.

"These are completely enclosed. Safer than being outside." He turned to the rest of the crowd. "But the rest of us? We need weapons. We need something to help us ward off any dinosaurs we might encounter."

Heads turned from side to side as murmurs spread instantly through the crowd, along with flickers of alarm. Maybe people hadn't really thought seriously about a dinosaur attack, maybe some of them were still in a state of disbelief about what was going on. They were in for a rude awakening – danger would soon become their reality.

People instantly looked scared. They automatically stepped back towards the open doorway of Silas's transporter – a few looked as if they were about to charge it.

Silas could barely contain his fury. His eyes shot pure venom at Lincoln, who wasn't in the least worried. *He* knew much more about this continent than Silas, who still sported the remnants of bruising around one eye. Lincoln was done with being bullied by the Stipulators. And even though Lincoln knew that most of the weapons might be next to useless, it really wasn't the point. In an environment like this, people deserved to be armed.

"Which transporter are the weapons in?" Lincoln was already fed up of waiting on an appropriate response from Silas. The murmurs in the crowd grew louder. "Where are the weapons? Give us some weapons!"

Silas waved to the transporter behind him, muttering

something and continuing to give Lincoln an evil glare. Lincoln knew he'd probably pay for this later, but Silas seemed less of a threat than the rest of Piloria.

The crowd moved to the second transporter, and Leif jumped inside as soon as the door opened and started passing weapons out to the crowd. Crossbows, spears, axes – much the same type of thing they'd had before. Once every adult had a weapon in their hand, the crowd dispersed a little, moving back around the transporters and staring at the area surrounding them.

They started to move slowly, first through some thinning forest and then across a hilly terrain. Leif and Lincoln were constantly on guard, looking for any nesting sites that could mean they were in imminent danger. But the rest of the group appeared to be in awe of Piloria. Sweat was already running down their faces and necks, as their bodies tried to acclimatize to the heat.

Lincoln frowned. "The evergreen leaves worked for Blaine. I hope they've worked for Storm and Reban. But how on earth do you disguise the smell of four hundred people from the dinosaurs? Do you even think that could be possible?"

Leif shook his head. "Not a chance." He wrinkled his nose. "Some of the people smells are getting to me already."

Lincoln nodded in agreement. "Right there with you."

Things were different this time. It was more difficult to filter out the mechanical transporter noises from the forest noises. Piloria was used to peace. To animal noise. To plant noise. The noise of life quietly finding a way.

The noise of the huge transporters and other machinery was ugly, a complete abomination amongst the gentle forest sounds. But more than that, it could attract attention – and not in a good way.

"We're too loud," Lincoln hissed, as he continued to look from side to side. "*They're* too loud," he said, waving his hand at the transporters ahead.

"Never mind the transporters," muttered Jesa as she moved alongside him and Leif. "What about the people? Haven't they ever heard of quiet?"

She was right. Four hundred people weren't quiet. No one seemed to have reinforced the necessity of keeping a low profile on Piloria. Maybe the Stipulators hadn't even thought that far ahead.

For the first few minutes, people had been silent as they'd started across the terrain. But the colours and smells of the forest had obviously distracted them from any thoughts of immediate danger. Now, they were all talking loudly, exclaiming at every new fruit and flower.

Lincoln couldn't blame them. After grey Earthasia, Piloria was information overload for the senses. Every turn revealed a new type of plant. Every step on the soft, moist ground was a new sensation. Aromas drifted easily in the air. Flowers, fruits and some animal scents assaulted the senses. The colours here seemed too bright to be natural. No wonder they were amazed by it all.

As the transporters crushed through the forest, insects

filled the air around them, saving themselves as the bushes they'd been resting on were trampled. Fluttering wings of bright orange and red made people gasp. Smaller blue-bodied buzzing bugs were curious about the new species on their continent and hovered around, eventually being batted away by hands and backpacks.

Kayna, Jesa's mother, tugged at her daughter's sleeve. "What's wrong?" she asked.

Jesa tutted. "Dinosaurs rely on their senses – sight, sound and smell. We're practically a walking buffet." She winced as one of the youngest members of the party – a kid of around four – pricked himself on a thorny bush and started yelling.

Lincoln stopped walking and turned to his mother and sister. "We might as well put out an announcement and just tell the T-rexes where we are." He shook his head. "Stay close. Right by my side."

All his senses were heightened. This was Piloria, land of the dinosaurs. Only three of them knew just how dangerous it could be.

There was a rustle up ahead. Lincoln stopped dead, and Arta walked straight into his back. "Oof! Wh—"

He lifted his hand with one finger raised and cut her dead. The rustle turned into a rampage. Seconds later, a whole herd of duckbills came squealing through the crowd.

Everyone screamed. People scattered. They had no idea what these creatures were. But Leif and Lincoln did. Duckbills might be harmless, but they only ran like that when they were being chased.

"Take cover!" yelled Lincoln. He grabbed hold of his sister's and mother's hands and yanked them into the bushes. His eyes quickly scanned the canopy above. They might need to climb.

He watched through the leaves as people ran in every direction. A few were frozen to the spot in horror. He glanced around, making sure Jesa's family and Leif were accounted for. It was bedlam. The duckbills were confused by the sight and smell of four hundred humans. Their squeals became higher pitched as their herd mentality deserted them and mayhem reigned.

The transporters ground to a halt – but none of the doors opened. The Stipulators were staying safely locked inside.

People were shouting all around Lincoln. He could hear some of the workers' kids crying. One guy got charged by five duckbills and was tossed up in the air, landing with a horrible crunch. Lincoln felt sick. If the guy was lucky, he'd only have broken bones, which might heal in time. Anything else could easily be a death sentence. They might have brought some medical supplies, but right now, they didn't have facilities to cope with anything other than minor injuries and a few broken bones.

There was a long bellow and a loud thudding. Anyone who was still in view froze in terror. Lincoln pulled Arta under his arm. Moments later, a huge triceratops crashed through the undergrowth, trampling everything in its path.

Triceratops were plant eaters, but the size, armour-plating and current mood of the animal made it almost as dangerous as the meat eaters.

If he was at a safe distance, Lincoln might have admired the three magnificent horns and large bony frill. Its colouring was a mixture of green and brown, with splashes of red on the frill. But what was terrifying about this creature was its pure physical strength. It crashed forward relentlessly, side-swiping one of the transporters as if it wasn't even there, leaving a huge indent in its metal bodywork. The guy who'd already been tossed in the air by the duckbills was lying on the ground nearby, his eyes wide and his mouth open.

His fear lasted only a few seconds before he was trampled underfoot by the stampeding triceratops.

The dinosaur continued its rampage through the far side of the forest, leaving a clear path in its wake.

For a few moments, there was complete and utter stunned silence. Then a few scared duckbills ran back through the flattened scene.

Lincoln motioned to the others to stay still, but not all of the group could see him. A woman ran over to the near-flattened body of the man and let out a blood-curdling scream.

Leif didn't hesitate. He ran over and clamped his hand over her mouth. She instantly struggled beneath his grasp. "Stop it!" he hissed to the people around him, his eyes flashing with anger and frustration. "We need to be quiet. As quiet as humanly possible."

There was a loud creak next to him, as the crumpled door of the transporter tried to open. The mechanism screeched and Lincoln crossed the space in a few long strides, slamming the door closed again with the palm of his hand. He walked around to the front of the transporter and motioned through the glass, shaking his head and urging the transporter to start moving again.

He waved to the rest of the crowd, dispersed among the trees and bushes. He had no idea if everyone had stayed close or run for their lives through the forest. There was a strong possibility that some people were already lost.

"Let's move, people. And Leif is right. Keep quiet. We don't want to attract any unwanted attention."

An older man pointed to the body on the ground. "What about him?"

Lincoln swallowed. He didn't know the guy. Had he been a friend, he would have wanted to take the time to bury him. But Lincoln wasn't even sure where any tools would be in amongst the loads, or how long it would take to find them. And who knew if there were any predators close by? Had something spooked the triceratops, or had the duckbills just antagonized it? "We leave him," he said firmly.

Leif shot him a glance. It was clear he was as torn as Lincoln, but then he gestured to Jesa and her family to follow him. Silence fell across the group – whether it was driven by shock or fear, Lincoln didn't know.

Nothing about this was how he'd imagined things while they'd been sailing here. He hadn't figured they would land in a completely unfamiliar spot, or set out without warning people what to expect. When he'd first arrived, he'd been downright terrified, and to be honest, he'd expected everyone else to feel like that too.

But most of these people had practically been laughing and joking since they got here. Admiring the jungle sights and sounds, with little thought about predators. It felt to him like they were showing a lack of respect for Piloria. The Stipulators were the same, carrying on with their usual arrogance, despite everything. It seemed that even Silas's bruises and black eye hadn't reminded him that people were now questioning their leadership and decision-making.

No one else here had experienced the Trials, like Lincoln and Leif had – where they'd been forced to show their mental and physical strength before they were even allowed to come here in the first place. They hadn't experienced that first, bloody encounter with the megalodon while crossing the ocean.

Even now, Lincoln was annoyed by how slow people seemed to be to move on and get away from here. He knew how quickly the scent of blood would be picked up by predators. He waved people on as the transporters started moving again.

SEVEN

STORMCHASER

"What's that?" Storm sat bolt upright.

Reban pulled back the sheet hanging between them, his other hand on his weapon. Storm pushed herself up into a crouch as silently as she could, listening intently.

They'd spent three days hauling as many of their supplies and parts of Blaine's shack as they could down the coast from where they'd been before. Reban and Storm had managed to use one of the old solar-powered transporters for the last part of their journey – the others were all in bits, looking as if they'd been tested for their tastiness by various dinosaurs.

They'd headed south. Away from the raptor and pterosaur nests. The site near the loch where Storm had once seen a deinosuchus battle a T-rex had seemed hauntingly quiet as they'd dragged their makeshift wagon past. Last time they'd seen a T-rex, it had chased them but disappeared beneath the quicksand somewhere to the north.

They were probably crazy. There could be just as many predators in this part of Piloria – but at least they hadn't come across any raptors so far.

Storm still wasn't used to the noises around them in this new forest though. It was odd. She'd always imagined that forest would just sound like…forest. But being on Piloria had made her more aware of the differing sounds of nature and life around them.

And this sound wasn't one of them.

Reban's brow had a deep crease. He turned to her and mouthed the words, "What is that? An engine?"

Storm frowned too. As her ears tuned the sounds of the forest out, the alien sound that had woken her took full focus. It was distant and rough. The more she concentrated, the more the sound amplified. Doubled. Tripled.

Now Reban wasn't silent. "What?" he said, moving swiftly to the entrance of last night's hastily erected shack. Today's plan had been to get the shack in better shape. Set up a water supply and encase the whole place in the ready supply of evergreens they'd found in this forest, to mask their smell from the dinosaurs.

It seemed like today's plans had just changed.

EIGHT

LINCOLN

Within a few hours, people were almost collapsing in the heat. Most hadn't thought to carry water with them, and the temperature and humidity of Piloria was very different to Earthasia. Here, at the slightest exertion, sweat dripped from every pore – and needed to be replaced.

Leif banged the side of one of the transporters again, signalling it to slow down and open. "Pass out some more water."

The Stipulator who opened the door had stripped off his black cloak. Perspiration dotted his brow. If it was hot out in the jungle, it had to be even hotter inside the metal transporter.

"Again?" he muttered.

"Welcome to Piloria," said Lincoln, with no qualms at all. "You'll get used to it."

He passed out the water amongst those closest to him. "How much further?"

The Stipulator scowled and spoke to the person driving the transporter. "Maybe another hour."

Lincoln nodded and surveyed the crowd. Most were already flagging. After the dinosaur stampede, the transporters had picked up the pace considerably. His leg muscles were aching, as were his shoulders from the packs he was carrying. Could these people really make it another hour?

"You'll need to slow down a bit."

Silas appeared at the door, his face much redder than usual. "We won't be slowing down. We need to make it to the site early enough to make a start on constructing the encampment." He sneered at Lincoln. "If you can't keep up, that's not my problem."

"You can't set up if you reach the encampment site alone," snapped back Lincoln.

Silas leaned out of the transporter and grabbed hold of Lincoln's tunic. "You've got a smart mouth, boy. Watch it, or we might use you as dinosaur bait."

Lincoln held his breath, cooling his nerves and the overwhelming urge to punch Silas in the face. He needed to stay calm. He needed to play Silas's game. His ultimate plan was to find Storm, but if he turned and walked away right now, he'd have no supplies and no way to ensure his mum's or his sister's safety.

He blinked, and in that instant something flashed into his head. A daydream. A wish. A desire. An image of one of

Storm's knives cutting through the air and landing between Silas's eyes. As quick as the thought appeared, it was gone. But that didn't stop a smile tweaking his lips.

Silas tightened his grasp on Lincoln's tunic. "What are you laughing at, boy?"

Lincoln shook his head and stepped back. If Silas wanted to keep a grip of him, he'd have to step out into the jungle with the rest of them.

But, just as he'd expected, Silas's hand broke free. He disappeared back inside the transporter, muttering to himself as the door slid closed once again.

They tramped on. At one point Arta's legs almost gave way. She still wasn't as strong as Lincoln would have liked, even though her blistering plague had much improved. Now, she only had a few small areas on her skin that were red and scratchy and still required the thick pungent green ointment. The constant drag of suffering from the condition seemed to have weakened her in general – Lincoln wasn't sure if she'd ever fully recover. But with his mother on one side, and him on the other, they managed to keep her going.

Around five hours after setting out, the jungle started to thin around them and the air started to feel a little less dense. He could catch some other kind of scent – was it the sea? Were they back near an area of the coast?

People started murmuring again. They'd been walking in stunned silence since the encounter with the triceratops. Lincoln led his family through the final few trees and out onto a wide plain. As he looked to his left, he could see the sea in the distance. To his right was a cluster of hills – bumps on the terrain with a small river running through the middle. The grass was fresh and green, and there was a clear view of the surrounding area.

The transporters ahead ground to a halt. Their dark-grey metal glinted in the sun. In the lush greens of Piloria, they looked totally out of place. But then so did all the humans.

After struggling through the sweltering jungle, the strong breeze coming from the distant sea helped make the temperature more bearable.

Jesa appeared at his shoulder. "I don't know whether to be happy or sad," she said quietly.

"What do you mean?"

"This place." She sighed. "When I left, I thought I'd never see it again. And yet sometimes I'd imagine that if the dinosaurs weren't here, I could exist and look after myself on Piloria. I could survive and make a life for myself, and for my family. But this?"

She held up her hand as the doors to the transporters opened and the Stipulators started to tumble out. It reminded Lincoln of when he'd looked down one of the microscopes in the lab at the multiplying virus cells.

"This isn't Piloria," Jesa said softly. "Not in my head, anyway. Can we really just pick up the way of life from Earthasia and bring it here?"

Lincoln nodded slowly. He understood exactly what she was saying. "I think we're going to find out," he murmured. "I still can't work out where we are," he went on. "But this looks like a good spot. A good vantage point, with a water supply – a river running right through the middle…"

"I guess so," Jesa replied, as she scanned the landscape in front of them.

Silas had pulled on his cloak again and it fluttered in the wind. He looked like a giant pterosaur about to take off.

People started to gather around him. These people weren't like the rebels back in Ambulus City. They were all so used to following every instruction from the Stipulators that no one really knew how to act in any other way.

After a few minutes' consultation with his colleagues, Silas climbed onto the roof of one of the transporters. "People," he shouted, "listen to me."

Every hair on Lincoln's neck bristled. Already he was tempted to turn and walk away. He pressed his lips together, telling himself to keep quiet. Since arriving on the ship, Silas appeared to have immediately forgotten he'd made it on there by the skin of his teeth. He was the only Chief Stipulator on board, and since Octavius had kept a low profile, he had immediately assumed command.

It was an odd set-up. While Lincoln had seen the inside workings of parliament, most of the other people here hadn't. They wouldn't know that the tiny man called the Captain Regent kept the Chief Stipulators of the four hundred zones in order. All of the other lower-ranking Stipulators on board the ship had been part of the Ambulus City contingent and were used to answering to Silas, so had just fallen back into line.

Silas held out his hands. "We're here, in Piloria. The continent that will soon be ours. We've already used viruses against the most dangerous predators. The T-rexes, raptors and pterosaurs are no more."

Leif shot Lincoln a glance. They didn't actually know that. They hoped it might be true. But who really knew?

Lorcan stumbled out of one of the other transporters as the last few words were spoken. *Of course…* Lincoln had suspected he would be here, but hadn't seen Lorcan on the *Endeavour*. The scientist must have travelled on the *Invincible*. He was clasping one of his pieces of equipment to his chest, and his forehead was creased. Was he in on Silas's plans?

Silas kept talking. "After careful consideration of the information gathered from previous visits to Piloria – such as the terrain, and where the most dangerous dinosaurs nest – we've picked this spot as the best place to set up our encampment. Our first priority will be to enclose ourselves and ensure our safety. We have a ready supply of trees in the forest and will use these to build a large circular outer-defence wall."

"That'll do a lot of good against a titanosaurus," snarked Leif.

Silas kept talking. "You will all be given instructions as to what your role is. In the first instance, most of you will be involved in construction. Once we have our outer defence wall, we have materials to build houses and labs."

Labs? Lincoln watched the crowd. In a place like Piloria,

didn't it strike anyone else as strange that one of Silas's first priorities was building a lab?

Octavius shuffled out of one of the transporters, ignoring Silas and looking around, scanning the horizon as if he were searching for something. He still had the dinosaur book tucked under his arm. It seemed he'd no intention of letting it go. He started a quiet conversation with Lorcan.

Lorcan seemed almost stunned by the surroundings. His daughter Tarin emerged behind him from the transporter.

Arta let out a little yelp. "Tarin! I haven't seen her since we were in the medico care centre together."

"They must have been on the other ship," said Lincoln quietly.

He'd stopped listening to Silas. He could hear something else. Something he didn't recognize.

And hearing something you didn't recognize on Piloria was never good.

NINE

STORMCHASER

They sped through the forest, weapons at the ready.

The sound was inexplicable. They'd used the only working transporter – and it was currently dumped in a small clearing, right where they'd left it. Of the rest, one had been bitten clean in half, another was missing a wheel, and a third had clearly been trampled by some passing titanosaurus or something equally heavy-footed. So what on earth was making that racket?

Reban was slightly ahead. He turned to Storm and waved his hand, urging her to slow down as they reached the edge of the forest. Their pace dropped as their ears tuned in to the noise. The noise that went against everything they knew about Piloria.

People. It was definitely people. People talking, murmuring.

One voice cut above the others as Storm and Reban

emerged from the forest. Both of them froze, trying to take in the sight before them.

It was like one of the dreams she'd had since she'd got here. Or maybe one of her nightmares.

There were hundreds of people standing in front of them – along with six huge transporters. There were also a number of Stipulators dotted amongst the crowd.

But one Stipulator stood out from the rest. Silas was standing on the roof of a transporter, talking loudly to the crowd and dictating instructions.

Reban moved – his reactions instinctive, his face dropping into an angry mask. Her father had been abandoned here by his fellow Stipulators, literally left to die. Deciding to stay with him instead of returning to Earthasia had been a split-second decision for Stormchaser, and when the rain had fallen in monsoon proportions, or she'd been trapped up a tree by a raptor, she'd obviously had moments of regret.

Storm hadn't missed the overcrowding of Earthasia, but she had missed the people. The small, inane conversations you had on a daily basis. The quiet, everyday interactions. Having only one other person to talk to on a continent was tough – particularly when the relationship hadn't begun well.

But now? Her hands clenched as an overwhelming sensation swept over her. This place was *hers*. Hers and her father's. How dare other people appear out of the blue? And why here, the very spot they'd scouted to try to make a home?

Storm tried to scan the people who were gathered here, searching desperately for any familiar faces, but she didn't have time to even look properly before Reban started striding through the crowd.

"You!" he bellowed, as he pointed at Silas and moved swiftly towards him. "What are you doing here? What on earth do you think you're doing?"

For a few seconds, Silas looked shocked, then his lip curled upwards into a sneer.

"Oh, look who has decided to join us – our own reprobate, Reban Don, with his offspring. I'm surprised you're still alive."

Every head in the crowd turned.

"Storm!"

The shouts were almost immediate. She turned in the direction of the voices and two seconds later was flattened by Lincoln, Leif and Jesa, as they ran over and threw their arms around her. All of them seemed to start talking at once.

"We were so worried about you!"

"Thank goodness we found you."

"I'm so happy to see you!"

Lincoln's arms were around her neck and his body pressed against hers. For a moment, she couldn't breathe. *Her friends. Her friends were actually here.* She hadn't seen them since they'd boarded the ship back to Earthasia. She'd honestly thought she might never see them again. For the briefest moment she was completely overwhelmed.

Storm had never been much of a hugger. Affection and

close relationships just weren't her thing. But as the scents of Jesa, Leif and Lincoln surrounded her, emotions and shock choked in her throat. The aroma of soap and clean clothes – things she hadn't experienced in months – mixed, of course, with a little sweat, which was normal for Piloria. How long were they here for? She stepped back, trying to drink in the sight before her eyes, to make sure it was real. That she wasn't really dreaming. But this couldn't be a dream, because even though it had only been a few months, she could see something different. All of her friends looked leaner, more bony.

She was conscious of a few hundred pairs of eyes currently on herself and Reban, but she had to catch up with her friends. She shook her head and stood back. "What's happened? What are you all doing here?"

They exchanged weird glances, as if they weren't quite sure where to start.

Jesa pulled a face. "Things haven't gone well at home. Once we took the cure back" – she paused for a second – "there wasn't enough food for the population. Everyone was starving." She leaned forward and clasped Storm's hand again. "You have no idea how glad I am to see you."

Leif cut in: "People'd had enough. There's been a revolt. It was board one of the ships, or starve."

"Ships, what ships?" The first part of Jesa's sentence was dancing around in her brain. Once they'd taken the cure home, there hadn't been enough food for everyone. Of course. It was so obvious, and she couldn't believe the realization hadn't knocked her between the eyes before now. That's why the Stipulators had never provided health care for everyone – they'd didn't want more people to survive. They'd never wanted a cure for the plague.

Earthasia had already been starving. It was completely overcrowded, and the tiny patches of soil that were left had been used so frequently they were depleted. In her head, the cure had been for Lincoln's sister, and Rune's and Kronar's brothers and sisters. The people she knew about. The only people on her priority list. She hadn't really imagined that the cure would go out to everyone. She hadn't believed the Stipulators would let it happen.

Lincoln was looking at her oddly, as if he couldn't quite believe she was here.

"There are two ships," he explained. "It seems they had another ship – the *Endeavour*, waiting in the wings." He gave his head a shake too. "Things happened so quickly. We barely had time for anything. But the ships? They were ready and waiting. This was always the plan – we just didn't know about it."

"You fool!" The voice came from behind them and Storm spun around at the angry shout. "You brought all these people here? You think they can live here?" Reban sounded incredulous. Even from behind, Storm could see that every muscle in his body was tensed.

"Well, you managed to," shot back Silas, his voice dripping with sarcasm. He held his arms open wide, playing to the audience around him. "And isn't it funny, how we've both ended up at the same spot?" His gaze narrowed. "Maybe Piloria isn't big enough for us both."

Storm could see the confused faces of the people around her. There were flickers of recognition as many of them realized the man in front of them used to be the Chief Stipulator of Ambulus City. He might not be wearing his black cloak, but his black vest, and matching dark waistcoat and trousers with multiple pockets, along with his more rugged look and defined muscles, made him seem even more formidable.

There was a movement to her side.

"Storm?" The voice was quieter, but she recognized it instantly.

"Arta?" she squealed. Storm didn't hesitate. Her heart gave a swell of relief as she hugged Lincoln's sister. As she felt the slim arms slide up around her neck, the change was immediately noticeable. Arta's arms were bare, revealing almost healthy skin. No cracks, no blisters, no bleeding – it was only a little rougher than her own. She turned her head to the side to focus on the skin directly next to her. "It's worked? It's really worked?" she asked excitedly.

Arta laughed and nodded as she stood back and ran one hand down her arm. "It seems so. I feel so much better. I finally feel normal again."

Storm gave her another squeeze, as her stomach dropped a little. Her fragile friend, Arta, on the continent of dinosaurs? There was so much danger here, so many predators. It didn't even bear thinking about. Her eyes darted to Lincoln, but he was too busy watching Silas taunt Reban.

"We're here, Reban," said Silas. "You always knew we'd end up here. Piloria is ours. Now we're here to take it. It's time to say goodbye to the dinosaurs, and take this land as our own." He pointed at the ground. "You're standing on the place that will be the first human encampment on Piloria." He put his finger to his chin. "Or should we call this a colony? After all, we're the first settlers on a new continent."

Every cell in her body bristled. "I hate him," said Storm quietly. "I hate him and the way he thinks he's master of all he surveys. I can't wait for him to meet a T-rex." She paused for a second. "If there are any left."

"What do you mean, any left?" Leif's eyes were wide. "You mean the virus worked?"

He looked hopeful, and her insides clenched. "Well, I'm not sure. I just know I haven't seen any since we planted the virus. Not since the quicksand at least." She put a hand on his arm. "But it's not the same for the raptors."

"Who said you could come here? And like this?" Reban swept his hand out towards the people standing on the green grass. "Disorganized chaos. Unplanned. Are you crazy?" Reban snorted and threw his hand back up again. "No, don't answer that. We all know the answer."

Silas couldn't remove the superior expression from his face. He seemed to be revelling in every second of this. Storm felt uneasy. Some of Reban's words sat uncomfortably. Was she ready to welcome all these people – most of whom were strangers – to Piloria?

But Reban wasn't finished. He'd spent years as Chief Stipulator in Ambulus City. And even though he'd been abandoned on Piloria, it seemed that some things were ingrained deeply in him. "How on earth do you plan on keeping all these people safe, Silas? How will they sleep tonight without becoming dinosaur supper or breakfast?"

There was a collective intake of breath from the crowd, as heads flicked from side to side and eyes widened.

It seemed that the reality of Piloria was actually starting to sink in. Storm had no idea what had happened back home, or on the journey across the sea, but she didn't doubt that Silas would probably have promised these people that the viruses had wiped out the most dangerous dinosaurs.

The anger and edge of fear emanating from Reban was real. It was palpable. She almost felt as if she could reach out and touch it.

A small figure broke through the crowd. "Enough. Enough of this."

Storm froze again.

The elderly man lifted his head and his soft, grey eyes locked with hers. He walked past Silas and Reban, instantly dismissing them.

She blinked. This wasn't really happening, was it?

TEN

STORMCHASER

Octavius Arange was moving swiftly across the uneven terrain, with his green cloak rippling behind him.

No, Octavius didn't belong on Piloria. He belonged back in the parliament building on Earthasia. On his high chair in his office, surrounded by the aroma of old books.

But his grey eyes were locked on hers, and they were all she could see right now. The man who'd treated her with the first glimmer of interest she'd felt in years. He'd shown respect for the place she'd been and what she'd learned.

But Octavius hadn't been truthful with her. He'd lied to her by omission. He hadn't told her that her mother, Dalia, had been his niece. And now…he was here?

His old, wizened hand reached out and touched her arm. His voice cracked. "S-Stormchaser…" All of a sudden he sounded old, so old. Although he was the oldest man Storm had ever met – no one usually lived that long on Earthasia

– in his office in parliament, or in the red chair at the end of the white pristine debate chamber, he'd fitted, he'd seemed strong…ageless. But here he seemed different. No longer invincible.

She'd forgotten how he used her full name. Hardly anyone did that. But from the second he'd met her, Octavius Arange had told Storm her full name was beautiful, and always used it. And yet…

"You lied to me." She snatched her arm back. Storm was glad to see her friends, even though she didn't truly understand any of this right now. But Octavius? That was more complicated.

She leaned forward as anger overtook her.

"We're blood, Octavius. But you didn't tell me that, did you?" She spat the words out. "You knew. And you lied to me."

Octavius shook his head wearily. He didn't seem to care that she'd shouted at him in front of everyone else. "I never lied to you, Stormchaser."

"You did. You knew we were blood. My mother, Dalia, was your niece! You could have told me at any point when we were in your office. Any time. But you didn't. No. And you let them send me here." She put her hand to her chest. "Am I it? Am I the last of the family? Or do you have more, and I'm just the expendable one?"

She was conscious of Reban walking back towards her, a deep frown on his face. Not a single person in the crowd was murmuring to each other. Every eye was on her. Every ear was listening.

For a flash of a moment, Octavius's eyes had the glint of steel she recognized from parliament. But she could almost see him give himself a shake.

He drew himself up to his full height, which was still well beneath Storm's shoulder. But even though Octavius was tiny, he had an aura about him. A regalness that she'd never seen in anyone else.

"I fought for you in the chamber. I fought for you, because you were my family." He looked her straight in the eye. "And I'd fight for you again. I came here because *you* are here. Not for anyone else."

It was the way he said the words. With authority. With belief.

Her skin prickled, and Reban came and stood by her side. He slid his arm around her shoulders and she stiffened. They didn't share contact like this. Not ever.

"This can wait until later, Octavius." She could hear the unconcealed anger in Reban's voice. She could feel the solidarity of his arm around her shoulder. It was like them against the world. The two of them against this horde of imposters who had just invaded their territory.

Silas jumped down from the roof of the transporter and started shouting orders at people. There was a moment's hesitation, as if people were trying to decide whether to follow his directions or not.

Octavius blinked, then turned, his cloak swirling out around him as he walked back to where the rest of the Stipulators had gathered.

Reban looked around. He nodded. "Leif, Lincoln, Jesa."

Jesa quickly introduced her family: "Reban, this is my mother Kayna, and my brother, Caleb."

Lincoln followed suit. "My sister, Arta. And my mother, Tamb."

Storm could see all their faces practically recoiling at being introduced to Reban Don. Back on Earthasia, no one wanted to be known by name to the Stipulators. It usually spelled trouble. Seeing Reban Don in his new capacity would take some getting used to for the newcomers.

Reban couldn't hide a sigh. "I'm not sure what your plans are, but you're welcome to come back to the shack tonight."

Lincoln looked around, confused. "Blaine's shack? It's here?"

Storm nodded. "Literally. We've just moved it. It took us more than five days to get everything here, so it's probably not quite as you remember." She shrugged. "It's much worse." Storm looked at the river, then turned to Reban. "We'd better hit the water supply before they claim it."

"Agreed."

Another voice sounded from her side. "Storm?"

Her skin prickled in recognition. Her eyes widened. "Dell?"

Storm's chest tightened as she turned towards him. He was her childhood friend – for a long time, he'd been her *only* friend. He'd been like family to her.

Dell's dark hair was longer than before. His eyes were sadder. But she was so pleased to see him that she wrapped her arms around his neck. "I can't believe you're here! It's so good to see you."

He pulled himself back a little awkwardly as he glanced at the rest of them. He'd met Lincoln and Leif at the camp for the Trials. He knew who Reban Don was, but he'd never seen them together before. He hadn't witnessed the revelation that Reban Don was Storm's father, or seen her since the last time they'd sat by the loch in Ambulus City.

She reached over and touched his cheek. "What are you doing here?" She gave a smile. "You hate dinosaurs, Dell."

He flinched. "Do you think I came here willingly? We were promised the dinosaurs were dead. We were promised food and the chance of a home of our own. All that, if me and my dad would help construct the encampment." He pointed to a strange machine sitting behind one of the transporters. "Apparently, it can strip a tree and prepare it for use quickly. If we all work, we can have the outside wall up in three days."

Storm tried to process what he'd just said. She glanced behind her into the forest. "You'll make the walls from what? Our trees?" She shook her head. She could already see a group of muscular, lean men taking instruction from Silas. "This is our forest. If you strip out the trees, we'll lose our protection around the shack. We'll lose the plants we need to disguise the smell."

Dell wrinkled his nose. "The smell of what?"

Storm could feel her frustration building. "Us, dummy. People. Humans. Dinosaurs work on their senses. You don't want them to be able to smell you – that's why we use the evergreen leaves. They can't pick out our scent when it's masked by the evergreen. The shack is covered in them." She reached out her hand. "I'm not sure how on earth you can cover a whole compound."

An insect with bright orange wings buzzed around them. Dell sighed and tried to bat it away, then shrugged. "But we shouldn't need them, should we? The T-rexes, raptors and pterosaurs are gone. It's just these pesky things that are left."

"If you think they're the only predators on Piloria, you're more stupid that you look," commented Reban as he walked away. "Let's go, Storm. We need to collect our water." His eyes narrowed again. "And we need to decide if want to relocate our shack. Again."

Storm licked her lips. She'd just found her friends again. All her friends. Faces that had popped up in her dreams for the last few months. People she'd daydreamed about during the long days here, desperate to talk to them again.

And there were others. People she hadn't met before. New conversations to be had.

Her head turned from side to side. Reban was already striding towards the river, ignoring everyone else.

"What are we going to do?" Lincoln's mother's voice sounded strained. She looked tired. In fact, they all looked tired.

Storm turned and looked at Jesa with her family. The only time she'd seen those faces before had been on the crumpled sketch glued to the wall in Blaine's shack. Both of them had clearly aged. Jesa's mother not so well. It was odd finally seeing them in the flesh.

She felt a little pang as she looked between Jesa's and Lincoln's families. The affection within each group was obvious. Years and years of growing together, supporting each other and loving each other.

Years that she'd never experienced with her father and would never get back. This was her first experience of sharing space with two people who were her family. Her relationship with Reban was still in the early stages. She'd gone from hating him completely to becoming intrigued by him. Reban liked to wear a hard shell, but every now and then she'd seen flashes of something else in him. Concern about her. Compassion.

As for Octavius? She was still angry with him. She'd always been curious about Octavius – about why he'd picked her to be his aide in parliament. Now she knew why. Because she was family. He'd kept her at arm's length, but treated her with respect; talking to her about parliament, Piloria and subjects that mattered. Would it really have been so hard to reveal their relationship to her? He wouldn't have been at risk. She was the daughter of his niece. While Stipulators weren't supposed to marry or have families of their own, there were no rules about sisters, brothers, nieces and nephews. *That* was what made her angry with him. And her anger still burned fiercely.

People were starting to move away from the transporters. One guy climbed into the seat of the tree-processing machine, and others collected large saws from another transporter and headed towards the forest. *Their* forest.

These newcomers meant it. They meant to set up home here and start building their wall, right now. It was late afternoon. Dusk and night-time were the most dangerous times on Piloria – it was when the majority of predators hunted their prey. When it was only two of them, they'd managed to stay relatively safe. Avoid any predators they knew about – and Storm didn't want to find out about any others with four hundred unprotected people near her. This was the prelude to chaos.

Reban walked back, his water canisters slung across his body. "Anyone who's coming with us, fill up your canister now."

There were a few seconds of hesitation. Then Lincoln and Leif gestured to those around them and strode towards the river. Storm watched as one of the Stipulators stopped them en route, angrily gesturing towards the work crew.

But the guys were firm. They shook their heads and continued on to the river, arriving back a few minutes later. Lincoln nodded towards the forest.

But Storm was watching one of the transporters being unpacked. She had no idea a transporter could hold quite so many supplies. There were low-slung camp beds in tight rolls, mats, blankets, a variety of foods and a whole host of other things.

She wrinkled her nose. "Do you think you guys should wait a bit? Get your share of the supplies before we go into the forest?" There were so many people walking in every direction. It was unlikely right now that anyone would realize Jesa's and Lincoln's families had disappeared.

Reban spoke gruffly. "We only have one bed and one mat. It might be an idea. And try to get your share of food. But be quick about it. We'll wait for you just inside the trees."

It was clear Reban wanted to get away as quickly as possible. Storm understood that. Maybe it was the amount of people now on the continent they'd started to consider "theirs" – or maybe it was the potential predators they could attract. After a few seconds' hesitation, the rest of them made their way over to the various transporters. Lots of people were unloading supplies. There didn't seem to be any process to it. Some were being dumped in the middle of the grass. Some around trees. One group had even started to erect a tent-like shelter.

It didn't take long for Storm and the others to gather what they could carry and dart back into the forest.

Reban was already tired of waiting, his foot tapping impatiently on the forest floor.

He led the way and Storm stayed at the back to make sure no one got lost on the way to their shack. The truth was, it wasn't too far from the clearing where the Stipulators planned to build the compound.

Jesa, Leif and Lincoln had all been to Blaine's shack previously. Reban and Storm had transported as much of it as they could – but things were definitely less than perfect, and the rest of the new arrivals couldn't hide the horror on their faces as they walked slowly inside. There would be enough room for everyone to sleep inside – but barely. All cooking and eating would have to be done outside.

Kayna spoke first. "This is where...Blaine stayed?" She was blinking back tears. Back home, Piloria was overcrowded. Lincoln and his family had been relegated to one of the cave dwellings complete with damp and no natural light, and had to share with another family. Storm had no idea where Kayna had stayed but it was clear that, however bad conditions had been for her, the thought of the father of her children living like this for nine years horrified her.

Storm pressed her lips together and tried not to be offended. Reban was already trying to strike up the fire. It was going to be a long, long night.

She sagged down and crossed her legs. The last few days had been exhausting. Being chased by super raptors, dragging the shack halfway across a continent, then having four hundred unexpected guests was more than a little draining.

Her relationship with her father was delicate. Having seven other people crammed into their tiny space could only cause conflict.

Storm rested her head on her knees for a second and hid her face.

One of those other people was Lincoln. When he'd left she'd really wondered if they would ever see each other again. But now he was back, right in front of her. And she couldn't quite work out why it made her so twitchy.

ELEVEN

LINCOLN

He still couldn't really believe he was here. And so was Storm.

She was alive. Her skin tone was deeper, her muscles more defined, her clothes a little more worn. But she was still Storm.

He pulled out some tunics from the pile he'd taken from the transporter to give to her later. Blaine's clothes had been a hotchpotch of different materials stitched together. He guessed that living on Piloria permanently was hard on clothes.

The curtain at the entrance to the shack was pinned back, and just outside Reban was stirring something above the campfire. Lincoln's mother was helping, adding some of the supplies they'd brought from camp. He could tell she was nervous. Reban had been the Chief Stipulator in their area for as long as he could remember. The Stipulators had been both terrifying and threatening, ruling Earthasia with ruthless, unchallenged discipline. It would be hard for his mother to see Reban in a new light, even though he'd been exiled here in disgrace.

Lincoln leaned back on his palms. He was sitting on the floor in the main part of the shack, staring outside. Most of the others were outside around the fire. He could see the differences in Reban, even if the rest of them couldn't. Reban's time on Piloria had actually taken the edge off his temper. What they'd witnessed earlier with Silas was nothing to the way Reban used to erupt.

There was a clicking noise to his left. He turned to see two insects about the size of his finger fighting with each other under a bush. He smiled. It seemed that everyone had a battle to fight on Piloria.

"You transported this whole place?" Lincoln looked around in wonder. "How on earth did you manage that?"

"Hard work," said Storm quickly. "And sweat. Oh, and one of the old transporters."

Lincoln shook his head. "I can't believe we've ended up in the same place."

"And I'm still not sold on it," said Leif as he thudded down next to Lincoln. He ran his fingers through his hair. "What on earth are we doing?"

Storm sat down on Lincoln's other side. She pulled her knees up to her chest and rested her arms and head on them, watching the flickering fire outside. "Leif, what happened when you got back? What happened with Rune's and Kronar's brothers and sisters?" Her words were hesitant – as if she were scared to even ask the question.

Leif didn't play nice. He was always direct and to the point. "As soon as we got back, and you weren't with us, the extra rations stopped and they got flung out of the medico care centre – just like Arta."

Storm winced and shifted uncomfortably. She opened her mouth to ask another question, but Leif kept talking.

"We were lucky that Lincoln managed to keep a hold of some of the ointment for them all. But within months of being back, there were virtually no rations left. I had to take them back to Norden."

Storm leaned forward. "So they weren't in Ambulus City when the riots happened?"

Leif shook his head. "No. But I have no idea what's happened to them, or how they are. Or how my parents are."

Lincoln could hear the pain in his voice. Leif hated this place. He'd lost two friends here, then came back to try to help their families. Now, he was back again.

"Why didn't you stay in Norden?" he asked.

Leif's eyes went automatically in one direction: Jesa. She was sitting to the side, twisting a lock of her hair around her fingers, obviously lost in her own thoughts. He sighed. "Things are bad everywhere. Norden haven't cut back on the rations as much, and at least in Norden there are rivers. There's at least half a chance of fish to supplement the rations. I knew the kids would be better off there. Kronar and Rune might not be there any more, but I could have got by."

He took a deep breath as his eyes fixed on Jesa again. "But when someone else you care about is already living on half the rations they should be, and starving to death, wouldn't you go back and share what you could?"

Lincoln swallowed and glanced at Storm. Her eyes were fixed on the ground. "I guess I would," he answered quietly.

Storm was silent for a few minutes, as they all sat and stared at the flickering fire beyond the shelter of the shack. Caleb had hardly said a word since he'd got here. He had moved over next to Jesa. Maybe it was all the overwhelming sensations of setting foot on the dinosaur continent. Or maybe it was the fact he was sitting in the shack his father had lived in for the last nine years, up until his death. Lincoln couldn't even begin to imagine how Caleb was feeling.

There was a noise behind him. A snuffle. Lincoln was on his feet in an instant, his hand slapping the ground next to him, searching for his weapon, his eyes on his mother and sister, wondering how best to keep them safe.

His heart squeezed. This was it. This was how things would be for the rest of their lives. They'd never be able to truly relax again.

Leif had twisted around, a large knife in one hand. They all froze in position.

A snout – or a something – stuck through the few leaf fronds on the sides of the shack, at ground level.

Storm leaned backwards. "Barney..." she whispered as she reached out her arms towards the snout.

There was a weird little noise, then a small creature –

only the size of a few hands, pushed its hooked beak and tiny head into their shack.

Kayna let out a squeal and jumped back. Caleb lifted up one of the clay pots with both hands, ready to smash it on the animal's skull.

"No!" yelled Storm as she rolled across the space, putting her back between Caleb and the creature.

But Caleb's hand was already moving. The pot smashed into Storm's shoulder, splintering all over the ground, and she winced, bending down to pick up the tiny dinosaur at her feet.

Kayna's eyes were filled with fear.

Storm tucked the animal under her arm and turned to the others. "Calm down. There's nothing to worry about. This is Barney."

"This is *what*?" Kayna looked horrified, but her feet couldn't take her any further away from the creature.

Storm stroked its thick skin. The creature had a hook-like beak at the front and deep-green colouring on the skin underneath its neck. There was red plumage along its ridged spine, contrasting with the dark grey skin elsewhere.

"This is Barney," explained Storm. "He eats plants," she said firmly. "He's from one of the families of horned dinosaurs."

"It looks more like a bird, and I don't mean a pterosaur," said Lincoln quickly.

"What's it doing in here?" asked Kayna.

Storm circled her shoulder, obviously trying to shake off

any remnants of the clay pot. "It lives here."

Caleb looked at the fragments splintered around his feet, then at Storm's obviously injured shoulder. "Sorry," he murmured.

Lincoln could see the tiny tic in Storm's jawline. She was trying so hard not to show how annoyed she was. He glanced around. To everyone else, this place was a mess. A shack. And certainly not a home. But over the last six months, that's exactly what this place had become – Storm's home. And right now it must feel as if they'd all ambushed her.

He stood up and walked over. It was the smallest dinosaur he'd ever seen. He reached over and touched it, the skin rough against his palms. The red fronds weren't as soft as they looked. But the creature almost seemed to nuzzle into his palm as he moved his hand around its strange beak. "Hello, Barney," he said.

Jesa appeared at his side, obviously curious. "Where on earth did he come from?" She frowned. "And is he a he?"

Storm shrugged. "I have no idea. He followed me from the watering hole one day, and just kept scratching around. It was almost like he found me instead of the other way around."

Reban made a snorting sound from the fire. "Everyone who wants food better come now."

He looked around, then shook his head. "We only have two dishes."

Storm shook her head and lifted a stack of grey plates. "Procured. From the supplies of the *Invincible*."

"What else have we stolen from them?" he asked.

"We haven't stolen anything," said Lincoln. Then he shrugged. "I might have acquired some extra tunics for you." He walked over and picked up the dark-coloured pile of clothes, then stopped and ran his fingers over the fabric. "How do you make cloth?"

"What?" Leif stared at him with a confused look on his face.

Lincoln asked again. "How do you make cloth? I don't have a clue. I don't even know where to start. Not for a second." He looked down at the pile again and then up at the watching audience. "What if the stuff we brought from Earthasia is it? What if no one ever gets to go back and bring more?" The realization started to scare him and he couldn't hold the words back. He walked around the remnants of the shack and pointed at things. "The plates and clay pots – could we make more? What about the paper?" There were still a few of Blaine's drawings of dinosaurs glued to the wall. Storm must have put them back up. "What about graphite?"

He stared down at his feet as he remembered the one item Blaine had asked for every year.

"Sneakers. What about sneakers? I mean, how do you even start to make things like these?" Even though the temperature was warm, his skin felt cool. He tilted one foot to the side as he gaped at the sole of his sneaker. "What is this even made from?"

Silence had fallen around him. He lifted his head and watched his mother swallow awkwardly. All of this had only just occurred to him and he couldn't pretend he didn't feel a little panicked by it. Everyone else was staring at him. Jesa's mother had wrapped her arms around herself and was running her hands up and down them. Caleb just looked confused.

"What about the dinosaurs?" he said out loud. "Being here for two weeks was one thing. But being here for life? How can we possibly stay safe? Every second of every day there could be a predator around the corner. Look at the panic we had earlier with something that doesn't come up to our knees." He glanced at Jesa and her family. "Blaine survived here for nine years." He gestured towards Storm. "You two have survived here for the last six months. One person, or two people, can live relatively quietly and avoid attracting too much attention. But four hundred?"

Reban cleared his throat loudly. His violet eyes were fixed on Lincoln's. The message was clear. *Shut up.* It was amazing how every now and then the briefest flash of his past life as Chief Stipulator came out. "I said, the food is ready."

Caleb and Jesa looked pale, and both mums were muttering quietly to each other. It was like reality was starting to hit. Storm started handing the plates out, while keeping her gaze on Lincoln. The rest of them moved towards the pot Reban was stirring over the fire, holding out their plates so he could pile some of the concoction onto them.

Storm held back.

"What?" he mouthed.

She moved alongside him as she handed him a plate. "Why did you do that?" Her words were barely audible.

He shook his head a little. "I didn't mean to, I just—"

"You scared everyone," she hissed. He started as her eyes flashed. "They don't need that, Lincoln. They just got here. They haven't even had a chance to acclimatize without you terrifying them about the dinosaurs."

He understood she was angry, but it wasn't fair to be angry with him. "Last time around, we knew we were going home. This time – we're not. It's different. And none of us had time to prepare."

Her gaze was steady. "Home just changed continent." She turned and walked over to the fire, holding out her plate to get some food.

Lincoln's feet seemed like they were frozen to the spot – no matter what the temperature around him was.

Home. That was it. The thing he hadn't really let sink in yet.

From now on, Piloria was home.

PART FIVE

THE CAMP

TWELVE

STORMCHASER

She hadn't slept a wink. How could she? All of a sudden she was surrounded by people. Noises. Other people's loud breathing in the middle of the night. Who made that weird grunting sound?

Storm put her hands on her hips and arched her back as she looked around.

Everyone else was still sleeping. Even Lincoln.

His hair had grown since she'd last seen him. He'd always had the shaggy blond look, but it had got even longer, touching the collar of his tunic now.

She watched as he slept. Every now and then he gave a little twitch, as if he'd just remembered something, or was being pulled out of his dream.

Arta was next to him, her skin so much improved. She had some colour now too. Her cheeks were a bit pinker and a little more filled out. That wouldn't last long around here, unless they'd brought extra food with them. Every single thing that Storm and Reban ate, they'd foraged.

Moving had been a pain. They'd just set up their own kind of vegetable plot back at the last site of the shack. Inevitably, like other things, it had been left behind. They'd brought a few of the plants with them in the hope they'd be able to start something similar here.

She looked over at Jesa and her family. Caleb was curled so tightly into a fetal position that Storm almost smiled. It was the ultimate sign that he didn't want to be here. Kayna looked exhausted, even though she was sleeping. And Leif? He looked angry. No change there then. In a crowded environment, Reban seemed to have found the only spot where no one was touching him while he slept.

It seemed that sleep would continue to be a stranger to Storm. No matter how hard she'd tried, she had only caught a few hours. The rising sun was starting to send orange and yellow streaks through the sky. She left the shack and walked towards the edge of the jungle, looking out at the campsite.

It was like a whole new world. Most people were lying in the open on bed mats around the remains of various campfires. There were a few hastily erected tents. Around twenty large trees had been stripped and then driven into the ground on the far side of the camp. The start of the camp wall. Would it really offer any protection? They'd need to cut down most of the forest here to have enough trees to finish the job.

It still made her catch her breath – around four hundred

people now breathing the air on Piloria alongside her. Was it really so wrong that the thought made her skin itch?

Even though it was early, lots of people were already awake. A few were close enough that she could hear them talking.

"What about Heba? Any sign of him?" muttered one man.

The guy next to him shook his head. "Lana too. No one has seen either of them since the incident with the duckbills and the triceratops." He gave a shudder. "Every time I close my eyes, I see Frok lying on the ground, trampled."

The other guy stared out across the grass. "I thought this place would be better – not worse. Three people gone already, and we've only just got here."

A shiver passed over Storm's skin. Lincoln had told her what had happened on the journey from the ship. Part of her wanted to go and look for the two people who had gone missing, but another part of her also knew it could be a very bad idea.

She looked out over the compound again. There were kids playing at the side of the river, splashing each other with the flowing water. There were seven of them, all of varying ages.

Some people were only just waking up, others still sleeping. A few were gathered at the river, watching the children. One man looked as if he were trying to hook up some kind of net at the edge of the river. In the centre of camp a fire had been started and a large pot was bubbling above it.

People were so busy with everything around them that they didn't notice the movement in the sky. Storm almost missed it too – it was only a flicker in the corner of her eye.

The first of the creatures swooped low, like a bolt from the blue. It looked similar to a pterosaur, with a sharp beak and broad wingspan. There was one loud squawk and before the kids had a chance to even look up, the slim man with the net next to them had been caught in the large claws of the terrifying creature.

Storm yelled and started running towards the river. Heads turned and people started to panic. The man was screaming and struggling, his legs scrabbling madly in the air. One of the children had been hit by the huge beating wings of the creature and landed face down in the water.

The weight of the man must have surprised the creature, as it struggled, dipping up and down in the air. Storm was still running, but she was too far away. She'd never reach them in time. She didn't even know what it was. As she ran towards it, she realized it wasn't a pterosaur – it was much, much bigger. Its body was smaller, a strange mixture of blues and reds, but the wingspan was huge, each wing double the size of an average human. The creature had an elongated pink neck, topped by a small head with a red crest, and a long yellow beak that looked razor-sharp. It had only managed to rise a little into the air but the ferociousness of the huge flapping wings stopped anyone getting close, flattening a man who'd been rushing to help.

But then another little figure barrelled forward – Octavius – throwing himself into the air and grabbing at the feet of the dangling man. The increased weight made the creature drop once more, then finally lose its grasp.

The two figures fell to the ground.

A head raised and a pair of grey eyes met hers as Storm continued to thud across the grass. Octavius gave the slightest shake of his head, as if he were trying to warn her not to get closer. The rest of the crowd were standing back in terror. Behind her, Storm heard a woman let out an ear-piercing shriek as she yelled the name of her husband.

The rescued man was lying unconscious and injured at Octavius's feet; the man who'd tried to help and the child who'd been knocked over were still face down in the river. There was another shout. Roban. He must have been near the camp and heard the commotion. She knew he would be hot on her heels.

The creature was still flapping above them, squawking in anger at losing its prey. But it was determined. Octavius had just bent over the injured man when it descended on him, its sharp claws digging into his shoulders. His head flew backwards and Storm's stomach clenched.

She was almost there. Her legs powered on.

Her head flicked one way, then the other. She glanced at the kids and the other man in the river. Should she help them first?

But the thud of the flapping wings focused her attention – that and the huge gusts of air.

People nearby were cowering, terrified of the giant creature. Another squawk sounded above her. Darn it. More than one. Octavius's face was gripped with pain...then the creature flapped even harder and rose into the air, taking him with it. Storm's heart lurched.

Up, up he went. Higher and higher, just as she finally reached the spot on the ground where he'd been. Reban arrived at her side, wading into the water to deal with the victims. Suddenly the large birdlike dinosaur seemed to stutter in the air, dropping from its great height, obviously still unused to the weight of a human. Storm didn't hesitate, she leaped up, grabbing fruitlessly above her.

Octavius wasn't even meeting her gaze. His legs weren't pedalling in the air like the man he'd just rescued. He seemed paralysed by fear – something that didn't equate with the Octavius she knew.

Pain shot through her chest. She'd shouted at him. She'd acted like she hated him. And she'd really felt it. That hate and anger had simmered in her chest, real and alive.

Octavius. Her great-uncle.

He hadn't hesitated. It didn't matter that he was the smallest man in the compound, he'd leaped to save that man. Where were the Stipulators? Where were the other, bigger adults? Men or women with more height and more muscle?

She leaped again, but it was no use, the creature seemed to be gathering its strength. The driving force contained within its thin body was powering those huge wings in a way she couldn't begin to understand.

She started shouting. "Octavius! Octavius! Fight back!" Even she could hear the desperation in her voice. She jumped again and again, conscious of the fact he was getting higher and higher, further and further away from her. The second creature was circling overhead, squawking loudly. It sounded angry.

There was thudding behind her. "Now!" came the yell.

Jesa ran in front of Storm, raising her crossbow in the air and taking aim. The first arrow was batted away easily by the creature's flapping wings, as if it was merely a feather.

Storm's hands went to her waist. Her knives – she'd forgotten them. She'd left them behind. She'd never done that. The whole time she'd lived here, she'd never left the shack without her knives. What was wrong with her?

"Storm!" The voice jerked her from her guilty thoughts. Lincoln was panting at her side, pushing her sheathed knives into her hands. She grabbed the first one as another arrow launched into the air. Jesa's aim was true, but the creature turned its head, batting the arrow away with its beak.

Storm took a deep breath as the creature climbed further in the air. There was a flash in front of her – her vision momentarily blocked. The second creature had swooped down, clawing in the air, trying to take Octavius from its rival.

Its attack sent the first creature diving closer to the ground, its large flapping wings catching Storm so she landed flat on her back. The second beast gave a squawk, furious at being unsuccessful, and turned its attention to

Storm, trying to grab her with its claws. Where was Reban?

Lincoln's axe sliced into the second monster's body from underneath, catching it by surprise. The creature let out a strangled, panicked noise, which seemed to distract its rival that was clutching Octavius. Storm found her focus. She gripped her knife and took aim.

For the briefest of seconds, she filtered out all the surrounding noise and images, focusing entirely on the slim body of the creature overhead. The knife flew from her hand. She could almost hear it whistle as it cut through the air, bending a little at the last minute and landing squarely in the centre of the creature's chest.

There was a moment where nothing seemed to happen. Then the claws opened and the creature plummeted towards the ground in one simultaneous motion.

Reban was ready, his legs bent and his arms outstretched. *That* was what he'd been doing. He'd positioned himself squarely underneath the monster.

Octavius's limp frame fell. If he hit the ground unimpeded, he'd shatter every bone in his small body. But Reban broke his fall, not quite catching him entirely, as the weight seemed heavier than he'd expected, but managing to deflect him towards the river.

It was as if the world came back into colour around Storm. The noise invaded her ears, people shouting and crying. Lincoln ran in front of her, dropping to his knees in the water and scooping Octavius up with his long arms. Reban was lying on his back, clearly winded, gasping loudly.

"Is he all right?" It was Leif. They'd pulled Octavius up the bank and the Norden boy was checking him over as he lay motionless on the grass beside her.

She bent down, not quite sure what to say, and took Octavius's frail hand in hers. She patted it a few times. "Octavius. Octavius, wake up. You're safe now."

Kayna pointed to the blood pooling around his shoulder. "Look. What can we use to patch him up?"

Leif caught Storm's eye. "I'll go get some leaves. They'll do for now," he said quietly.

She looked around. The place had erupted into chaos – mainly around the two bodies of the creatures that were now lying half-in, half-out of the river. A mother was screaming, rocking back and forth in the water, cradling a small child in her arms.

Someone Storm recognized from the medico care centre rushed over.

Octavius gave a groan as his eyes flickered open. His complexion was deathly pale and he looked even older than before.

Storm leaned over and pressed both hands firmly down on his shoulder to try to stop the bleeding.

"Aargh!" Octavius yelped in pain.

"Sorry." Storm winced.

Reban crawled over next to her. "Is he okay?"

As she turned to reply, the dark shadow of a figure cast over them. "What on earth was that? I thought the pterosaurs were dead? We poisoned them. You said you poisoned them."

Storm looked up. Silas was pointing at Lincoln. He was wearing his black cloak as if he were still back on Earthasia, still part of the government.

Lincoln scowled. "No, we planted a virus – and we have no real idea of the effect of it. And that? That wasn't a pterosaur like we met before. That was nothing like them. It was completely different colours and at least three times the size."

"Quetzal...coatlus." Octavius's voice came out as a wheeze. All their heads turned. "What?" queried Storm.

"Quetzalcoatlus," he gasped again. "That's what they are."

Storm didn't even try to repeat it. She just glared at Silas. "Different creature. Different virus."

Leif reappeared with a pile of thick leaves in his hands. He didn't even wait for anyone else to move, he just bent down and started stuffing them in around Octavius's shoulder wounds.

"How's the kid that landed in the water, and the two men?" Leif asked.

Jesa frowned. "What?"

"The kid – and the man that Octavius saved. That thing had a hold of him too. Here." He thrust some of the leaves towards her. "Go find the man and patch him up. Check on the two who landed in the water. We'll need one of the medics to take a look at these wounds. Somehow I don't think leaves are going to cut it."

Reban sighed. "I pulled one of them out of the water. He didn't look good." He pushed himself up, and stretched out his back. He was moving slower than normal – obviously injured, but not admitting it. He turned to Silas. "This place is a mess. You need to get things better organized. Those kids were unsupervised. You left them vulnerable."

Silas sneered – not the least bit worried about anything Reban was saying to him. "Who could have predicted those…things? And we have other weapons – we just haven't had a chance to get them set up yet. Once we have our outer posts, we'll have guards who can spot any predator that comes from the land or the air. We'll be ready."

Reban stepped forward and poked his finger at Silas's chest. "And in the meantime?" There was silence. "That is exactly what makes you a fool – the fact you think that's how you should do things. The dinosaurs aren't going to wait for you to get ready to defend your nice new camp."

Silas let out a hollow laugh. "What do you want to do, Reban? Hide in the forest? You're a great leader, aren't you?" He gestured to the thinning trees behind them. Already the forest was looking less dense. The more the newcomers stripped it of trees, the less cover and protection Reban and Storm's shack would have.

People were starting to crowd around them. A few were helping with the wounded, but the rest were more curious about the obviously strained dialogue between the two Chief Stipulators.

"You there!" Reban's voice was fierce as he pointed at one of the medics. "Come with me and help patch Octavius up."

Reban gestured to Leif and Lincoln, and between the two of them and the medic, they picked up Octavius again, moving in long strides back towards the forest. Reban watched for a moment before turning to Silas.

"You're a fool, Silas. You still think that you're back on Earthasia. These people aren't yours. You're not the leader. Octavius is and always will be," he said angrily as he moved past. "You're in the middle of a dinosaur continent, and you haven't even unpacked your weapons?" Reban gave a snort. "I give you three days. Maximum."

Storm's stomach clenched. This was a flash of the old Reban. The Chief Stipulator who'd ruled Ambulus City with a reign of terror. It was almost like he was enjoying this – enjoying making a fool of Silas – and it made her distinctly uncomfortable. It wasn't that she didn't hate Silas too – of course she did. But the Reban she'd stayed with the last few months had been different. More fierce, but somehow also soft. More amenable. Staying alive was a full-time job on Piloria. Everything else really had to be left aside. There was no time for anger and resentment. And there was definitely no time for power struggles. There were four hundred people here whose lives were at risk. People had to learn to work together, not bicker amongst each other.

She sighed as another medic stared down at the pack in his hands, glanced once at Silas, then hurried after Reban. It seemed he was more inclined to follow the old Chief Stipulator than the new one. Interesting.

Jesa and her family turned to follow, leaving only Storm

in the centre of the circle of spectators. People moved past her carrying the coughing and spluttering kid from the river, and supporting a pale-faced man who was bleeding as badly as Octavius was.

Some of the people started to murmur. "Does Silas really know what he's doing?"

"Maybe we should stick with Reban Don. He's at least lived here already. He knows what we're facing."

Storm smiled. Even though Silas was now standing in the middle of the encampment, dressed in his ridiculous Chief Stipulator uniform, it seemed that his authority was diminishing by the second.

She shot Silas a look of disgust before striding back to the river, splashing through the shallows and yanking her knife from the chest of the quetzalcoatlus. She stared down at the knife, then wiped it on her trousers as she strode back past the onlookers and Silas.

"Did I forget to say?" She raised her eyebrows as she walked past Silas. "Welcome to Piloria."

THIRTEEN

LINCOLN

It had taken over an hour for the medic to stitch Octavius's wounds. They'd all just sat around the shack watching, and feeling generally helpless.

Lincoln hated the expression on Storm's face. It was clear there was so much bubbling under the surface. By the time the medic had finished, given Octavius something for the pain and let him sleep for a number of hours, the sun was starting to set in the sky.

Jesa had gone back to camp to check on the other survivors. When she came back, her face was streaked with tears.

"The man who got hit by the wings and knocked into the river? He died. They think he broke his neck. The kid should be okay in a few days. The other man – his wounds are really deep, like Octavius's. I took them some of the evergreens and some of the yellow vines so they could make some fresh ointment, to see if it would help."

Lincoln nodded. Of course. They'd brought some ointment with them, but on Piloria they literally had a fresh supply at their fingertips. It had helped those with the blistering plague back home but the rest of the people here wouldn't know it was what Blaine had used when he'd been bitten by a T-rex and had deep, festering wounds on his legs. Now, they would discover just how incredible the ointment really was.

Storm appeared at his side. "I'm going to take a walk to the beach. Want to join me?"

"Is it safe?" Last time he'd been here they'd been reluctant to move anywhere at night, since it was the time most predators hunted.

Storm nodded. "So far. It's a clear path to the sea. I was there last night and never encountered anything."

"Okay." He felt Reban's eyes burn into his back as the two set off towards the beach.

They'd spent a night on a beach in Piloria once before, after they'd raided the pterosaur nest, but this beach was different. The sand was darker and more shingly.

Storm walked down to the water straight away and waded in.

"No tylosauruses here?" Lincoln asked.

Storm shook her head. "Nope. I have something that keeps them away." She glanced over her shoulder. "Have a seat, and wait a while."

Lincoln couldn't help but frown. What was she talking about?

He settled down on the shore and ran his fingers through his hair. Storm was silhouetted by the setting sun against a purple sky. The ocean stretched out in the background. The ocean that led back to Earthasia.

"I wonder what's happening back home," he said.

"What do you think's happening?" she asked over her shoulder while keeping her eyes on the ocean. "Just how bad were things when you left?"

"I've never seen anything like it. My last sight of Ambulus City was watching it burn as the ship left. There were riots. Everyone was starving." He picked up some of the sand and let it run through his fingers. "I never knew..." His stomach tightened. Now he was here with Storm, he felt as if he could finally say the words that had been circulating in his head for so long. "I never knew just how delicate a balance it all was. I knew about the food shortages. Everyone did. But I never imagined the impact of bringing the ointment back."

Storm turned around in the water to face him. "But that was always your intention."

He sighed and shook the sand off his hand. "I know. I needed it for Arta. But I didn't know how quickly things would change. They never really told us anything. I mean, just how many people were actually dying from the blistering plague? Hundreds? Thousands?"

She frowned. "Surely it couldn't have been that many?"

He shook his head again. "I think it was more than any of us really understood. As soon as the ointment got out there..." His voice tailed off.

Storm was holding her arms wide, fingers trailing on the water. Her forehead creased in a deep frown. "How did the ointment get out there? What happened when you got back?"

He didn't get a chance to answer, as at that moment a smooth head broke the surface of the water near to Storm.

He leaped to his feet, before realizing that she hadn't jumped back. Instead, she was stretching her fingers out to the creature and moving towards it.

No. It couldn't be. It just couldn't.

Her soft voice carried in the wind towards him. "Milo. Come here, gorgeous. Where have you been these last few days? Did I throw you off by moving down the coast?"

He watched, almost hypnotized. Their shapes were black in the twilight. Storm dipped her head to Milo's, putting both hands on either side of the plesiosaur's head and touching her own forehead against it.

Could he really believe what he was witnessing? This was the creature that had saved Storm back on Earthasia, when she'd been caught underneath a boat. This was the creature she'd swum with on a regular basis back at the lake in Ambulus City. The creature that had helped Storm in the sea for the final Trial that had made her the winner.

He'd never really understood their bond. Storm had told him about Milo, and he had witnessed a few things himself. But this? This was different.

Now, he was able to witness everything first-hand.

Storm was talking softly, stroking Milo's head. The beach

near the shore would be too shallow for such a creature and Storm hooked one hand around Milo's head and neck and floated, allowing herself to be pulled further out to sea by the dark grey creature with its large flippers. Lincoln watched in wonder.

It was almost like a choreographed dance. The creature glided through the water, allowing Storm to tread water as it circled her. He could hear Storm laugh. She seemed genuinely happy and at ease.

Lincoln shifted on the sand. Would he enter the sea here, day or night? After his last few experiences, probably not. But Storm seemed unafraid. It was clear she trusted Milo. She trusted that the creature would know if there was danger in the sea around them.

He stood up and brushed the sand from his hands, taking a few steps closer to the waves. Storm was still laughing and splashing. Watching her was mesmerizing. For Lincoln, every dinosaur was a predator. Even the plant eaters, like the titanosaurus or the diplodocuses, were so big that one swipe of their tail made them nearly as dangerous as the meat eaters.

Lincoln thought about the little aquilops Storm had claimed was also a friend. That was it. She was making *friends* with dinosaurs. It was something he never would have contemplated. Not really. They were surrounded by a continent of dinosaurs. He knew they weren't all bad, but he'd secretly hoped that when they'd got back here the worst of the dinosaurs would be dead and the rest could just be avoided. Storm was the only person who'd ever suggested trying to live in harmony with them.

He kept watching, sitting there for a while. A tiny seed of warmth spread through him as he watched the silhouettes in the water against the backdrop of the midnight-blue sky, which was now speckled with stars.

But then Lincoln remembered that far, far across that water was another land, another home, which was probably in turmoil. Turmoil he'd created.

The warmth left him, chasing itself from his insides and evaporating into the breeze coming from the sea. Storm let out a whistle and he lifted his head in time to see her wave her hand and wade back out of the waves, water streaming from her hair and skin.

She shivered as she approached and he shook his head, pulling his tunic over his head to hand to her. His body was still adjusting to the increased temperature here.

"How long have you been doing this?" he asked her.

She shrugged. "Since I got to Piloria. I've made my way to the shoreline as often as I could and just…waited. Eventually, he showed up."

Lincoln shook his head. He still couldn't really understand. "But, how on earth did…?"

She laughed and stepped forward, putting her finger unexpectedly to his lips. It stopped any other words dead. "I don't know," she whispered, "and I don't care. All I care about is that he's here. He's my friend. I trust him. He's the one little piece of back-home I still have."

The words sent a ripple across his skin. She was talking about a reptile. She wasn't talking about a family member or a *person* who was dear to her. Because Storm had never had that. Not really. And even though she now had two family members on the same continent as her, Milo seemed to mean more to her than ever.

Lincoln hadn't wanted to leave Storm behind, and had worried about her all the time he was back on Earthasia. On the way back to Piloria his nerves had been on edge, as he fretted about what he might find once he got here. So that first initial sight of her had filled him with relief. But now he realized that while, for him, Piloria had always been about survival, Storm hadn't only survived here, she'd thrived. Her skin had darkened and her eyes were brighter. Storm was more *alive* here. No matter how tough things were, it seemed like Piloria was the place she was meant to be.

But while Storm felt at home here, could anyone else feel the same? Could Lincoln? He couldn't shake off the swathes of guilt that had wrapped themselves around him. All of these people were here because of him. Because he'd taken the ointment home and thought only of curing his sister. He hadn't looked at the bigger picture, because he couldn't see beyond his own family. They'd only just set foot on this continent and already people were dead.

He felt so confused right now. And Storm was still the person outside his family he felt most connected to, most protective of. One of the only people he felt he could talk honestly to.

She frowned. "Hey," she said, lifting her hand to his face.

Lincoln stepped back. He had to put some distance between them. He had to say these words out loud. "I did it," he said as he ran his fingers through his hair. He looked out over the dark undulating ocean. "All this has happened because I wanted to save my sister."

She shook her head, drops of water showering around them. "You didn't know what would happen with the ointment. There were no guarantees." She put her hands on her hips and arched her back. "This was always going to happen, Lincoln – whether they found a cure for the blistering plague or not." She pushed her wet hair back from her face. "I don't think any of us really knew what was going on. I'm not even sure how many of the Stipulators knew how bad things were."

She reached out and touched his arm, her voice low.

"There hadn't been enough food for years – our land was stripped of anything good, we might as well have planted our crops in sand. Things were always going to come to a head." She lifted her hand and pressed a finger into his chest. "You couldn't control that. I couldn't control that. And it seems like neither could they."

He tried to listen to her words, but he couldn't push the feelings of guilt away. "What have we done? Who have we left behind? What if we never get a chance to go back?" He turned and looked behind them. "How on earth can we live here? We can't even last a day without losing someone."

Storm twisted her hair in her hands and squeezed the

water out onto the sand beneath their feet. She tilted her chin upwards and looked him square in the eye. Even though there was only the moonlight above them, he could see the determined edge in her violet eyes. "We live here because this is home now, Lincoln. It has to be. For us, and for them. This isn't a battle. It's a partnership. And the sooner you and the rest of the Earthasians realize that, the better chance we all have of survival."

She started to take a few steps towards the shrubs and bushes that would lead them back to the shack, before stopping and turning to face him.

The moonlight reflected off her sun-darkened skin. "I'm glad you're here," was all she added, before she turned on her heel again and strode into the distance.

Lincoln hurried after her. It was dark. It was Piloria.

No one should be left behind.

FOURTEEN

STORMCHASER

It was fully dark by the time they got back. Storm felt awkward. She'd understood what Lincoln was saying. She could practically see the guilt emanating from him. But he hadn't seemed to realize that she was part of it all too. She'd sent the ointment home with Lincoln, as well as the plant samples. She'd wanted Arta to get better too. She hadn't really thought about the rest.

But instead of feeling guilty, it made her angry. Angry that people were supposed to die instead of having the right to a treatment. Angry that now they had a treatment, they would still die – only this time from starvation.

As they approached the shack, they could see everyone sitting outside around the fire. Jesa, Leif and Caleb were slumped next to each other – all looking as if they were ready to sleep. The two mothers were working together on something, next to the fire. Octavius was huddled near the flames, with a blanket wrapped around his shoulders, talking intensely with Reban, who glanced up and scowled at her.

He didn't need to say anything. She knew exactly why he was glaring at her. And he was right. By nightfall it wasn't truly safe to be walking in Piloria.

She ignored his scowl and moved next to the fire, loosening out her damp hair and fanning it across her back and shoulders in an attempt to get it to dry.

"You know it makes sense," Octavius said quietly to Reban as she sat down.

"Sense to who?" hissed Reban. "To Silas?"

Octavius seemed unperturbed by Reban's anger. "Sense to everyone," he replied firmly. "We can't have two camps. We need a united front. Everyone has to work together."

Reban lowered his face towards Octavius. "I will not work with Silas." He spat the words out through gritted teeth.

Octavius ignored him and kept talking. "This isn't just about you any more, Reban. It's about the people of Earthasia. It's about finding a way for all of us to survive." He paused for a second and lowered his gaze. "It might even be about saving the human race."

The words sent a chill across Storm's skin.

She was struck by how fragile Octavius looked. He'd always had this remarkable presence about him. Power. Strength. Energy. Tonight, huddled in front of the fire, he just looked...old. Lincoln's words on the beach struck a chord.

No one was safe here. She'd just found her great-uncle, but how long would she actually have him for?

Octavius picked up a stick and poked at the fire. "It's not all about you, Reban," he repeated. The words were so quiet it was almost as if he were talking to himself.

But Reban heard them. His jaw was clenched and she could see the tense muscles around his neck. She wondered if he would argue some more, but instead he just threw up one hand and stomped off into the shack.

Storm swallowed awkwardly, but she couldn't help feeling curious.

"What was all that about?" she asked.

Octavius gave a tiny shrug. "The camp. We have to join the main camp. This won't work."

She straightened. Now she understood why Reban was defensive. "This isn't Earthasia. I don't answer to the Stipulators. Silas has no say about what we do here."

Octavius's face broke into a smile and he shot her a sideways glance. He almost looked like himself again. "Spoken just like her."

"What?"

"Your mother. Dalia. You sounded just like her then."

She stiffened, one finger reaching up and twisting around a strand of hair as she shook her head. "Don't say that."

"Why not? Dalia was my favourite niece. My only niece."

"But you didn't stay in touch. You didn't look out for her." The words shot out of her mouth.

Octavius let out a hearty laugh, followed by a series of

coughs. "Dalia didn't let anybody look out for her. Especially not her crotchety uncle."

Storm pulled her knees up to her chest. Her memories of her mother were fading. Every night, as she lay in bed, she'd try to remember as much as she could. Little things. Like the way her mother had spun around in what was left of the forest back then, her long brown dress billowing out and her straight dark hair streaming in the sunlight. Her laugh. The way she smelled. The constant worry that she always tried to hide in her eyes.

Storm swallowed, trying to ignore the pain in her chest. "Tell me about her," she said simply.

She kept her eyes on the flickering flames, knowing that Octavius had turned his head towards her. There was silence for a few seconds, then he started speaking.

"Dalia was headstrong. She came into the world screaming, letting no one doubt that she was there. She hated school. When she was a child, she had to go three days a week. She spent most of her time fighting with the instructor – telling him, or her, they were wrong. Dalia asked questions." He let out a gentle laugh. "Dalia had what was known as an 'enquiring mind'. But even though she was brighter than most of the people around her, she wasn't interested in academics. She didn't perform well in the tests at school."

Storm turned her head slightly to half meet his gaze. So much of this sounded achingly familiar.

Octavius lifted one eyebrow. "I heard someone else was a bit like that too."

She blinked, trying to hide the emotions welling in her chest.

Octavius leaned back a little. "And she was beautiful." He gave an appreciative nod. "You're like her. Very like her – you have your father's eyes, but your mother's colouring."

The emotions were still building. She'd wanted this for so long – the chance to talk to someone about her mother. Reban had told her a few things, a few memories he had of her mother – but Octavius had known Dalia when she'd been a child. These memories were different, more precious, and no matter how angry she'd been with Octavius, he was the only person who could share these with her.

"How come you never met me? You're the Captain Regent. Even though you said my mother disappeared, surely you knew where she was? Surely you knew she'd had a baby?"

He shook his head and looked at her with his grey eyes. "You give us far more credit than we deserve. The Chief Stipulators couldn't even tell me how many people lived in their zones. Without consistent birth records, how on earth can we keep track of things?"

He shook his head again.

"When Dalia disappeared, I had no idea if she was still in Ambulus City or not. How do you find someone in a city with millions of people?" He reached over and touched Storm's arm. "The first time I saw you – when you came to hand that message in at parliament? It didn't feel real. I thought I'd imagined things." He gave a laugh. "I'm getting old, you know? So I pushed it all away and didn't think about it again."

He met her gaze again.

"Then the rumours began." He glanced towards the shack. "And Reban started acting strangely. I never heard about the Trials, or that you were one of the Finalists who went to Piloria. It wasn't until you came back that I realized who you might be."

Storm shifted and rubbed her eyes. The smoke from the fire was getting stronger – at least, that's what she was telling herself. Octavius gave a little twitch and she frowned. His hands were trembling. Was he cold? The air around them was warm. He seemed to realize she was staring, and hid his hands back under the blanket.

He gave a smile. "As soon as I heard what your name was, I knew. I knew you were Dalia's daughter."

Storm sat up a little straighter as something clicked in her brain. "You said something to me back at the parliament, about using my full name. No one calls me Stormchaser. Only you and my mother."

He raised his eyebrows. "She never told you why she chose your name?"

Storm shook her head. "No, never." All the little hairs at the back of her neck stood on end and she blinked furiously. A few people had commented on her name throughout her life, but at first she'd been too young to notice and she'd never thought to question her mother until it was too late.

Octavius cleared his throat. "When Dalia was young –

much younger than you are now – I sometimes told her stories. She liked that. She always used to say that she wasn't tired and needed another story before she could get to sleep." He gave a soft kind of smile, as if he were lost in a memory. "And there was one that was her most favourite."

"Which one?" The words practically flew out of her mouth. Storm couldn't help it. She almost wanted to tug the words and memories out of Octavius's mind.

Octavius seemed to settle a little into his bones. His body had been tense, even a little tremulous, but now it was as if some of the pent-up tension finally left his body.

"I told her a story about four sprites." He looked into the dark sky littered with stars above. "It was a world very different to this one. One ruled by the weather. The king of the land had no children – no heirs. So he looked to his four sprites and told them whichever one could conquer the weather would be the one to inherit his kingdom."

Storm shifted position on the hard ground. Her mother had told her stories as a child, but never this one.

"The sprites had always been friends. They worked hard to keep the weather under control. They enjoyed it. One used to catch the sunlight in glass jars, and keep it for dull days. Another collected rainwater, and used it when the sun dried up the land. A third chased the storms away, stopped them from stripping the land of their crops and resources. But the fourth was a little less focused – more of a dreamer, and used to spend her time chasing rainbows and trying to find the pots of gold at the end of them."

Octavius gave a sigh.

"But when the king made his declaration, the sprites were excited. The thought of ruling the kingdom was all that most of them could think about. The sun-catcher worked even harder, trapping every possible second of sunshine. But instead of sharing the sun on dull days, she kept it all to herself, vowing that when she became ruler, she would decide when the sunny days should be. The rain-collector worked hard too. Every single drop of rain was collected, but instead of replenishing the land, she let the crops wither and die, deciding that when she became the ruler she would decide whose crops would grow, and which would die. Meanwhile, the storm-chaser kept chasing the storms away. She didn't worry about the others, she was too busy trying to keep the land productive and animals safe. She even told the rainbow-seeker where to find a rainbow, leading her to the end of one, once she'd chased a storm away. For the first time, the rainbow-seeker found gold at the end of a rainbow, and once she found it, she was so delighted that she ran straight to the king to show him her prize. The king was overjoyed, and rewarded her by declaring her the new heir to the kingdom."

Storm wrinkled her brow. "That's it? That was the story?"

Octavius laughed and shook his head. "But it didn't end there. By the time the rainbow-seeker took over the kingdom, the land was scorched and dry. The rain-collector had hidden away any rain she'd collected, and the sun-catcher had opened her jars of sunshine, out of spite at not winning. Only Stormchaser had continued to do her job. And because she worked so hard, she developed powers she didn't know that she had."

"What kind of powers?"

Octavius gave a little smile, as if he could tell she was anxious to reach the end of story. "Without the weather sprites working together, things got worse. Even fiercer storms whipped up, and it was then" – he emphasized the words – "that Stormchaser's powers became even more apparent. She had an aura about her. Because some of the storms were now too powerful to be chased away, she developed a protective shell. She could seek those people out who were most at risk from the storm, and protect them. As the weather grew worse, she saved hundreds of lives.

"Still the storms got worse and worse. The rainbow-seeker grew lazy. She'd found one pot of gold, but now she was on the throne she didn't bother looking for more. In the meantime, the sun-catcher and rain-collector were jealous. They started plotting to overthrow the rainbow-seeker and made their way to the palace.

"When the worst storm ever hit the land, all three of the sprites were trapped within the palace walls. Stormchaser stayed outside, trying and trying to chase the storm away, with no luck. When the castle walls started to fall down, she used her aura to protect the other three sprites from the toppling stones. But her aura had grown weak from overuse and from being extended to include those far away from her.

She didn't have enough power to keep the heavy castle gates from crashing down on top of her."

Storm held her breath. "What happened?"

Octavius's face was tired. "The sprites were desperate. They knew their actions had cost the life of their friend, but they couldn't do anything to save her. But, with her last, dying breath, Stormchaser pointed to the sun streaming through a set of clouds misted with light rain and showed them a new rainbow. She told them they would find another pot of gold and to use it wisely to protect the land from the storms she wouldn't be able to chase away."

Octavius rubbed a hand over his eyes and pulled at his blanket. The air was colder now, the temperature dropping as a brisk breeze came in from the ocean.

"That's it?" Storm could feel the resentment in her chest. The ending seemed so unfair. "But none of them deserved it. They'd been selfish. They'd thought only of themselves."

Octavius nodded. "But they learned their lesson. They dug up the gold, protected the people and ruled the kingdom together. They looked after the parts of the weather that they could, and accepted the parts they had left themselves vulnerable to." He pressed his lips together for a second and looked thoughtful. "They learned to look at the bigger picture and respected Stormchaser's sacrifice."

His grey eyes met Storm's. "It's not always about one person. Someone wise once said, 'The needs of the many outweigh the needs of the one.'"

"But she died," said Storm, feeling the pressure in her

chest as she said the words out loud. It was ridiculous. This was a child's story that she'd never heard before, but it had obviously meant something important to her mother.

Octavius nodded. "She did." Then he gave a little sigh. "And that was the story that Dalia asked me to tell her time and time again." There was a little glint in his eyes. "But often, just before the end, she asked me stop."

"She did? Why?"

He let out a soft chuckle. "Because Dalia had a vivid imagination. She often wanted to change the end of the story to suit herself. Sometimes, she had Stormchaser cut off the heads of the other sprites – she could be quite bloodthirsty, you know. Other times she had the three sprites caught up in one of the storms and whipped away to another world. In a few others, she didn't protect them at all, just let the castle walls fall on top of them."

Storm smiled as her hand came up to her mouth. "My mother was ruthless!"

Octavius gave a slow nod. "She could be. But at other times she let me finish the story with its original ending. She loved the character. She admired her. She often wanted to fight for injustice – that was the type of person your mother was." He gave Storm a smile. "So, when I heard your name, and saw you – your build, your skin colour, your hair" – he gave another smile – "and then met you, and realized how tenacious you were… How could I ever doubt you were hers?"

Storm stared at the flickering fire for a few minutes. She'd missed out on so much. The years without her mother just seemed…lost. The emptiness where her mother should have been felt as though it echoed inside her, amplifying in the still night air. It sent a surge of resentment through her.

"But you never said." The words came out bluntly.

Octavius nodded. "How do you tell a teenager – one you never knew existed and who's just had a terrible experience – that she's had family all along? And, with all the backstabbing in our parliament, would that make life easier for her, or harder? Would it actually put her more at risk?"

Storm tried to let his words sink in. It was so much easier just to be angry with him and Reban. But some of what they both said did make sense – even to the lonely teenager she'd been.

Octavius's gravelly voice cut through the quiet. "She would be more proud of you than you can ever imagine."

Storm blinked back tears. "Wh-what?"

"You're like her in so many ways, but different in others."

"What do you mean?"

"You have her strength, both mentally and physically. You have determination. You ask questions. You think for yourself." He shot her a sideways glance. "And you have resilience, in spades."

The last words prickled at her. "I didn't have much choice about that."

Octavius kept his voice steady. "But you have more too, Stormchaser. You have a big heart – one that you try to hide. Sometimes that's good, sometimes it's bad. Don't let it stop you forming the relationships you should. Your mother?

She didn't have the same warmth you have – the warmth that sneaks out, even though you try to hide it. Don't." He held up his arms and tried to hide a wince. "Particularly around here. Particularly around your friends. It makes you more…" He gave a smile. "Human."

Storm was deep in thought. So much was swimming around in her head. She sighed and pulled her knees up to her chest. The rest of the camp was still engaged in other things. Jesa looked as if she might fall asleep on Leif's shoulder. Caleb was already gently snoring. Lincoln, his mother, Kayna and Reban were bent forward in quiet conversation. "Named after a fairy story," she said. "But this place isn't a fairy tale," she added wryly.

Octavius gave a brief nod. "This place will be what we make it." He paused for a second. "But we have to make it together."

Her breath stalled. She knew what he was saying. "I know." It came out automatically.

"There can't be two camps. There has to be one. You have to join with the people of Earthasia. They're your people, after all."

Storm sighed. It had been playing in her thoughts since the others had arrived. She'd watched the labourers of the camp start construction at an alarming rate, and she couldn't help but be curious. Solar panels had gone up on the first day, to start a power supply. Drainage had been dug. A system had been put in place to get a fresh water supply from the river – much better than the one she'd been planning in her head. The shack they'd transported across Piloria wasn't exactly good. It seemed that neither she nor Reban had developed the same set of skills Blaine had possessed. The idea that the camp might actually build toilets had more appeal than she could possibly admit.

"I'm not sure Silas and Reban will ever see eye to eye," she said.

"Neither am I. But we have more to worry about than two men butting heads together," he replied.

She looked at the people near her. She couldn't hide the fact that she wanted them all to be safe. Some of them she knew well, some of them she'd only just met. But they were the closest thing to a family that she'd ever had.

And the other people – Dell and his father, not to mention everyone else. The kids. She'd spent so much time taking care of herself, isolating herself from everyone around her, that to be here now, with four hundred other people, might be overwhelming. But it was also…something. A community.

It would be different from the faceless millions back on Earthasia; the first real community of settlers on Piloria. Maybe this could work. Maybe if they stuck together, they could actually build something here. Try to live in harmony with the dinosaurs. Would that really be impossible?

The idea made her stomach flip over a little. A tiny seed was blossoming in her mind. She'd like that. She'd actually like it if she could help these people adapt to life on Piloria. Teach them how to respect the land in a way they'd never done back on Earthasia. Because it wasn't only about surviving the dinosaurs, it was also about learning to make a sustainable life for themselves on Piloria. Learning to survive and not destroy each other, or the land.

A smile danced across her lips. She wouldn't be ruled by Stipulators. Life didn't have to be like that. They had the chance at a whole new world here.

"Is that a smile of agreement?"

Storm raised an eyebrow. "I want to make things crystal clear."

He didn't look at all surprised. "What?"

"I'm an outdoor girl. I'll help with the construction. The water. And teaching the kids to stay safe. I'll teach them how to hide, how to climb and how to disguise their scent."

Octavius nodded. "Skills that everyone will need to learn."

"But I'm in charge of me. No one else."

His eyebrows lifted. "I would never expect anything else."

She pushed herself up and gave him a smile. "And don't make any mistake" – she winked – "I only agreed because of the plumbing."

FIFTEEN

LINCOLN

The camp transformation moved at a staggering pace – all motivated by the overwhelming urge to feel safe. It seemed the attack by both the triceratops and the quetzalcoatlus had quickly focused minds to the dangers on Piloria. The trees from the forest were stripped and hammered into the ground, forming a tight circle around the compound, with four covered towers – manned day and night – as vantage points to keep a watchful eye for any potential predators. Half the trees were now missing from the forest that Reban and Storm had temporarily called a home, leaving their now-vacant campsite looking exposed and vulnerable.

The building that had been constructed first hadn't been any type of home. Silas had prioritized the lab, and its walls and roof had gone up in two days, giving Lorcan somewhere to start work. But people were asking questions about why a lab was the priority over shelter. Lincoln already had suspicions that Silas was on a one-man mission to wipe most of the dinosaurs from Piloria. DNA from the quetzalcoatlus had been easily available and he'd heard Lorcan had been instructed to move as quickly as possible on creating a new targeted virus.

In amongst the chaos of the construction, Lincoln had been assigned to one of the work teams, instead of the lab. At first he hadn't questioned it and working with the heavy-muscled labourers was a revelation. They didn't hold back their thoughts on Silas, Reban or any of the surrounding events. And it seemed they had a curious admiration for the young man who'd already survived on the dinosaur continent twice. Lincoln, in turn, was keen to develop skills he'd never had the opportunity to learn before – and he knew how to work hard. It made slipping into their team easier.

After a few days, he started to wonder why he hadn't been assigned to the lab. Since Storm and Reban had told him about the scary changes to the raptors, he was conscious that he really needed to have a conversation with Lorcan about the potential damage their last viruses had caused. Both had emphasized strongly how important this was. But since Octavius had been injured, Silas seemed to be taking as much control over the camp as possible and, try as he might, neither he, Reban or Storm had managed to get into the lab to have that conversation with Lorcan.

Storm wasn't afraid of hard work either, but she found it

difficult to ingratiate herself into the various work streams around her. The men eyed her with suspicion. Lincoln couldn't help but feel sorry that her bravery on Piloria had been pushed aside. Now she was only viewed as the daughter of a former Chief Stipulator and great-niece of the Captain Regent.

Nothing was helped by the tension simmering between Silas and Reban. With Octavius taking some time to recover from his injuries, the camp was fast dividing.

But despite the tension, Lincoln liked the sense of community that had already developed in the new camp. After Octavius's conversation with them all, his friends and family had agreed to try to make things work by joining the main camp. In some ways it was good. It made Piloria feel less barren. Less empty. There were people to talk to, people to work with and people to laugh with. Although he suspected that Reban had only agreed as a way to keep an eye on Silas and to try to keep the people safe.

In the next few days, the plan was to start constructing the buildings that would become homes. So instead of sleeping outside under the stars and next to a campfire, they would eventually live in something resembling a proper house. On Piloria. It still felt so unreal.

Lincoln was finishing off chopping down some more trees with the work crew, ready to start work on the new homes. The first thing they heard was the crashing, which was quickly followed by the ground trembling beneath their feet.

The trembling amplified with every passing second, changing rapidly into a thudding noise. Everything around them shook.

Lincoln knew instantly what it was. "Leif, Storm!" he shouted, not quite sure where either of them were.

People were acting on instinct – and running away from the sound. But Lincoln did the opposite. He ran towards it.

Leif appeared alongside him. "What we gonna do?"

They'd only heard one creature make a sound as loud and slow as this before: the titanosaurus – the largest dinosaur they'd ever seen.

"We need to try to divert it somehow. We both know it's harmless in theory, but the sheer size means it could trample the entire camp."

Feet sounded behind them. Storm, wearing not many clothes. Lincoln did a double take.

She ran up alongside them, a red tunic flapping in her hands. She was wearing her trousers but only underwear on her top half. She scowled at the side glances from both of them. "I was just getting dressed," she hissed. Then she waved the tunic. "We think dinosaurs can see colour, remember?"

Of course! They weren't sure, but last time Storm had worn a red tunic she'd pretty much been a target for the dinosaurs they'd encountered.

"I'll try to get its attention." She stumbled as she pulled the tunic over her head.

Lincoln shook his head at himself as he ran alongside.

He'd just started running towards the sound – knowing what it was – with no plan. Storm? She'd taken a few seconds to think, even if it did mean appearing half-dressed. Was that what happened when you stayed here as long as she had? Did your brain start working faster – because it had to?

They approached the edge of the thinned-out forest, just as the creature emerged. Trees had been trampled in its wake, crushed like mere twigs beneath its giant feet.

He saw Storm shudder. No wonder – last time they'd encountered a titanosaurus it had stamped on the spot where she'd been sleeping only moments earlier.

Lincoln glanced behind them. People had gathered near the edge of the compound, their eyes wide with fear. Ahead of them the titanosaurus stopped and lifted its head, which had previously been low amongst the trees, extending its long neck. The gasps of the people behind him were carried through the air as they realized the true size of the creature. It was higher than most buildings back on Earthasia and at least five times the breadth. One footprint alone was bigger than a human. And right now, its path would take it straight towards the compound.

Storm shot a panicked look at Leif and Lincoln. "We can't let these people think that all dinosaurs are bad. We can fix this. Help me! Make some noise, distract it away from the compound!"

She ran straight in front of the titanosaurus, shouting and waving her hands in the air. After a few seconds of confusion,

Leif put his fingers to his lips and let out an ear-piercing whistle. Lincoln joined them, shouting at the top of his voice.

The titanosaurus moved its large head and neck in the most graceful way, sweeping through the air as if trying to locate the sounds.

There was a shriek from the crowd behind them as its head swept low, just above where Storm was standing. Lincoln and Leif instantly stepped backwards, but Storm stayed deadly still. The creature's head was almost at the ground now. Its head alone was the same height as Storm. The eye on the side nearest to Storm seemed fixed upon her.

Lincoln knew the titanosaurus was a plant eater. It didn't hunt. Its only danger to Storm was its size. But that was terrifying enough. Then she did something completely unexpected. She lifted both hands towards the creature's head, leaving them only a few millisectars from the rough dinosaur skin.

Leif and Lincoln sucked in their breath. From just behind her, Lincoln could see Storm's hand trembling. The creature's dark eye was staring right at her, bigger than her outstretched palm. It gave a long, slow blink. It seemed curious. Lincoln wasn't sure if it had been the noise, or the coloured tunic, but somehow Storm had managed to attract this giant creature's attention.

"I think we run now," she said. She was trying to keep her face from moving as she spoke. He had no idea why. But the titanosaurus was still staring at her. Its gaze was kind of hypnotic. She spoke quietly. "I'd love to be able to have a conversation with one of these creatures. To know what it was thinking. To know how much it notices the world that it tramples on. To find out if they even understand that humans have invaded their land."

If Lincoln hadn't been so tense, he might have smiled. The whole compound was facing danger and Storm's thoughts were all about talking to and understanding a dinosaur.

"What do you think will happen if we run?" hissed Leif.

"Hopefully it will follow us," breathed Lincoln. He'd started to sweat. None of them had thought this through. It was ridiculous. This creature could kill them in one step, or with a sweep of its giant tail.

"You think we can outrun a titanosaurus?" choked Leif.

"We only need it to be distracted and head in a different direction from the compound," said Storm quietly. She took one step back towards them. "So, on my count, let's go." She turned her head and gave both of them a wink. "If you're not fast, you're last." And in a flash of red she was gone.

Lincoln blinked. "She didn't count..." he started to say, but Leif was quicker than him and took off after her.

Lincoln swallowed. He knew he should run. But the titanosaurus had raised its head a little, as if it were wondering what was happening. It started to lift the leg nearest Lincoln and something surged through him. "Run!" came the shout from behind him.

So he did. As fast as he could. Storm and Leif had covered the open space in front of him swiftly.

The earth shook as the titanosaurus's foot hit the ground behind him. He swerved sharply to the side as he continued running. Within a few thumps, the creature was alongside him, allowing him to see the true majesty of its size. Its massive stride meant it kept up easily. Leif and Storm were still running ahead, well away from the compound.

Lincoln kept veering to the right, conscious that the dinosaur's tail could be swinging in his direction. He glanced to the side, then flattened himself to the ground, dirt splattering over him as it swept just above his head.

The creature kept heading in the same direction as Storm and Leif. There was another portion of forest off to the far right, and after another few thundering steps, the titanosaurus halted. It seemed to lose interest in Leif and Storm ahead on the open plain, and then changed direction towards the thicker forest in the distance, probably on the hunt for food.

Lincoln pushed himself up on to his hands and knees, spluttering dirt from his mouth. He raised his head. Storm and Leif had stopped running and were bent double, watching the titanosaurus thudding off into the distance.

His heart was hammering in his chest and his tunic was sticking to his back. He stood up, trying to catch his breath. Storm and Leif started to walk back towards him. It took them quite a while to reach Lincoln. Storm's hair was plastered around her face, and Leif was distinctly red.

"It worked." Leif was shaking his head. "It actually worked!"

Lincoln shook his head too as they walked back towards the compound. "What on earth were you doing – whispering to it?"

Storm smiled, she had a far-off look in her eyes. "It was looking at me. Maybe it was wondering about us – I know I was wondering about it."

Leif put one hand on his hip as they kept walking. "So what, you're the dinosaur whisperer now?" He started laughing. Storm started laughing too and so did Lincoln, a mix of nervous energy and relief flooding through him.

"Just don't ask me to whisper to a raptor," joked Storm.

They headed back into the compound, gaining a few nods from people who had witnessed what happened.

"Let's get some lunch," Lincoln said to Storm and Leif. "Nothing like chasing a titanosaurus off to work up an appetite."

"I should find Octavius," murmured Storm, "see how he's doing." She brushed her hand down her red tunic. "And I probably should get changed. Don't want to continue to be a target."

The boys nodded, ready to head back to the campfire, where they hoped that someone had food cooking.

As they sat eating, Lincoln heard a noise behind him and turned around. Black cloaks. Again. Doubtless the heavy cloth would be stifling in Piloria's unbearable heat. It seemed the Stipulators were more concerned with keeping up appearances than comfort.

There was quite a crowd gathered round. One figure amongst them seemed familiar. Dell.

Since their arrival on Piloria, Dell had almost been conspicuous by his absence. He'd been busying himself with any of the preparations going on in camp rather than spending time with his former best friend, Storm.

Lincoln had noticed how hurt Storm was by her friend's actions and he hated it. Over the last few weeks, she'd become quieter and less fiery when she was around other people. It was almost like Dell ignoring her was draining her confidence bit by bit, along with others who were suspicious of her because of her relationship to Reban and Octavius. Maybe, after her latest actions, people would start to treat her with a little more respect.

Lincoln was curious. He strode over and tapped the nearest guy on the shoulder. "What's going on?" he asked.

The guy had a weapon clutched to his chest. "We're going hunting."

"What?" Storm's voice was clear behind him, tinged with anger. She'd changed into a black tunic and had obviously come back to join them for lunch. "Why on earth would you need to go hunting?"

Most of the men shrugged. One of the Stipulators gave her a dismissive look. "We need to eat. And we need to get a better idea of the surrounding area."

"Who said you should go hunting?" asked Lincoln.

"Silas," replied one of the Stipulators. Lincoln felt a flare of annoyance. Since Octavius had been injured, Silas was trying to make himself seem like the man in charge.

Storm shook her head. "You already have food. I've seen the supplies you brought from Piloria" – she waved her hand to the left – "and you've already made plans to plough some of the land for crops." She planted both hands on her hips. "Plus, if you want to know about the surrounding area, why don't you just ask the people who've been here longer than you?"

The Stipulator's lips turned up in a sneer. "Maybe we don't think they're a source of reliable information."

Lincoln put his arm out automatically. He knew Storm too well. She jumped forward just as Reban approached from behind.

"Still an idiot, Larkin?" he commented. "Some things never change."

Larkin tried his best to keep his sneer in place. He waved his hand unconvincingly. "Get back to whatever you've been assigned to do, Reban. You're not in charge here."

Lincoln could see the fire simmering in Reban's eyes. He almost expected him to lash out, but instead Reban stepped right up to Larkin's face. "I've got news for you. Neither are you." He gave a little smile. "And, strangely enough, no one has been brave enough to try to assign me any kind of job. Why do you think that is?"

Reban looked at the crowd gathered around as he let the words hang in the air. He nodded.

"Storm, Lincoln, it seems we would be poor hosts if we let these people go out alone." He raised his eyebrows. "We can escort them." Reban gave Storm a half-smile. "I've heard you shouldn't be left unsupervised. Apparently you start chasing dinosaurs."

Dell muttered something under his breath, his eyes never leaving Reban. It was clear he was still intimidated by the former Chief Stipulator. Larkin opened his mouth, about to object, but Lincoln got in there first.

"Sure thing. It's a dangerous world out there. We wouldn't want to disturb any nest sites and end up with you all being breakfast, lunch and dinner."

One of the burliest guys sneered. "You mean *you'd* be breakfast, lunch and dinner."

"Me? No way. I can sprint, climb a cliff or tree, or swim to the bottom of the ocean." Lincoln smiled and used Storm's phrase from earlier: "If you're not fast, you're last." He looked the guy up and down. No one from Earthasia was overweight, but this guy had muscles to spare. "And if it comes to it, I can outrun you any day."

He nodded back to Storm.

"Let's gear up. This could be interesting."

She fell into step beside him as they made their way over to where the weapons were stored, tilting her chin in the air and sniffing.

"What?" he asked. "What is it?"

"I think it's testosterone," she joked. "You know, one of the scents we try to hide from the dinosaurs?" She shook

189

her head. "You guys need to let it go."

She winked and walked on ahead, leaving Lincoln laughing behind her.

SIXTEEN

STORMCHASER

She was almost amused. The two Stipulators looked as if they could expire at any moment. It had taken her a few months to adjust to the climate on Piloria – the extra heat and humidity just seemed to drain every bit of energy. Lincoln had dressed lightly and held his water canister in his hands. But the rest of the scouting party could barely see through the streams of sweat running down their faces.

Reban seemed to be relishing their discomfort, and strode quickly on ahead, pressurizing the others to keep up.

"I'm not going to let them hunt," Storm muttered under her breath to Lincoln.

"You might have a hard job stopping them," he replied, glancing around the twenty-strong party.

"Watch me." She grinned back, full of determination. "Give them another ten minutes and they won't have the energy to make it back to camp, let alone hunt anything."

Lincoln pulled a face. "If Reban goes any faster, soon I won't be able to keep up either."

She kept grinning as he wiped a thin trickle of sweat away from his temple. She nudged him. "You've got soft, city boy. Time to get back in shape."

Reban stopped just ahead of them. They'd already crossed quite a bit of grassland, and a steep hill lay ahead.

"Okay, guys," he said, smiling at the men wilting around him. "You want to scout this area? Where better to do it than from a high vantage point? I suspect there is either forest or marshland on the other side of these hills, but we won't know until we look." He waved his hand in front of him, his eyes fixing on Larkin. "Maybe it's time to take off that cloak. Don't want to wear anything a predator could get hold of, eh?"

He spun back around as Storm stifled a laugh, watching Larkin gulp and finally remove the heavy cloak, tucking it under one arm.

The climb uphill was slow. The sun had risen high in the sky and the steep hill had no cover, making things even hotter. By the time the group had all reached the top, most fell to their knees.

But Storm didn't. She was taken by the view beneath and beyond. A huge dark lake stretched out in the valley below, surrounded by dense jungle. Across the other side was a herd of stegosauruses, drinking from the water, their spikes glistening as they caught a few of the sun's rays. She smiled and spun around to look back over the open green space they'd just crossed. It was almost like two separate planets. The valley below would be sheltered from the winds that continued to drift in from the ocean.

She kneeled down next to Dell, who was panting. She'd tried to engage him in conversation a few times on the trek, but each time his answers had been curt and to the point. Dell hated this place. He hated everything about it.

"Don't you see it?" she said quietly. "Don't you see how beautiful this land is, how alive?"

Dell looked up through heavy, tired eyelids. "All I see is a place we're clearly not meant to be."

Disappointment overwhelmed her. But she tried to push it aside, still anxious to make him see the world through her eyes.

She shook her head. "Look, Dell. The grass, the lake, the jungle. The smells." She threw her hands up into the air. "The colour! Have you ever seen so much colour before? This is it, Dell. Don't you remember when we still had a little patch of forest and we played in there as kids all day? Don't you remember how much we loved it?" She was desperately trying to raise a tiny bit of enthusiasm in him.

His voice was flat. "There wasn't anything in our forests that could kill you."

Storm's heart clenched in her chest. "Why did you even come? Why did you even come here if that's how you feel?" Frustration was making her angry now. She'd seen the look on Lincoln's face when he'd told her about back home and the burning city. How could Dell think it was better than this?

Now it was Dell's turn to look angry. "Why do you think I got on the ship, Storm? I got on the ship because my dad was promised the world if he came here to help build. He was one of the few people left on Earthasia who knew how to work with wood. What was left for me? Who did I have to stay there for?"

Now she saw it. His anger was directed at her. There had been glimmers during the original Trials – when Dell insisted they were only there for the food, but Storm had been gripped by something else. He couldn't understand her fascination with what might lie on Piloria. He'd always said he never wanted to set foot on the place.

And yet here he was. Angry. Annoyed. But still here.

A sharp caw made them all jump, and something soared up from the trees into the sky above them. Several of the men crouched low and put their hands above their heads, waiting for the attack.

Storm didn't move, she just stood with her hands on her hips, watching the elegant creature glide in the air above them. "It's a dimorphodon," she murmured.

"A what?" snapped the nearest guy.

"A dimorphodon." She recognized it instantly from Octavius's book, which she'd had the chance to study these last few weeks. "Look, the bright-blue body, grey wings and yellow beak."

"Shoot it," snarled one of the guys. "Shoot it before it tries to eat us."

"What? No." Storm spun around. She pointed to the

creature sailing in the winds above their heads. "Why on earth would you want to shoot it? It's not doing anything to us. Haven't you learned anything from this morning? We can live alongside these creatures."

All eyes turned to the dimorphodon. Its movements in the air were elegant, like some kind of dance in the sky. Storm realized she was holding her breath as it swooped low, skimming the treetops of the jungle, then rising high and heading towards the sun burning above them.

There was a crackle beside her. Storm turned instantly, in time to see Reban flatten the man just to her left, as the gun he had pulled to his shoulder misfired. "Why?" she shouted at the man.

A few of the other men started running down the hill automatically, fright and adrenaline surging them away from the noise and down towards the thick trees. Storm's stomach clenched. Dell was amongst them.

"You idiot," growled Reban as the guy's gun tumbled across the ground and the dimorphodon gave a loud caw and disappeared into the distance.

Storm couldn't help herself. She crossed the space in seconds and grabbed hold of the guy's tunic.

"What on earth were you doing?"

The guy pushed her back, sending her sprawling on her backside and knocking the air from her lungs. Storm barely had time to look up before she heard something else – a loud crack, as Lincoln's fist connected with the guy's jaw.

"Don't you touch her!" he yelled.

She was stunned. Stunned by what had just happened, and by Lincoln's reaction.

Reban hauled the guy to his feet, a surprised and amused look on his face. But before he got a chance to speak, there was a click behind his ear.

Storm froze. Larkin had pulled a gun from his hip and was aiming it at Reban's head. Her brain whirled.

Lincoln looked panicked – he was breathing fast, his hands in fists at his sides. His eyes darted between Storm and Reban, clearly unsure of his next move.

Storm saw a flash of something in the glinting sun. A glass vial slid from Larkin's hand as he adjusted his grip on the gun and it bounced on the grass at Reban's feet.

It was bright yellow, a liquid she hadn't seen before. But the size and type of container was horribly familiar. No. It couldn't be. She went to move but Lincoln got there first – the gun temporarily forgotten.

"What's this?" he demanded, lifting the vial with its sloshing yellow liquid.

Larkin laughed at them all, exchanging glances with the other Stipulators as the rest of the group watched uneasily. "What exactly is it you think we're doing out here?" He laughed again, his voice echoing around the hilltop. "Did you really think we were just hunting or scouting?"

Storm couldn't help herself. The anger that had been bubbling inside spilled over. "You want to plant a new virus? You're even more stupid than you look, then. No one has asked us about the original viruses. Do you have any idea of the harm they can cause?" Her stomach squeezed. No wonder they hadn't been able to speak to Lorcan. He'd obviously been busy following Silas's commands. She glanced swiftly at Reban, who nodded in agreement and spoke before she could continue.

His top lip curled as he stared at the yellow vial. "What is that – one virus fits all?" He didn't seem at all intimidated by the gun, which was now pointing at his temple.

Then suddenly he took a step back and kicked out, sweeping Larkin's legs from under him. Larkin yelped and the gun fired into the air as he landed on his back.

Reban grabbed it and leaned over him. "My daughter is right, it's like being handcuffed to a bunch of idiots. Do the viruses work? Who knows? Because we don't. What we do know is that they definitely didn't work on the raptors. Or maybe they did? Because ever since we planted the virus for the raptors they've become stronger, faster, more intelligent. We've made an already terrifying predator virtually invincible." He shook his head and kicked at Larkin. "But hey, let's do that to them all. Because no one will let us near Lorcan to tell him that some of his viruses have had the opposite effect. Do you think he would keep doing this if he'd any idea?"

One of the other Stipulators was looking between Larkin and Reban, his weapon held in his shaking hand, as he tried to decide who to point it at. The other men were muttering to each other, unsure what to do.

There was a noise below them on the hill. All turned

their heads. Two seconds later, Dell and two of the other men who'd disappeared came streaking out of the jungle, yelling.

For a few moments, Storm was frozen, watching the three men running up the hill towards her. She'd been on Piloria long enough to know exactly what that meant – but she'd never been here with Dell before. All the things he'd said about this place, all the ways he hated it... She'd spent the last few weeks trying to convince everyone there was more to Piloria than monsters – particularly this morning. Her clenched stomach told her that was all about to blow up in her face.

SEVENTEEN

STORMCHASER

Four creatures emerged from the forest, running on their strong hind legs. With their high curved sail-backs, they were instantly recognizable from Octavius's book: spinosauruses.

Their skin was shades of yellow – which was ironic considering the colouring of the latest virus – with bright red tips on the array of spines sticking up from their backbones. Their snouts were long and narrow, with rows of sharp teeth. These dinosaurs were bigger than a T-rex, and every bit as terrifying.

Reban didn't even blink. He bent down and yanked Larkin up from the ground.

"Run," he said, without sparing the man another glance. "You too," he hissed at Storm. The rest of the men needed no further instruction, abandoning their packs and weapons and taking off as fast as they could.

Lincoln's eyes darted from hers to Reban. It seemed Dell and the other men had disturbed a whole family of spinosauruses in the forest and every one of them was currently in pursuit of what must be strange, new creatures to them.

Storm pulled a knife from her belt. She wanted to run. She did. But already she could see that the powerful legs of the spinosauruses were more than a match for the three small men. The dinosaurs were catching up fast.

"Run!" Reban's face was directly in hers, spit coming from his lips.

"I won't leave Dell," she insisted. She was currently fighting every natural instinct she'd honed on this continent. She'd never come across a spinosaurus before. And she couldn't pretend she wasn't terrified. But would she sacrifice her former friend?

The slowest guy was taken out by a quick flick of the largest spinosaurus's snout. He flew through the air, landing with a crunch as another spinosaurus trampled over him as if he wasn't even there. Storm squirmed at the squelching sound, knowing instantly there was no point trying to help him. One of the smallest spinosauruses stopped running, instantly intrigued by the possibility of an easy dinner.

Dell's eyes were wide, his face bright red and sweat staining his clothes.

"Run," she screamed as Lincoln grabbed her arm and tried to pull her in the opposite direction.

"We have to go," he growled.

Reban grabbed the nearest gun from the ground and fired it wildly in the direction of the rampaging spinosauruses. Most shots clearly missed but one took a tip off the bright red edge of a spine. It seemed like the dinosaur didn't even notice.

Lincoln picked up another gun and started firing too. But nothing was stopping these creatures. It was clear they were angry. "I thought these guys ate fish," yelled Lincoln, as he automatically took some steps backwards. "That's what it said in Octavius's book!"

"Guess they can adapt," said Reban briskly. "Let's move, people!"

Storm's palms were sweating. She crouched, getting ready to take aim with her knife. The guns might not be working well, but a knife aimed at a mouth or eye could surely do some damage. Her eyes fixed on Dell's face, which was scrunched up, his eyes now just tiny slits. It was obvious that every single bit of his strength was concentrated on running. Concentrated on getting away. Her friend. The only true friend she'd had back on Piloria.

Yes, they had different views. Yes, they'd had plenty of fights. But when Storm had been left alone as a twelve year old, and had to move into one of the misnamed Shelters for orphans, Dell and his father were the only people she could really consider friends. They'd always looked out for her, always been on her side – even when she'd tried to push people away. How could she go back and tell Dell's father that all his worst nightmares had come true?

Her first knife sailed through the air, missing the spinosaurus leading the charge completely.

Her hands moved automatically, pulling another from her belt. The second missed its eyes and glanced off the side of its head, making it shudder for the briefest of seconds. She didn't get a chance to line up the third before she was yanked from behind.

"Move!" This time Reban wasn't taking no for an answer.

Dell was only a few sectars away, the dinosaurs catching up fast. She grabbed her pack and another gun from the ground, and started running. Reban's face was like stone. He stood rooted to the spot, waiting for her to go past him before he started running too. She couldn't help but keep looking over her shoulder. "Keep going, Dell," she yelled, praying he wouldn't look behind him and see how close the spinosaurus was. The guy behind was slowing, his face beyond scarlet from the uphill run and heavy air. His footing slipped and he stumbled but didn't quite fall. The spinosaurus didn't miss its chance. It snapped at his heels with its teeth.

She could feel the thud of their giant feet on the ground just behind hers. She shouldn't have waited so long. She shouldn't have delayed Lincoln and Reban from escaping. They were only here because of her. Selfish, stupid behaviour. But she couldn't leave Dell behind. She just *couldn't*.

There was a snap and a yell. Reban was alongside them by now and he turned, holding his gun behind him and firing wildly. She knew her heart was still beating, she could feel the thump in her chest, but it felt like it had stopped. She opened her mouth to shout, but nothing came out. She was too scared to turn. Too scared of what she might see. Adrenaline was still coursing through her veins. Her skin was coated in sweat and her clothes were sticking to every part of her body. Lincoln was just in front of her. She could tell he was slowing his pace to stay with her. There was a dark flash to her left. Dell. He was wheezing. His body now barely capable of drawing breath. Relief that he was still with them swept through her as she kept running, her hand grabbing wildly for his in an attempt to pull him along.

"Go right," shouted Reban. Her body swerved automatically. She was used to this. The behaviour instinctual. No time to question. Most of this area was open. Reban was directing them towards a more covered part, somewhere they might have half a chance of hiding.

Lincoln was still just ahead, shooting anxious glances over his shoulder. As they ran, he moved his gun to his chest, preparing to shoot. Storm followed his lead, reaching for another knife on her belt. She had no idea what had happened to the other guy and could only hope that, despite the earlier yell, he was keeping up.

Her legs ached, all her muscles screaming. The gorse and bushes were closer, some trees amongst them.

The thuds continued behind them. How many now? Was it only the smallest who'd stopped its chase? She didn't even want to think about what had happened to the man left behind.

Reban disappeared into the high bushes ahead of them, leading the way. Storm didn't slow, she kept a tight hold of Dell's hand and yanked him through the closely crammed foliage. "Stay upright," she hissed between her teeth, knowing that the ground on Piloria was frequently wet and treacherous.

She kept going, then moved sharply to the right. Spiked branches scratched her face and arms. Behind her, the noise level increased. The first spinosaurus had reached the bushes. It just seemed to crash forward. Then something made it stop.

Storm held her breath as she crouched in the bushes. Dell was next to her. Sweat dripped from his nose and his breathing was ragged. She shook her head and pressed a finger to her lips, willing him not to speak or to breathe too noisily.

She peered through the bushes. She could only see one spinosaurus now – the largest. The rest must have become bored with the chase or been distracted by the fallen man. The creature had its head in the air. Listening. Or smelling.

She'd long since learned that some of the most predatory dinosaurs relied heavily on their senses of smell and hearing.

The only noise around them was the wind rustling through the bushes. Reban and Lincoln would be hiding too. They knew exactly how this worked.

But the other guy who'd been with Dell didn't. A loud

groan came from somewhere in amongst the thick green foliage. It had to be from him – all the others had escaped well ahead of them.

The spinosaurus's head turned quickly to the noise. It rose higher on its hind legs. Her heart was racing in her chest. Spinosauruses were supposed to live mainly on fish. And yet this spinosaurus's actions reminded her of the raptors. She licked her dry lips, not moving a millisectar.

The groan sounded again. She wanted to shout and tell the guy to be quiet. But she had no idea where he was in here. She could only imagine he was nowhere near Reban or Lincoln. Both of them wouldn't hesitate to put their hands over his mouth to keep him quiet.

There was a rustle beside her. She frowned, ready to give Dell trouble, and turned just as he crumpled next to her. She reached out her arms automatically, wrapping them around his limp body. Her senses were already on alert but now she had an awareness of something else – a metallic edge in the air.

A horrible feeling swept over her. It coincided with a wet sensation at her fingertips. She bit back the wave of nausea as she stared down at Dell's blank face. She moved her hand as carefully possible, trying not to make a single sound.

Dell's leg was badly bitten. It was a wonder he'd managed to keep running – adrenaline and fear must have kept him on his feet. But now? He was bleeding badly. And she couldn't even move to find some leaves to pack the wound. The bush she was crouched in only had small spiky leaves.

There was another groan. This one much louder. A dead giveaway.

The spinosaurus moved quickly, crashing through the bushes to her far right. A few moments later, a scream rang through the air. Storm pressed her lips together, trying not to shout out. It couldn't be Lincoln or Reban. It couldn't.

There was a snuffle and a thrashing sound. Every instinct made her want to grab one of her knives, but her arms were full. Dell was a dead weight in her grip. She could tell he was alive, his chest was rising and falling rapidly – at least for now.

She closed her eyes and just listened. This was sometimes the most important action to take on Piloria. The spinosaurus moved again – this time closer to her. It was obviously bored by whoever had screamed. The large footsteps thundered closer. It was shocking how big and heavy these creatures were. Before today, she'd only seen them on the pages of a book.

Storm opened her eyes as it snuffled nearer to her. It was displaying inquisitive behaviour, as if it hadn't quite worked out what these strange new creatures were. She watched carefully. Its skin was coarse in places, the shades of yellow varying across its body. The neural spines were mesmerizing. She could see the ripple of the long thin projection of bones beneath its tightly stretched skin – it almost resembled the sail on one of the old fishing boats. The tips of the sail looked as if they had been daubed with splashes of red paint.

The head moved closer and she flinched backwards. Even

though, by walking on its thick hind legs and holding its shorter arms up in front, it resembled a T-rex, the long thin skull and snout were far closer in appearance to the marsh-living deinosuchus.

It lifted its head from the bushes – obviously not finding what it was looking for – and spun around sharply, its muscular tail missing her by millisectars.

The spinosaurus seemed bored now. It wandered back through the bushes and out across the grass plain, heading back towards the valley with the forest and lake.

She waited long enough for it to be out of earshot, then let out her breath.

"Lincoln? Reban?" she whispered loudly.

It only took a few moments for them both to appear. Reban lifted one hand. "Wait here," he commanded before disappearing in the direction where the scream had been heard.

Lincoln pushed through the bushes and dropped to his knees beside her. "Dell? Dell, are you okay?" he said, trying to elicit any kind of response from Dell.

He shot her a worried glance, looking at the small pool of blood by her feet. Lincoln moved swiftly and started pulling thick leaves from a nearby bush, bringing them over to help patch the wound.

Reban came back shaking his head. "Great. We've managed to lose two Stipulators now. People will think I've done this on purpose."

Lincoln wrinkled his nose. "What happened to him?"

Reban sighed. "I think he was stamped on. I don't think the spinosauruses were actually hunting us to eat. But we aroused their suspicions. The gunshots must have put them on edge. I suspect that forest is their territory and we disturbed them. I think they were defending themselves." Storm could see his brain processing. "When they appeared at first – it was almost like a family. A mum, dad and two kids."

Not everyone has a family like that. She squashed the thought and gave a gentle nod. "When it was searching for us it seemed...curious, more than anything."

Lincoln nodded too as he sat down beside her and started to pack leaves around Dell's leg, tying them on with thin yellow vine, similar to the one they used when making the ointment. Dell flinched and groaned at the touch of his leg.

"How are we going to get him back?"

Reban looked at her. "We'll carry him. I'm sure between the three of us we can manage." He sighed. "Here's hoping the rest who ran ahead have made it back safely."

"The virus." It came back into her head. "They brought another virus with them. One we haven't used before. What happened to it?"

A deep frown creased Reban's brow. He pulled something from his pocket. The glass tube with the yellow liquid. He must have picked it up in all the confusion. "Leave this with me. I'll speak to Silas about it – and Lorcan. He must have made it. But we have no idea what it's based on, or which creatures it's supposed to target."

Storm's mouth was dry. "This is what I was always afraid of, that they wouldn't only kill the predators – they'd kill them all."

Lincoln shifted uncomfortably next to her. She knew he'd been fine with stealing the dinosaur eggs to create the viruses at first, and he'd been pretty much fine about planting them. He hadn't had all the same worries that she had. And now? With his mother and sister here, would he want to help wipe out all the dinosaurs too?

He took a long, slow breath. "We need to talk about this. We need to talk about this together – at camp. How much do we really know about this land? There are virtually no creatures left on Earthasia. Do you think there's a chance that wiping out the animals helped worsen the damage to our land? What if we make the same mistakes again here? This is it. This is our last chance. We have to try to get to Lorcan somehow, find out what the plans are. Even if he's the most closely guarded person in the compound. We'll never get a straight answer from Silas." He met Storm's gaze with his bright-green eyes. "These decisions should be made together. Discussed, debated." He seemed to be thinking hard. "And we should do something else. We should try to find the diplodocus. The duckbills. More Barneys – more aquilops. The people in camp have to be shown that some of these creatures are safe." He emphasized his words. "We *can* live safely with some of these creatures."

She was listening to his words. She knew they made sense. But he still hadn't said certain things out loud. He still hadn't said that he disagreed with killing some of the dinosaurs. And that made her distinctly uncomfortable.

Reban bent down and wrapped an arm around Dell's waist, pulling him up onto his feet. "Lincoln," he said, nodding, "take the other side." He waited until Lincoln moved into position and took some of the weight. "Storm, get the weapons. Stay on guard. This will be a slow journey back to camp."

She knew that. Storm slung one of the rifles over her shoulder and held another in one hand. "Where did everyone else go?" she said quietly, as they pushed their way through the thick bushes.

The group had started out with around twenty people. Two men were definitely dead. But the rest?

Lincoln shrugged. "I guess everyone took off in different directions. We won't find out who is still alive until we get back to camp."

Reban still looked mad. "What a waste. The camp can't work like this. Every time we send people out, they're at risk. What was the count? Four hundred? If we keep going like this, there won't be anyone left in a year."

Lincoln shot Storm a look, but he nodded in agreement. "The trouble is, people still don't really get it. This is the dinosaurs' continent – not ours. We just need to find a small space and try to get on with life. Silas, he can't seem to get his head around the fact that we're not here to take over the world. We're here to survive. It's hard enough doing that, without taking stupid risks."

Storm nodded as she scanned the immediate horizon. It was clear. "Let's push on," she said. "We don't want to end up stuck out here at night."

The trek across the plain was more than slow, the three of them swapping positions every now and then to try to take Dell's weight. He managed to stay on his feet, but his eyes were closed most of the way and he didn't speak. It was clear he was weak. Storm couldn't help but wonder how much blood he'd actually lost.

Eventually they came across two stragglers – both with minor injuries – who'd got disorientated and wandered in the wrong direction for a bit.

"Where is everyone?" one of the guys asked, his eyes wide.

Storm glanced backwards. "I guess we're it. I hope some of the others have gone on ahead." She wrinkled her brow as she looked at the rips in the guy's clothes. "Didn't you run off into the jungle with Dell?"

He nodded. "It was almost like the spinosauruses were lying in wait. I scrambled up a tree as quickly as I could and stayed up there until the coast was clear. By the time I came down" – he pulled a face and shuddered – "there were two bodies. One halfway up the hill, that was the Stipulator – Larkin. He looked as if something had bitten him. And there was somebody down next to the lake too. He wasn't moving and I didn't go and investigate."

"Did you check if they were alive?" asked Lincoln.

The guy retched, the question obviously bringing something to mind. "Since they didn't have heads any more

I took it for granted they weren't. What even lives in the lakes around here?"

Storm, Lincoln and Reban exchanged glances. Another lake to mark as dangerous on the map. So far they'd only came across one that looked safe. It seemed that creatures like the deinosuchus seemed to lurk in many of the marshes or lochs on Piloria.

By the time the camp came into view, they were all exhausted. One of the lookouts spied them and shouted for help. The gates were opened and a few people spilled out, taking Dell from their arms and helping him towards the newly erected care centre.

Silas appeared at the back, his black cloak billowing behind him.

"Is this it?" He couldn't hide the surprise on his face. "A few stragglers came back earlier, I thought the rest would be with you."

Reban pulled the yellow vial from his pocket and flung it at Silas's feet. "It's a jungle out there, Silas. I can't keep everyone alive when you send them out there unprepared. Especially when it seems like everyone didn't have the same plan. If they aren't already dead and they don't get back here before nightfall, I guarantee they'll die out there. You've cost us more lives today. This can't continue."

Silas's face changed to its usual sneer. He picked up the vial from the ground, examining it in the dimming light. The yellow liquid seemed almost luminescent. "What a shame there wasn't opportunity to plant it. Still, at least it hasn't gone to waste." He tucked it back into his pocket. "There'll be another chance soon."

The anger and frustration that had been building in Storm all day erupted. "You're an idiot," she yelled. "You have no idea what you're doing. You have no idea how to keep people safe. I need to speak to Lorcan!" One hand clenched into a fist and the other tightened around the gun in her hand. She couldn't help but move forward. Reban caught her from behind, wrapping his arms around her waist and shoulders to hold her back. "The most dangerous thing on Piloria is you!"

Silas threw back his head and laughed. People had gathered around them, everyone watching the exchange. There were murmurs in the crowd, people obviously wondering what had happened to the rest of the scouting party. Silas liked nothing better than an audience. "Put your little creature back in her box, Reban. Or I'll leave you both outside the camp wall." He looked down his nose at them both. "As for Lorcan? He's not available. Work in the lab is so busy right now…" He turned on his heel to stride off.

Reban's voice rose clearly amongst the mutterings of the crowd. "People died today because of you, Silas. Be careful. Soon you won't have anyone left to boss around."

Silas didn't turn back – he just kept walking towards the lab.

Reban let his grasp loosen. He gestured with his head. "Come on, Storm. This is a battle for another day."

She sagged down, all the pent-up energy depleted from

her body. Running on adrenaline wasn't good for anyone. Storm ran her fingers through her knotted hair. She was exhausted. All she really wanted to do was go to bed. They had water now. They had somewhere they could wash properly and actually get clean. They'd been allocated one of the newly constructed buildings to call their home. But she and Reban still hadn't actually slept in it. Reban was looking at it now. Eyeing it with suspicion.

They'd stayed in Blaine's shack together since they'd been left on Piloria. But the shack had been different. Always a bit ramshackle. Always like a temporary solution. The home they'd been allocated wasn't. It was permanent. It had a kitchen, a bathroom of sorts, two sleeping areas and a sitting area. It was six times the size of the room Storm had slept in at the Shelter back on Earthasia. Yet right now it just felt wrong. It felt…awkward.

She drew in a deep breath and looked across the compound. "Dell," she said. "I need to check on him and find his father." She turned and pressed the guns she was currently carrying towards Reban. "Take these, we'll talk later."

And she walked away as quickly as possible. Her brain was spinning. Silas was quickly ruining their chances of making a life on Piloria. He couldn't see past the "kill everything" agenda. Just how far would he go? And what about Lorcan? She'd asked around. Virtually no one had seen him. Was he being kept a prisoner in the lab, or was he as invested in killing the dinosaurs on Piloria as Silas was?

Storm sighed, stopped walking and looked up at the sky above her. The sun was going down and the stars were starting to emerge. Somehow she knew she wouldn't get a wink of sleep tonight.

EIGHTEEN

LINCOLN

He still couldn't get used to it – walking into a home, instead of a cave.

It was the first time in years that everything his family owned wasn't permanently damp. Not that they owned much here. One of the labourers called himself a carpenter. He had a real talent for making things from wood. So far they had a table, chairs and a large wooden bench that his mother had covered in cushions stuffed with some kind of strange dried leaves from the jungle. It was lumpy, but still oddly comfortable.

The power was the other strange thing. Power on Earthasia had been limited, with frequent power outages – particularly in the caves. Most things had been done by candlelight. On Piloria, things were entirely different. Sun was in plentiful supply and the solar panels had been set up the first day they arrived. Lincoln couldn't get used to being able to turn a light on or use the kitchen any time he wanted.

The labourers had even laid wooden and stone paths between the houses, to counteract the torrents of rain that came every few days to replenish the land around them.

His footsteps slowed as he reached their family home. Space. A room of his own. A food supply – the fruits from the surrounding bushes. Even the cornup that grew in the ground around here tasted better than back on Earthasia. Lots of things on Piloria were good. As long as you didn't take into account the kind of day he'd just had.

More men lost. Needlessly. There was a certain kind of arrogance and ignorance amongst some of the would-be settlers. They had so little respect for the creatures on this continent. It didn't matter that some of them were deadly, not all of them were – and that's what they had to remember. Did Silas really mean to wipe out all the living creatures? Lincoln tugged at his dirty tunic. Maybe it was time to get into the newly erected lab and see what Lorcan was actually doing there.

He pushed open the door to his new home and walked in, his footsteps faltering straight away. The heat in here was overwhelming. His mother and Arta were crouched over the large bench.

"What is it? What's wrong?"

His stomach growled automatically at the smell of food. His mother was obviously cooking something.

Arta looked up, lines creasing her forehead. "Oh, Lincoln.

You're back." Her gaze narrowed at his dishevelled appearance. "What happened?"

His answer was automatic. "Nothing." There was time for all that later – doubtless someone would tell them about the losses from the scouting party. He walked around the bench. Octavius was lying on it, shivering even though a fire was blazing in the room.

"Octavius?" He kneeled down beside the bench. His mother had a cloth pressed to the old man's forehead.

Tamb spoke quietly. "I was with him earlier today. I knew he wasn't well, but he wouldn't go to the medico care centre." She gave a weak smile. "Said there was nothing they could do for old age."

Lincoln shook his head. "This isn't old age."

Octavius wasn't even talking. His eyes flickered open then closed again with the occasional mutter coming from his lips. Lincoln reached out to touch him and Octavius flinched.

"His shoulders. It must be the wounds on his shoulders. Have you looked at them?"

Lincoln's mother shook her head. "How could I? He's the Captain Regent. I can't take his clothes off." His mother was clearly intimidated, either by Octavius's position, or by the fact he was an unrelated male.

"But I can. Get me a basin with some water, then leave us."

His mother and Arta moved quickly, bringing some clean water and some cloths, before retreating to one of the bedrooms.

"Come on then, Octavius. Let me help you out of these."

He lifted the frail man easily, pulling back the blanket while Octavius tried to cling to it. "I'll only be a moment."

He lifted the edge of Octavius's undershirt and gently manoeuvred it upwards. The first thing he noticed was the smell. The next thing he noticed was the old leaves almost fused to Octavius's skin.

"Oh no. Hasn't someone been cleaning this for you? It's infected. Didn't you have any ointment for it?"

As soon as the words left his mouth he felt a wash of shame. Who would clean Octavius's wounds for him? He was a proud old man, with only one living relative – a young teenage girl. Of course he wouldn't ask Storm to help him. Storm said Octavius had waved her off the last few times she'd visited, saying he needed to sleep.

Lincoln almost choked as he tried to soak the old leaves off Octavius's shoulders. Now, he was angry. He should have thought about this. It just hadn't even entered his mind. As soon as Octavius had been injured, he should have made sure that someone was taking care of him. But there was just so much else going on here. And Octavius was so used to being in charge, and seemed so invincible. He hadn't imagined him actually being ill.

Lincoln took a deep breath. This was going to take some time. He walked through to the bedroom. "Mum, there are some things we're going to need. I'll give you a list. Find Jesa, Leif or Storm. They'll be able to help you."

His mother looked confused. "Is it bad?"

"It's really bad."

"Shouldn't we take him to the care centre?"

"We probably should," he glanced over his shoulder, "but if he'd wanted to go there I think he'd be there already. Let me clean his wounds and you can give him some food while I try to make some fresh ointment."

His stomach was churning. Octavius had been the Captain Regent of parliament. He was used to telling everyone what to do. But right now Octavius just looked like a frail old man. A very sick, old man. Would the fresh ointment even work?

Octavius was the person who had got Lincoln and his family on the ship. They owed him. If they'd stayed in the burning city there was every chance they would have died. At least on Piloria they had a chance to fight for survival.

He gently eased off one edge of an old leaf. The wound on Octavius's shoulder was putrid, with yellow pus leaking out, and the smell...

Lincoln breathed in through his mouth. He had to do this.

Octavius needed to be around. This thing between Reban and Silas would come to a head at some point and there needed to be someone who people respected to help settle it. Someone who they might listen to, in amongst the fighting and taking sides.

He owed Octavius. He owed Storm. And he owed the people outside.

If they wanted to survive, they needed to work together.

And if they didn't have Octavius, would that even be possible?

NINETEEN

STORMCHASER

"I have an idea."

The faces around the campfire looked up. It didn't matter that they'd all finally settled into their new homes – at the same time every night, one of them started a fire outside and they all sat around in the safety of the enclosed compound. Sometimes they brought food they'd made in one of the kitchens, sometimes they cooked something on top of the fire, but the important thing was the sitting together. Keeping hold of their own little community. Jesa and her family, Lincoln and his, Storm, Reban and Leif. Somehow, now, the group felt like her own family. The only person missing was Octavius – but the last few times she'd visited his home, he'd waved her away, claiming to be busy. It was odd, she had a sense that he was almost... avoiding her.

The daily ritual set them apart from the others, who eyed

them with suspicion for sitting outside at night, rather than hiding away in their homes.

It was a clear night, with the bright stars twinkling in the dark sky above. The wind was brisk but the air warm. The orange fire flickered, sending a plume of twisting smoke dispersing in the air around them.

Jesa leaned back on her hands, her legs stretched out in front of her. "Go on, then. What is it? Hit me with it."

They were all tired. Construction was almost at an end. The only person who hadn't worked outside today was Lincoln, who'd disappeared for a while saying he was trying to track Lorcan down.

Leif leaned forward. "Tell me this is something interesting. Some of the people around here are idiots."

Reban let out a snort. He'd been strangely quiet these last few days.

"Pity there wasn't some kind of test before everyone got on the ship," he commented.

Lincoln's mother spoke quietly. "There wasn't time for anything like that, Reban. People were fighting for their lives. Earthasia wasn't like anything you remember."

Tamb's voice was haunting, and the others exchanged glances. She rarely spoke, unless it was about day-to-day things. Reban shifted uncomfortably on the ground, his sarcastic quip put firmly in its place.

Storm tried to hide a smile. Of course she shouldn't smile. Not with the way Tamb had said those words. It was clear she was still troubled by the way they'd left Earthasia. But watching someone set Reban right? She liked it. He was a little uncomfortable and a little embarrassed now – these were sides of his character that she'd rarely seen. In the last weeks, she'd learned so much more about her father, by watching how he interacted with others. Before, when it was only the two of them, it had taken a few months before they'd reached some kind of alliance.

Leif broke the silence. "What's the idea, then?"

Storm plunked herself down on the ground next to him, and glanced around at her companions. She was getting used to this; the point at night where they were all comfortable enough to sit in each other's company. There were other people on watch. They didn't have to constantly look over their shoulders, and that was new to her.

The only other people she also wished were sitting around their circle were Octavius, and Dell and his father. But Dell had hardly spoken to her since he'd been released from the medico care centre – even though in the face of a dinosaur attack, she'd refused to leave without him, she'd waited to help him. It wasn't that she wanted praise or thanks, but the fact he couldn't even seem to acknowledge it hurt.

It was almost as though Dell blamed her for every dinosaur that was alive on this continent. Like Storm stayed up all night and created some new hideous creature that they would all have to run from. It was ridiculous, and she knew it. But somehow she just couldn't have that "get over yourself" conversation with her only old friend from back home.

Lincoln sat down beside her and gave her a rough nudge. "Come on then, don't keep us in suspense."

She took a deep breath. It was easier to stare at the fire than the surrounding faces. Particularly when she wasn't sure if they would agree with her. "We need to help them."

"Who?" Jesa frowned.

"The people here. All they know about dinosaurs is fear. We need to show them that there's more than that. Lincoln already suggested we should and I think he's right, so I've been trying to work out how." She sighed as she hugged Barney close. "I caught one of them today pointing a gun at Barney. They didn't seem to care he was tiny, or that he was harmless. All they saw was a *dinosaur*."

"So what's your plan?" Leif asked.

Storm pressed her lips together. "We know they're not all predators. We know that some of them are harmless herbivores. Just maybe a little ungainly. A little too big."

The idea was forming more completely in her mind now.

"I think it's time we had a scouting party of our own. I think it's time we showed people in the camp how beautiful some of the dinosaurs really are."

There was silence for a few seconds. It was clear she'd caught them all unawares. Jesa was the first to speak, her voice a little high. "You and Lincoln obviously think the same way. I like it. Did you have somewhere in mind?"

Storm nodded, glad of the first bit of enthusiasm. "Sure. When Reban and I came here first, we staked out a huge watering hole. It's a couple of hours' walk from here. But the diplodocuses seem to nest around the area. The watering hole seemed safe, and there were lots of other gentle creatures there too. It would be a good starting point. A relatively safe starting point." Safe. She'd said that word twice now, but it was the one she was trying to emphasize, even though she still had a few doubts herself.

Reban was watching her carefully with his violet eyes. For a minute, she thought he might actually disagree. But it was almost like something clicked in his brain. "You know, that might not be a bad idea." He nodded to Arta, Tamb, Kayna and Caleb. "Apart from the trek in from the ship, you've never really got a chance to see the land. This way, if we go together, and everyone follows our instructions, we can show you how to move around safely. We can give you tips. What to look out for. What to avoid. Ways to make yourself less visible to a dinosaur."

There were a few anxious glances. Jesa nudged her brother. "Don't you want to get out of here? Get a chance to explore a bit more?"

He gave a reluctant nod. "I guess so."

"And it will be safe?" Tamb's eyes settled on Reban instead of Storm.

His eyes flickered to Leif and Lincoln. "As long as you all follow instructions, there's no reason it wouldn't be." He leaned forward, putting his hands on his knees and facing Storm. "How are you going to convince the others to come? And do you really want them to come?"

It was a fair question. There were a few people in camp

she'd rather not take along. There was no way they would follow instructions, and she couldn't trust them around the watering hole – not after last time on the hill.

She gave a careful nod. "How about we start small? We ask a few groups, a few families, if they want to come along. Convince them that they'll be safe – they might even have fun! When we get back, they'll start talking to others, and hopefully word will spread that there's more to Piloria than Silas portrays."

Lincoln nodded and smiled at her. "I can think of a few people who might want to come along. People who are more" – he took a moment to choose his words – "sympathetic to what we're dealing with. People who might actually want to live peacefully with the dinosaurs instead of slaying them all."

"Leif?" She wanted to hear from him. In a way, he would be the hardest to convince. Leif had never had any love for the dinosaurs.

He gave her the briefest glance. "You're sure about this?"

Storm nodded quickly. "I wouldn't suggest it if I wasn't. I'd never put you all at risk."

His gaze was steady. "You're *sure*?"

"I'm sure."

He let out a sigh. "Well, okay then." He wrinkled his brow. "Anyone got an idea of how to get past the Stipulators?"

"We're not prisoners. We can leave whenever we want. This isn't Earthasia." Reban's voice was firm. So firm it sent little goosebumps up Storm's arms.

She gave a hesitant smile. "Okay, then. It's agreed. Let's

plan, talk to people, garner some interest, then in the next few days we go on our own expedition. Let's show these people that not all dinosaurs are bad." She leaned over Barney. "What do you think, Barney, want to come?"

He gave a little grunt and snuffled off. Storm fixed a smile on her face and lifted up her water canister. "To having fun."

There were a few muted murmurs around her. Not exactly the enthusiasm she was hoping for.

Storm leaned back and looked up at the dark night sky. She had to make this work. She just *had* to.

TWENTY

STORMCHASER

"**A**nd where do you think you're going?"

Sneering Silas. She was starting to think the guy had eyes in the back of his head. Storm tilted her chin.

"Out," was all she replied.

She could sense the nerves from some of the rest of the group. A few had taken a bit of convincing to come along in the first place. But finally they'd managed to persuade around thirty people to join them. It was a start.

"Got them." Reban strolled easily through the group, clutching a variety of weapons to his chest. He looked up. "Oh, Silas." He said the words as if Silas were something on the bottom of his boot, and Storm had to stifle her laugh. Reban started passing the weapons out. A crossbow for Jesa, extra knives for Storm and guns for Lincoln and Leif. Reban gave a nod. "More than enough." He turned back around and shook his head. "You still here?"

Silas's jaw clenched. "Where do you think you" – his eyes swept over the group – "and your little stragglers are going?"

Reban smiled and bit into a piece of fruit he had in his hand. "Out," he said simply, repeating Storm's answer.

This time, she couldn't hide her smile.

Reban gestured with his head. "Open the gate, Silas. Some of us have things to do."

Silas exploded. "You're not going anywhere. None of you are! No one gets to leave the camp without my permission."

Reban was as cool as could be. He raised one eyebrow, clearly provoking the Chief Stipulator's well-known fury. "Since when do I need your permission to do anything?"

It worked like a charm. Silas erupted, his pent-up anger and frustration spilling over. "Everyone has to do what I say! I'm the Chief Stipulator here. My word is law. No one makes a move without my say-so!"

Reban continued eating his apple as more people started to gather around, curious about Silas's outburst. "This isn't Earthasia, Silas. This is Piloria." Reban held out his arms. "A whole new world." He looked around and gave a little nod of his head. "We need to work together to survive. But there's no need for Stipulators here. What we need is a new kind of government – *elected* officials amongst the four hundred or so people here, so we can make decisions together for the welfare of our community."

Something flashed before Storm's eyes. A vision of Reban from the past. On Earthasia, where his actions were never questioned. Where he'd ruled, partly, by fear. In parliament – where he took no prisoners. Now, she was seeing a whole other side of him, and she knew she shouldn't really be surprised. She'd witnessed how he'd been treated by his peers before he'd been banished to Piloria. Awkward as it had been, they'd learned to work together on Piloria. They'd had a few months of doing only what *they* wanted while learning how to survive here. Going back to being governed by someone else seemed almost alien to her – and obviously to Reban too.

But as she watched the scene unfold before her, Storm was learning more about her father than she ever had before. This was deliberate. He was goading Silas deliberately. Setting out the questions he wanted the people here to start asking themselves.

She couldn't help but be impressed. He was right. The people of Earthasia had already revolted against the Stipulators and their rules. There was every chance that it could happen again here. Silas had survived by the skin of his teeth the last time. What about now?

She could hear people start to whisper behind her.

But Silas seemed to focus only on the current object of his hate. "I can throw you out of here anytime I want, Reban. You aren't that important. In fact, you're an instigator." He put his hands on his hips and looked around. "Maybe the next building we construct should be a prison." He nodded to himself, as if he were imagining approval from the people listening.

A few of the scouting party started to look angry. But it was Jesa who spoke up first.

"What exactly is your issue, Silas? None of us are prisoners here. We don't have time to build prisons, or to rule over each other when we're still trying to work out how to survive. If we want to go outside the camp, then that's exactly what we'll do." She gestured towards Storm and Reban. "They're going to show us areas that are safer. They're going to teach some of the people who haven't been here before how to scout, how to move safely in a land with creatures we aren't that familiar with. How dare you try to stop them? I mean, are you crazy? Shouldn't this be the kind of thing we make compulsory? Learning to live with other creatures – rather than hunting them and scaring them into attacking us? After all, my father managed to survive here alone for nine years with no help from you – and without your rules."

She pointed to the towers.

"Yes, we need protection. Yes, we need to be vigilant. But we also need to remember that we've come to their continent – not the other way around. Put yourself back in your box, Silas. We're done listening to you."

Storm's mouth fell open. She couldn't help it. She moved over next to Jesa. Reban's eyebrow had gone up a further notch.

Jesa had always been feisty, but clearly she had a line in the sand that Silas had just crossed. She was right. Jesa's father – a former Stipulator – had been left here for nine years and survived.

Silas went to open his mouth again, but Reban lifted his palm in front of Silas's face. "Save it. I think Jesa covered everything."

He turned towards the crowd. "Okay, then. We're armed and ready to go. Who wants to go and see a little of Piloria, without the danger? If you're coming, wear walking boots and bring plenty of water. We'll be gone for a few hours."

A few people nodded at each other. "Wait for us," was the cry, and they headed back to their homes to get what they needed.

Reban moved towards the gate and gestured to one of the guards. "I expect we'll be back mid-afternoon." He smiled at the furious Silas. "Just be glad I didn't demand we take the transporters with us. But people need to learn how to survive on the land, not in a metal box."

The guards started opening the gates, not waiting for Silas's approval. It looked as though Reban's words – or Jesa's – had connected with some people. There were still a few angry faces, standing shoulder to shoulder with Silas. But as Storm's group waited patiently at the gates, other people joined them.

When everyone was ready, Reban gave her a nod. "Okay, Storm. Let's go." He lowered his voice for a second. "And let's hope nothing else has staked a claim on this watering hole – otherwise we're all in trouble."

He pasted a smile on his serious face and lifted one hand in the air as he surveyed the waiting group.

"Come on, guys, let's see some Piloria!"

Storm waited at the tail end of the group with Lincoln, signalling to the guards to close the gates behind them and getting the full, furious glare of Silas until they were fully closed.

She adjusted her backpack on her shoulders and gave Lincoln a wry smile. "Looks like my good idea has grown arms and legs." She raised her eyebrows as she started walking. "Here's hoping they all stay attached."

TWENTY-ONE

LINCOLN

Over the course of a few hours he could see the mood and attitude of the group changing. Their wariness and fear as they set out was easily understood. But the altercation with Silas actually seemed to have worked in the scouting party's favour.

People were annoyed by him. Lincoln heard snippets of conversations he hadn't heard before. *Who put him in charge? Why do we have to do what they say? I liked that idea of elected officials – a group of representatives we choose to make decisions.*

He couldn't help but smile. Things were changing. Hopefully for the better.

Because their group had swollen to around sixty, Reban had broken them into three parts. Leif and Jesa leading one, Reban leading another, and Lincoln and Storm leading the third. It made it easier to teach the survival skills along the way. Storm was as agile as usual – teaching a few doubtful people how to scale a tree if they had to.

As they trekked through a forest, Lincoln pointed out some signs of other creatures, some food they could eat, and some foods they couldn't – which was all information Blaine had given them months before. They pointed out the evergreen leaves and yellow vines they used in the ointment for the blistering plague and a whole host of other ailments. Storm showed them the plants that created the gum Blaine had used, along with places to find water if they ended up lost or stranded.

Halfway along, they came across a little pack of aquilops. The creatures were small, only ankle height, as well as being curious and friendly. Several of the people recognized them as being the same as Barney and asked Storm whether they could take them back to camp as pets. But the aquilops had other ideas – they were playful but fast, and when a few camp mates tried to lift and capture them, they squealed and darted off into the jungle.

They stopped at various vantage points and talked everyone through things they should try to observe before deciding on a route. It was basically a quick survival course on how to try to stay alive if, at any point, they found themselves outside the camp. They'd already lost a few people who'd wandered away from camp, never to be seen again.

After the initial few minutes of terror on their faces, the group members realized this was all just about staying safe. By the time they were halfway to their destination, their spirits were bright. People were laughing and joking, remarking on the scents and colours of Piloria. Several picked flowers or plants to take back to camp.

They found a thicket of berry brambles and carefully dug up some of those plants, in the hope they'd be able to find somewhere closer to camp for them to grow and thrive – another new food source.

Storm was a natural teacher, and people listened. They respected her. In fact, it seemed they'd started to respect all those who had been on Piloria before. Lincoln could see the pride on Arta's and his mother's faces as he answered questions and demonstrated survival techniques across the varied landscape.

Storm fell into step next to him all along the route. He could see her occasionally glancing towards Reban, watching how he was interacting with his group. Eventually she realized Lincoln had noticed. She gave a shrug.

"It's weird. It's weird seeing him as something other than a Stipulator. That's what he's always been." She waved her hand. "I mean, not here – not for the past few months. But when you all first appeared, I wondered if…"

"You wondered if he would turn back into that person?"

She nodded. "It crossed my mind. And to be honest, I think it probably crossed his." She gave a sigh and ran her fingers through her hair. "He'd just started to seem…normal, if that makes sense. We were having conversations. Real conversations. But as soon as he set eyes on Silas, it was like a black veil descended."

Lincoln could see the concern laced across her face. "But," he said carefully, "things seem better now. There will always be a rivalry between Silas and Reban. It's been there so long it's probably ingrained in their blood."

He'd meant it as a casual throwaway comment, but Storm's face fell. "But some things *are* blood. And they should be more important."

Now he felt bad. He put his hand on her shoulder. "He became a father to a teenager, literally overnight. You both have a way to go. Sometimes he gets it right, sometimes he gets it wrong." Lincoln smiled. "I think that's normal for parents, don't you?"

"Hmm…"

It wasn't exactly a positive response. But before he could ask something else she turned to him, walking backwards as they headed up a hill. "Hey, have you seen Octavius? I was looking for him these past few days. The house that's supposed to be his is almost untouched." Lincoln's skin prickled. Lying to Storm in the past had caused problems. He'd promised he wouldn't do it again. But Octavius had purposely said he didn't want people – and by "people", Lincoln was pretty sure he meant Storm – to know he was sick. Did lying by omission count?

"Yeah, I've seen him around."

He waited for her to question him further, but she turned back around as the hill got a little steeper. The two other groups had stopped at the top of the hill, and when Lincoln got there, he understood why.

It had to be one of the best vantage points in Piloria. From here they could see for hundreds of sectars. The shallow watering hole was nestled in the valley, the sun glimmering off the surface so it looked almost silver.

But it was the creatures around the watering hole that were capturing everyone's attention. The vulcanodons were small sauropods that lived in family-sized packs. From here, it was easy to see their dark-grey skin, four column-like legs, round bodies and long necks and tails. They weren't big enough to be too intimidating, roughly twice the size of an average man. And there were other creatures too, skirting around the edges of the watering hole – the duckbills with crests on their heads, which looked like bulky lizards, and the smaller aquilops, that seemed to run between the rest of the creatures' feet.

"Look – more Barneys," said Storm with a smile.

The people around them seemed frozen in wonder. They all stood in silence, watching the scene. The surroundings were lush green with bright bursts of colour around the watering hole. The creatures moved companionably together. The aquilops looked as if they were having fun, running around the edges of the rest of the creatures. The duckbills were oblivious to their surroundings, occasionally nudging at another creature as they snuffled around the ground for food or waded into the broad watering hole to drink. But it was the vulcanodons that were the most entertaining.

Everyone watched as one of the fully grown vulcanodons seemed to be tending to the younger ones in the middle of the watering hole. The smaller ones were flicking water with their heads and tails, showering every creature around them.

"Are...are they playing?" asked the guy standing next to Lincoln.

Storm grinned as all faces turned expectantly to her. She shrugged. "Who knows?" She pointed to the sun, high in the sky above them. "Or maybe they're just as warm as we are? They come here every day around the same time. They're peaceful, plant-eating creatures. Apart from their size and being a bit ungainly, they aren't any danger to us at all."

The three groups had congregated together at the top of the hill. "Have you been near to them?"

Leif spoke first. "I haven't met these ones. But their bigger versions – the diplodocus – were at another watering hole the last time we were here. We filled our watering cans at one and washed next to them at another."

Lincoln took a deep breath. It felt good to hear Leif say something positive. He understood how angry he was at being stuck here. But what other option was there? It seemed as if Leif was reluctantly accepting that Piloria was their new home, and trying to make the best of it. And from the way his friendship with Jesa was continuing to develop, that could only be a good thing.

"They didn't mind you being here?" asked another guy, his brow creased into a frown.

"They don't seem to." This time it was Reban who answered, making the guy jump a little. "Storm and I have been here a few times. We always check the surroundings before we go down to the watering hole, but we've never had any trouble here." Reban stretched out his back, then turned to either side. "Anything?" he asked Leif and Jesa.

They shook their heads. He turned to Storm and Lincoln; they shook their heads too.

"Okay then." Reban was standing in the middle of the group now. "If you feel ready, we'll go down to the watering hole. In previous days, this was essential for me and Storm. You don't have that problem. Back at the camp we're getting clean water from the river. But, if you're ever out here, places like this might be your best source of water." He pulled a silver packet from his rear pocket. "If that does happen, you need these. Sterilization tablets. Put one in your water canister once you've collected your sample and leave it for an hour. It will be safe to drink after that." He put the tablets back in his pocket. "Okay, lesson over. Remember to always observe the surroundings for a while before you go down. Make sure – like today – it's safe."

Lincoln could see a few anxious faces in the crowd. "If you don't want to come down, feel free to stay up here. It's a great vantage point."

Leif and Jesa started the slow walk down the hill. Their easy manner seemed to reassure some people, who started after them. Reban nodded approvingly as most of the rest of the group started too, leaving only a few individuals on the top of the hill.

Lincoln murmured to Storm. "Let's go. They might join us in a while."

Storm nodded and they walked, side by side, down the hill.

A few of the vulcanodons looked up at the approaching strangers. They appeared curious for a few minutes, obviously waiting to see if the strangers meant them harm. The duckbills completely ignored the humans, though the aquilops were more than a little interested. Around ten of them snuffled at the feet of the group. People were still wary. One woman let out a little yelp as an aquilops touched her foot. Storm ran over next to her and touched her arm.

"They're harmless." She gestured at Barney, who was sniffing around her ankles. "He's followed me around since I first got here." She bent down and held out her hand to the snuffling aquilops, letting it smell her skin. "See?"

The woman gave a hesitant nod, but stepped back. Lincoln was watching everyone with interest. People were naturally curious about the dinosaurs, but maybe didn't quite believe that they weren't a danger. He could tell Storm was anxious for this to work well, and he understood why. She wanted to convince people that not all dinosaurs were deadly, that they could actually cohabit here.

Reban seemed a bit more relaxed, talking to people, pointing out some things about the dinosaurs around the watering hole. Lincoln had no doubt that the scene at the gate had worked in Reban's favour. More people were questioning the apparent authority of the Stipulators on Piloria. And they were right to. His visit to the lab yesterday had been fruitless. The Stipulators wouldn't let him anywhere near Lorcan, no matter what kind of excuse he gave them to get in the lab. They'd only muttered about how they couldn't take the risk of contamination, and that the lab was only open to authorized personnel. But Lincoln had worked in the lab before, he knew how to avoid contamination. It all felt like a cover story to keep him out. And what about Lorcan? He must have realized that Silas wasn't allowing people to see him. Had he even been allowed to leave the lab? No one had seen him – or his daughter, come to that – for the last few weeks. And Lincoln wasn't entirely sure that Lorcan would want to spend all his time here developing dinosaur viruses. Maybe Silas was threatening him, or his family? It was the only explanation that made sense.

Storm appeared back at his side and sat down at the edge of the watering hole, pulling out some food from her backpack. She handed part of it to him. "Here, I came prepared."

He smiled and opened his backpack too. "So did I. I picked some fruit along the way." He pulled out one of the orange fruits they'd tried before and started to peel back the thick skin.

Storm pulled her knees up to her chest and rested her arms on them, watching the interactions of the group around the watering hole. Jesa and Leif were splashing at the other side, Arta and Lincoln's mother was with them, laughing and joking. A few other people were watching closely, and, with a careful eye on the vulcanodons, they paddled into the clear water too.

One of the teenagers was kneeling down, holding out his

hand the way the Storm had a few moments earlier, allowing an aquilops to smell it. He laughed as it kept nudging his hand.

Storm sighed and Lincoln turned towards her. "This is it," she said. "This is what I want for Piloria." Her eyes were fixed on the scene ahead.

Lincoln could almost feel her longing.

"Look at it. This place is beautiful. The green, the clear water, the fruits and flowers." Her eyes were sparkling as she talked. "And the gentle creatures. What harm could they possibly do us?"

He understood. He did. But he had to say the words she didn't want to hear. "But they're not all like the sauropods, Storm. You know that." He didn't say any more – he didn't have to. They'd both witnessed enough on Piloria to know that a life here would be a life constantly spent being vigilant. Having an off day could cost you your life.

She nodded her head and pressed her lips together for a moment before she turned to face him. "But I have hope. Hope that this is the kind of life we can have here. Have you ever seen anything so beautiful? Think of what we came from. A bland, grey city. Virtually no living creatures. No viable land. We destroyed our own continent. This – this is a whole other kind of beauty. One I want to be part of. One I want to take care of."

Lincoln swallowed and spoke carefully. "So…if we heard that things had calmed down back on Earthasia, and we had a chance to return?"

He barely got to finish before she shook her head and patted the grass they were sitting on. "No way. This is it. This is it for me. I want to stay here. I want to stay here – with this." She lifted her hand again and smiled. The sun had changed position and a faint rainbow had appeared in the distance behind the dinosaurs. Storm sucked in a breath.

"What? What is it?" Lincoln instantly scanned the horizon, checking for any movement that might signal trouble, but he couldn't see anything at all.

Storm had her hand up to her chest, and when he looked at her again her eyes were wet.

"What?" he asked again. "Have I missed something?"

She smiled and shook her head. "No. It's nothing. It's just…"

Her eyes were definitely glistening with unshed tears. She steadied her breathing. "It's the first rainbow I've seen on Piloria." She gave a thoughtful kind of smile. "It reminds me of something. A story from my past."

"What story?" His curiosity was piqued. Storm rarely spoke about her past.

She picked at the grass with her fingers. "It was from a long time ago. A story that Octavius, apparently, used to tell my mum."

"A kids' story?"

She nodded and he frowned. "But your mother never told it to you?"

Storm shook her head. "That's the strange thing, because it's kind of special. But if she did tell me it, I don't remember."

She stopped talking and stared out at the horizon again. This was the point where he wanted to ask more questions. What was the story? What did Octavius tell her?

But Lincoln knew better than to push Storm. Anyone who pushed Storm learned quickly that prying was the best way to get her to slam all her shields up at top speed. She had so many layers. It was part of why he liked her. That, her conviction and her strong beliefs.

Lincoln knew she meant it when she said she never wanted to leave – no matter what the dangers were here. He was having a tougher time adjusting than she was. But Lincoln's issues were all about keeping his family safe. He'd brought them here – they were his responsibility. He watched as his mother and Arta laughed and ate fruit with Jesa and Leif at the other side of the watering hole. It was the most relaxed he'd seen any of them, and he'd love it if this could be their new "normal". But would there really ever be a chance of that?

He looked sideways at Storm. She'd let her hair down. Her skin was darkening every day. But it was her violet eyes that always made him catch his breath. They were the one thing that had made him connect her to Reban when they'd all first met. It was amazing how things had changed, how far they'd all come since that initial, frosty meeting.

Lincoln leaned back on his hands. "I still can't quite believe all this. It seems unreal. And look, Reban's even managing to be sociable."

Storm laughed as she glanced over to where her father

was standing with some of his group near one of the vulcanodons. "Maybe this is the person he wants to be, instead of the one he was on Earthasia."

His heart gave a pang. It was a hopeful thing to say. And from what Lincoln could see, Reban was trying his best to leave his cold-hearted Chief-Stipulator past behind. Yes, there was still frustration. But, like Storm, he'd never heard Reban once wish he could be back on Earthasia. It seemed his intention was to make his life here.

"Do you think there is anyone else?" Lincoln asked Storm.

"What do you mean?"

He paused for a second. "I mean, those two ships – the *Invincible* and the *Endeavour*. Do you really think across the whole of the continent, Ambulus City was the only place to send out ships?"

She looked thoughtful. "It hadn't really crossed my mind. But now you mention it, no, of course that doesn't make sense." She sat more upright. "Maybe there'll be a ship from Norden, or from Tarribeth City?" She ran her fingers through her hair and wrinkled her nose. "Or maybe those places were fine. Maybe there have been no riots there."

"Do you even think that could be true?" His eyes had fixed on Leif now at the other side of the watering hole.

He had to be worried about his family back in Norden, and for Rune's and Kronar's families too. There had been no time to get in touch. No chance to see if they were safe or not. But was there a chance they could be headed to Piloria too?

"The thing is," he went on, when Storm didn't reply, "Piloria is a big continent. If anyone else does come, they could land at the other side of it, and we would never, ever know. Never find out." He leaned his chin on one hand. "And we might never find out what's happened back home."

She shot him a sympathetic glance. "You're still worried about that, aren't you?"

He nodded and swallowed. "You didn't see it. You didn't see the chaos. The panic. You didn't smell the fires burning, and wonder what else might be—"

His voice broke off. He couldn't say any other words out loud. He ran his fingers through his hair. "You've no idea how glad I felt when I saw Octavius at the ship. If it hadn't been for him…we would never have got on board. We would have been left behind."

Storm's voice was quiet. "We have to look forward, Lincoln. This place can be good for us, not just a way to escape the bad. I didn't see the burning city. I made my own choice to stay here. I wasn't left with only one option – this was the one I picked."

He shook his head. "You say that, but you were, Storm. You'd just found the only person you knew of as family. And if you wanted to have any kind of a relationship with your family, you had to stay. Coming home to Earthasia would have left you with a million questions that you would have had no way of answering."

He noticed a slight tremble in her hand on her knee. Her head gave the tiniest nod of acknowledgement. "I wanted to stay." Her voice was a bit shaky. "Whether it was with Reban or not. But maybe it was partly because I don't feel as if Earthasia is my home. I never have. I have no connection to that place. No reason to ever want to go back." She lifted one hand. "This is where I feel settled. This is where I feel I belong."

"But what about what we're doing?"

"What do you mean?"

"I mean, we got here, and within a few days, we practically stripped a forest to create our home. We dug up the land to make drainage. We built watchtowers and walls to protect us. We started creating power for electricity."

She looked puzzled. "You think we should all just live in the forests like Blaine did?"

"You don't?"

She shifted a little awkwardly on the grass. "I don't think the evergreen shacks would work with so many of us. The whole point of Blaine's shack was to blend in, to not be noticed. Four hundred people can't exactly blend in. Do you really think it's possible to hide the scent of four hundred bodies? We've already seen the titanosaurus. We've met all these dinosaurs today – they're not so far away. How long before more come to camp? Piloria is big. But is it really that big that we can hide?"

He started pulling at some blades of the thick, soft grass. "You know what the next step is, don't you?"

Her eyes narrowed. "No. What?"

"They want to find a way to electrify the outer rim of the wall."

"What?"

He nodded. "I heard some workmen talking when I was trying to get into the lab. They think the solar panels can create enough power to electrify the fences. They want to use it as a line of defence, in case we get attacked."

She shook her head. "I don't get it. It's not as if there've been any T-rexes prowling about – and an electrified fence is hardly going to do anything if the quetzalcoatlus decide to come back."

"Yeah, they're looking at a new kind of weapon for them, too. Same principle. Some kind of electric shock to zap them."

"Will that even work?"

He shook his head. "I'm not entirely sure. Maybe it's worth a try. They don't seem to think that bullets or arrows will pierce the thicker skin of creatures like the spinosauruses." He raised his eyebrows. "Not everyone has your throwing skill with a knife, or Jesa's accuracy with an arrow."

She still looked a bit puzzled. "But an electric shock, I still don't get it. Could that really protect us from the predators?"

"Maybe. They haven't sorted everything out yet. I don't know much about power supplies and generators. They were talking about needing to lay some more cables and a junction box outside of camp."

"How much more did you hear at the lab?"

He shook his head. "That was it. They wouldn't let me in."

He could tell she was itching to ask something else and he could guess what it was. "I haven't been able to find out about the viruses. But leave it with me. I'll try again. I have to be able to get through to Lorcan somehow."

She gave a nod and stood back up, dusting herself off. "We should start to pack up and head back. We've disturbed these guys long enough."

He gave a thoughtful nod as he looked back around the group. Everyone seemed happy. "Do you think your little publicity trip has worked?"

Storm put her hands on her hips and looked around, shooting him a cheeky glance. "It better have. Remember, I even talked *Reban* into taking part."

She winked and walked towards the nearest group of people, asking them to start packing up so they could head back. Lincoln waved over at Leif and Jesa, then to Reban, so they could gather everyone and make sure no one was left behind.

He stood for a few seconds, with a weird feeling in his chest. Lincoln knew how important the success of this trip was. He'd seen the yellow virus. He'd guessed what Silas's plans were, and he hadn't yet managed to get near Lorcan to persuade him not to make any more of the virus. It was so important that people felt this could be a home, in harmony with the dinosaurs. Slowly but surely they had to find a way to persuade them that Silas's deadly plan wasn't the right way.

His mother and sister looked happy. They hadn't been ready at all for Piloria, but they seemed to be embracing it now. Leif's hard edges were being eroded little by little, too. He, above anyone else, could hate the fact he was here. But Jesa and her family seemed to have welcomed him and helped him finally embrace the place.

He watched as Storm continued her journey over towards Reban, her hair swinging like a dark sheet in the sun. Her footsteps slowed just a bit. Was he the only person that noticed her confidence always swayed a little in front of her father?

His stomach gave an uncomfortable twist. He knew Storm was still desperate for Reban's approval, but the funny thing was that at times Lincoln could also see that Reban was desperate for Storm's approval too.

Lincoln slung his backpack over his shoulder. It was time to escort these people home. It was time to hope that they would spread the word that there was beauty outside the camp walls – and friendly dinosaurs.

All it would take was for a few conversations – a few whispers to start other people in the camp becoming curious. To start questioning Silas's authority and his beliefs. To plant the seeds for people to think on their own. For the good of Piloria, it was inevitable that at some point this would all come to a head. At some point, people might have to make a choice about who they would follow and what kind of life they wanted to lead on the dinosaur continent. And when it came to that, Storm and Lincoln could only hope that enough people would support them, and want to live the way they did – with the dinosaurs, rather than without them.

Lincoln looked up at the sky. That was all they could hope for. That, and some kind of miracle cure for Octavius, of course. Because it was Octavius who should lead this fight for them. People liked him. People respected him.

Lincoln sighed. It was time to get back and see how Octavius was doing.

TWENTY-TWO

STORMCHASER

Security around the lab was tight, but Leif and Jesa were keen to have a little fun. Two men were standing at the lab doors. No one seemed to get in unless they worked there. On Storm's signal, Leif and Jesa started an argument a little way in front of the guards.

"Don't you steal from me again!" shouted Jesa. "I planted the bramble bush, so the fruit is mine!"

"Get over it," yelled back Leif. "We all have to live together and share what we have." The shouting continued, with both of them getting closer and closer to the other's face.

"They're enjoying this," Lincoln whispered quietly in Storm's ear.

She nodded in agreement. "Absolutely."

The guards were curious and started towards Leif and Jesa. As they got closer, Jesa's face dropped. "Is that a T-rex?" she screamed, pointing to the wall behind the guards.

"Run!" shouted Leif. He turned on his heel and both him and Jesa set off at high speed.

The guards glanced at each other for the briefest of seconds.

"What do we do?" asked one, looking behind him and scouring the edge of the compound. Fear was written all over his face.

"I'm not hanging around," said the other, and took off after Jesa and Leif.

Within a second, the other followed.

Storm nudged Lincoln. "Quick. Now."

They ducked through the thick door, slamming it behind them.

Storm had never been inside a lab before. She'd never had reason to. But the bright-yellow virus had imprinted on her brain. She needed to ask questions, and she needed an opportunity to speak to Lorcan Field.

As she pushed open the second door, she was struck by how quiet the lab was. The surfaces gleamed, a few machines whirred and there was a massive whiteboard, with figures all over it, on one wall. A few people were inputting data into machines, and some others were peering down into microscopes.

There was a large glass wall, and behind it she could see two white-suited figures. She walked over and pressed her hand against the glass, pulling it back instantly. It was cold. She stared at the palm of her hand for a second, surprised that they'd managed to achieve such a temperature on Piloria

– it was so humid and hot. Lincoln stayed behind her, keeping watch for the return of the guards.

Lorcan appeared from behind a metal door, his white hair in a shockwave around his face. He frowned for a second, his head tipped to the side, as if he were trying to place her.

"Stormchaser," she said, holding her still-cold hand out towards him. "I'm Reban's daughter, Octavius's great-niece." She glanced to her side. "And a friend of Lincoln's."

He gave a curious nod. "What can I do for you, Stormchaser?"

She waved at the microscopes. "You know that I've been here on Piloria before. I was part of the team who planted the first viruses." Storm didn't tell him she'd been against the idea. She was trying to get the information she needed from Lorcan. Storm pasted a smile on her face. "I also helped source the plants for you, so you could recreate the ointment back on Earthasia, for your daughter."

A frown creased his brow. "What is it that you want?" He leaned forward and lowered his voice. "And how did you manage to get in?"

She kept the smile on her face. "I wanted to talk to you about the new viruses you're creating. And the success of the old ones." She leaned forward too. "And we might have played a little trick on the guards. Let's talk quickly, I'm sure they'll be back."

Now, he looked interested, but the frown got deeper. "The viruses, yes…" he said slowly.

"The new virus. The yellow one. Is it dinosaur-specific?"

Lorcan paused for a second, as if he were thinking of the answer. "Well, it started out that way."

"But?"

"It was supposed to be based on the quetzalcoatlus DNA. You know we had the specimen after the attack. But…Silas changed his mind."

"Why?"

"He decided it shouldn't be so specific. There had been talk of this before – when we'd been creating the first dinosaur viruses. But the DNA was so complicated, so different for each species, that we didn't think it would be possible to create one virus that would affect all dinosaurs." He shook his head. "I still don't think it's really possible."

"What happened with the yellow virus, then? Is it just for the quetzalcoatlus?"

Lorcan sighed. "Maybe…maybe not. He rushed us. Told us not to specify it so much. But that doesn't really mean anything, in the world of science."

Storm bit her bottom lip and walked around the metal countertop, tracing her finger along it as a few conversations from the past floated into her mind. "If you do that, isn't there a chance you could make it so non-specific it could also affect humans – and plant life?"

Lorcan's head shot up. "No. That couldn't happen." But the way his frown increased told her there was at least an element of doubt in his mind.

"But you're making a virus to affect a living, breathing

creature. Isn't that just what we are? Living, breathing creatures."

Lorcan took some brisk steps over to the board and picked up one of the markers. She could almost see the rapid calculations in his head as he tried to reassure himself that she was wrong.

"There's something else we need to speak about," she added.

"Hmm?" He was already too busy for her.

"We think the virus did something to the raptors. It didn't kill them. It seemed to make them stronger."

"What?" His marker fell from his hand. "What did you say?"

Storm wanted to scream out loud. "You all arrived here in such a hurry and started to throw up this camp. Silas obviously has his own plans. But nobody stopped to talk to us about what happened when everyone left before. We don't even know that the T-rex and pterosaur viruses really worked. We think they might have – because we saw some bodies. But we weren't sure. What we are sure about" – she took a deep breath – "is that the raptors changed."

"What do you mean they changed? That's impossible."

"Is it?"

Lorcan's face paled. His voice was quiet. "Tell me how they changed."

Finally. "It didn't happen straight away. But after a while we noticed that they seemed bigger, stronger. And it wasn't just that. They seemed" – she actually didn't want to say the words out loud – "they seemed more intelligent. We always thought they were communicating, but it seemed even more pronounced. Their tracking skills improved. They could jump higher than before. We thought we knew the skill set of the raptors. But suddenly they became so much stronger."

Lorcan was still shaking his head. "But how on earth could our virus do that to them? And so quickly?"

"You're tampering with DNA. Doesn't it make sense that as well as killing cells, it can strengthen them?"

Lorcan rested one hand against the wall. "I-I…" He looked at the calculations on the board. "I'll need to go back over things. To look at them all again."

Storm straightened her shoulders. "Until you find out what went wrong, I don't think you should make any more viruses. We've moved five days' travel away from the closest raptor site we know of, but that doesn't mean they won't still find us – especially now there are so many of us. We don't even know anything about their mating patterns, or if they move with different seasons. Apart from Blaine, no one has really taken the time to try to get to know these creatures."

Lorcan was staring off into space. "Stronger. Smarter. It's like our worst nightmare."

Storm nodded slowly. "That's why I wanted to speak to you. That's why I wanted to tell you to stop. No matter what Silas orders you to do. I've tried to get in before today – we've all tried – but Silas has this place guarded so much it's been near impossible to get to you."

She could see the flash of fear behind Lorcan's eyes.

"He's been telling me my work is too important. Implying I shouldn't leave the lab at all. I have my daughter, Tarin, here. If I don't do as he says…" His voice tailed off.

She reached out and grabbed his arm. "He's not a man of science, Lorcan. Not like you. He doesn't understand how dangerous this could be. Imagine if we wipe out all the dinosaurs and ruin the whole ecosystem of Piloria? We could destroy this land, just like our own, in a matter of months. This beautiful green and vibrant continent could become as grey and lifeless as Earthasia. We could starve again, only on a different continent." She kept going, not giving him a chance to speak. "Or what about if the opposite happens – and we make all dinosaurs faster, stronger, more intelligent, more terrifying? We won't have a chance of survival. Is that what we want to do here?"

She tightened her grip on his arm.

"What if the virus you make hurts us, as well as the dinosaurs? What if *you* kill every living creature on this continent, including us? Your daughter's here as well, didn't you bring her to Piloria for a better life?"

Lorcan flinched as she said the word "you". Storm had said it deliberately. She was trying to manipulate him, trying to make him think again and to stop him following Silas's orders. According to Lincoln, he'd done it before, so surely he could do it again.

She released the pressure of her fingers on his arms, letting her voice get a little gentler. "Why can't we just take a moment? Think about things. You don't have to do what

Silas says. Or, you can let him think you're doing it, while you find out a bit more." She pointed to the board. "I don't know a single thing about what's up there – and I don't imagine he does either." She closed her eyes for a second, letting herself calm down. "This could be the most important decision you ever make." Her voice tailed off to a whisper. "For Piloria, we've got to get it right."

When she opened her eyes again, Lorcan was watching her carefully. "Do you know what you're asking me to do?"

She looked him straight in the eye. "I know that you were brave enough to do it before. I'm asking you to be brave enough to do it again. This isn't just about Tarin. This time, what you do will affect every single one of us who lives here. It could also affect the land and the creatures that live here. We need to fight for our survival, but let's do it the right way."

She stepped back. There was nothing else she could say. She'd done what she came to do. Storm had to give him time and space to consider his actions.

She gave a little nod of her head. "I won't tell anyone we had this conversation," she said briskly, "and I expect the same from you."

Lorcan blinked. He looked as if he might be physically sick.

He nodded towards a door behind him. "Go out that way. It's the way to the bathroom, but there's an exit next to it. They haven't thought to put a guard there." He beckoned to Lincoln, who was keeping watch at the other door. He reached out and grabbed Lincoln's arm as he approached.

It was the first time Storm had noticed a flicker of a smile on Lorcan's face. "She's persuasive, isn't she?" He squeezed Lincoln's arm, and for a second she got the hint that they might have discussed her before. "Be careful. Keep an eye on her. I've a bad feeling that Silas has it in for you two."

Storm's stomach clenched as they hurried to the exit.

"What does he mean?" she asked Lincoln.

He shook his head. "I've no idea. Let's just hope we don't find out."

TWENTY-THREE

LINCOLN

The camp was really taking shape. The lab had been finished first and a range of other buildings had been completed. Everyone had a home now. A huge communal centre had also been built for use as a school during the day, and a meeting place at night.

Crops had been planted both inside the camp and outside, in the area that used to be forest. Lorcan had been strangely quiet in the lab. He'd sneaked Lincoln into his office and questioned him relentlessly about the developed raptors – but it was useless. Lincoln had never set eyes on the raptors since he'd come back to Piloria. He could only recount what both Storm and Reban had told him.

The most interesting things were the plans for the power. The solar panels had been supplying power to the camp with ease, but it seemed that Silas wanted to proceed with his plans to electrify the outer wall of the camp. Men had been laying cables to a power box outside the camp. Lincoln was curious. He wandered over to the nearest labourer.

"Do you really think this will work?"

The guy gave a nonchalant look. "Put it this way, once the power supply is connected, I wouldn't touch the outer wall."

Lincoln looked questioningly at the large box being constructed outside the camp walls. "How come the power box is outside the camp?"

The guy tugged at his shirt. "There have been problems before."

"What kind of problems? Where?"

The guy looked a bit uncomfortable. "Back on Earthasia. There were a few problems with the power boxes. Electrifying the fence means we're using more power than we originally planned. It could cause issues."

Lincoln folded his arms across his chest and asked the question again. "What kind of issues?"

Sweat was running down the guy's brow. He stopped what he was doing and scratched at his beard. "Last time we overextended a power supply back on Earthasia, the box exploded. The power supply was limited anyway and the Stipulators made us load the power for more streets than we should have into one supply box."

"What?" Lincoln couldn't believe his ears. "Where did that happen?"

The guy's voice was low and he glanced over his shoulder. "On the outskirts of Ambulus City. Took out a whole street. That's why Silas said we had to build outside the camp walls."

He shrugged. "You know, just in case."

Lincoln watched for another few minutes, then walked swiftly back to his house. Octavius was still there.

It had been two weeks. They were fast running out of excuses for Storm. Each member of Lincoln's family had told her that they'd seen Octavius at some point or another.

In the last two days, he seemed to have picked up. He'd been more awake, more lucid. It seemed the mountain of soup that his mother had been feeding Octavius had started to have some effect – that, as well as the daily cleaning of his wounds, along with the application of a few different ointments.

It hadn't taken long for the people here to start exploring the plant life on Piloria and experimenting the same way that Blaine had. A number of people had the blistering plague and the fresh ointment kept the symptoms under control and their skin unbroken. His mother had tried to source some of the other leaves and vines that they'd noticed Blaine using, too. Lincoln wished he'd paid more attention – but one of the pastes she'd concocted was red, pungent, and seemed to have done the trick on Octavius's shoulders. The wounds had taken a while to finally clean out – for the first week, yellow pus had just flowed from them – but eventually they'd started to heal.

Maybe it was his age. Maybe it was the fact the quetzalcoatlus's talons had been so long. Or maybe it was the new and strange bacteria that lived on this continent. But Octavius's healing process had been long and arduous.

He'd been insistent that he didn't want Storm to know he was unwell. For the first few nights, Lincoln had sat up with him in the main room, as Octavius had thrashed around, delirious with his fever.

Frequently during the night, he'd cry out for Storm or for Dalia. Sometimes he'd just mutter away for hours under his breath. Other times he'd started conversations with Lincoln, as if he believed he were someone else. Sometimes those conversations were fierce, with Octavius angry and shouting. Sometimes they were quiet and his brow was creased with lines of worry.

In the last two weeks, Lincoln felt as if he'd been exposed to the world of the Captain Regent in a way he could never have imagined. The parliament on Earthasia had always been distant. The Stipulators had seemed an unstoppable force. Now, he knew so much more about what had gone on behind the doors of parliament over the last fifty years.

Some of the information horrified him. Families being sent to the mines for minimal crimes. A Stipulator who was murdered by his aide. Another Stipulator who'd killed numerous people but been protected by parliament.

But now the fever had passed. Octavius was sitting upright on the bench, drinking some kind of strong-smelling tea. He gave Lincoln a smile and lifted his cup to him as he walked in.

"It's not as good as bartoz tea, but I'm acquiring a taste for it."

He had *The Continent of Monsters* open on his lap in front

of him, the book that had been written by Reban's great-uncle – Magnus Don. No one had fully explained how he'd managed to get the details of quite so many of the creatures on this continent, though. Octavius had a graphite stick in his hand and was making notes in the book.

Lincoln was instantly intrigued. He crossed the room and sat down next to Octavius. "I'm glad to see you're feeling better. What are you doing?"

Octavius gave him a smile. "I'm updating the book of monsters. It wasn't quite as accurate as we thought, was it?"

Lincoln looked down at the pages. There were already a few scribbled notes next to the T-rex, along with sketches of feathers. His fingers itched to touch the pages. "I guess not," he said simply.

He settled back and watched as Octavius flicked from page to page, stopping occasionally to consult with Lincoln, and adding more notes.

Many of the creatures were still new to Lincoln, but lots of them he'd now seen.

He gave a sigh. "If you'd shown me a book like this a few years ago, I would have been horrified."

Octavius lifted one eyebrow. "And now?"

"Now…I guess I'm just curious about the ones I've still to meet." He pointed to a page with a terrifying armoured creature labelled with the name *Ankylosaurus*. "That really eats plants? Are you sure? Why all the armour?"

Octavius laughed. "Have you looked outside? 'Why all the armour' indeed." He turned to the back page of the book and shook out a map. This one looked relatively new in comparison to the one he'd seen Storm carrying.

"You drew this? A new map?"

Octavius nodded. "We're learning so much more. It's important we keep our findings up to date. Things change so quickly."

Lincoln leaned forward to study the map. It showed every place he'd been. The T-rex nest, the cliffs, the pterosaur nest, Blue Bay, the raptor nest, and the deep pool where they'd escaped the dilophosauruses – the dinosaurs that spat acid and had scarred his back. He pointed to the camp, which had been sketched on the map. It had yet to be labelled. "So, what are you going to call this place?"

Octavius shook his head. "The first real settlement on Piloria? I have no idea." He sat back for a moment. "Maybe we should let the people here decide what to call their new home."

It was the way he said those words. It sent a little tingle down Lincoln's spine. "I heard, you know."

"You heard what?"

"All the things you said when you were sick. Things about the parliament. About decisions that were made."

Octavius sucked in a deep breath and looked at Lincoln carefully. Here, he wasn't the Captain Regent any more. Here, he was just the oldest living man on Piloria – maybe even on the whole planet.

"Things have changed." Octavius's voice was strained. "We can't go back to how we were before."

Lincoln couldn't help himself. "Well, someone better hurry up and tell Silas. He thinks we're back home on Earthasia. I wake up each morning and expect to walk outside and see some parliament building constructed in the trees again." He sighed and leaned back. "And maybe someone should tell Reban too. One minute he seems fine, the next minute he goes back into full Chief Stipulator mode. And I've always had the impression he doesn't like me much, but I've no idea why."

Octavius looked up in amusement, his pen poised above the paper. "Oh, that's easy. I can answer that."

"What?"

"Storm."

Lincoln shook his head, momentarily confused. "What about Storm? I don't get it."

Octavius's grey eyes sparkled. "Don't you?" He still seemed amused. "Well, I guess in time, you will."

Lincoln shook his head as he pushed himself back up. "You do know you talk in riddles sometimes, right?" He straightened his tunic. "I better get back to work before they come looking for me."

He headed to the door, then paused. "Let me know if you need anything – or if you want me to take a look at your shoulders again."

Octavius gave a gracious nod then an unexpected wink. "Reban might not approve, but I do," he said, before turning back to his map and starting to detail it further.

Lincoln paused again and opened his mouth to say

something else, but Octavius was already back at work.

He shook his head. It must be his age. Lincoln had never met anyone as old as Octavius before. Maybe this was what happened to them all, they all just became a little weird, a little kooky.

He smiled as he kept walking back to the lab. Now he was better, who knew what the old guy would do next? Maybe he could work with them to put a stop to Silas's virus scheme for good?

PART SIX

THE JUNGLE

TWENTY-FOUR

STORMCHASER

They leaned over the map together.

The original map that Octavius had given them was in four pieces now, weathered around the edges and faded in some places. It was spread over a large table in Jesa's family's kitchen and had been painstakingly recreated in some parts, and amended in others where they knew that things had changed. Leif, Lincoln, Storm and Jesa were crowded around the table next to Octavius. Caleb had pulled an early morning shift with the construction team and was already gone.

"What about over here?" Leif asked. "We haven't looked over that ridge. It could just be more jungle, but what do we know?"

Jesa gave an encouraging nod.

"Yes, let's go somewhere new," she agreed. "We've explored mainly to the west." She looked at Storm. "You and Reban came here from the east, so you've charted that part.

273

It's about time we pushed north. Let's explore more of the middle of this continent."

She adjusted the backpack on her shoulder. Lincoln and Storm exchanged a glance and smiled. It made sense to them too.

Octavius was positioned on a stool next to the table, a pen in his hand, ready to start on the map again. His face was screwed up – he'd lost his reading aids during the rushed move – and his hand moved subconsciously to push up the aids that were normally perched on the end of his nose. He gave a little shudder and looked at his hand in frustration.

He spoke with caution. "We have absolutely no knowledge about that area. It's possible you'll find creatures that no one has encountered before."

Jesa leaned against the table and counted off on her fingers. "So make sure you get the size, the colour, the description, the movement, and…" She paused significantly. "What they eat."

Octavius raised an eyebrow and gave her an amused glance. "You sound like you've heard this before somewhere."

Storm leaned on her hand and smiled too. "I wonder where from. Could be we have someone in this camp who is bit obsessive about their map." She hovered her hand above the paper, shaking it a little, taunting Octavius as if she were about to touch his precious map. He pulled it closer to him. "Stop it." He was half serious, half joking.

It was obvious that Octavius was still tired. Maybe it was just the higher temperature and more humid atmosphere on Piloria. But in the last few weeks, the lines had seemed deeper on his already wrinkled face. His frame had seemed smaller. Almost like he was slipping away.

Storm's stomach gave an uncomfortable twist. Until she'd met Octavius, she'd barely seen anyone with grey hairs or wrinkled skin. She had to face the fact he'd die at some point. But the one thing she knew for sure was that she wasn't ready for that.

Being here, in the camp, had opened up a whole new world for Storm. It wasn't only Piloria, it wasn't just the dinosaurs. It was the sense of community. Knowing that she could walk a few steps to another house and find Octavius. Knowing that in the next row she'd find Lincoln, Jesa and Leif.

"We need somewhere new to explore. Somewhere else we can take people to show the best parts of Piloria, where the creatures are safe to be around. Silas is up to something. I can sense it. And I haven't been able to get back into the lab to speak to Lorcan again. The back door is guarded now. We need to get more people on our side, to stand with us if we need them to."

Even though tensions were sometimes high – Silas and his men seemed to spend most of their time muttering and looking at everyone else through hooded eyes – living in camp was a whole new experience for Storm. A positive one. And she wasn't going to let Silas ruin that for everyone.

Introducing the rest of the camp to the quieter dinosaurs had only been the start.

Things had been going well since then. They'd taken four more groups on expeditions to the surrounding area – always to places they'd already scouted and knew were as safe as they could be. And people talked. Attitudes were changing. Humans were naturally curious. They wanted to know more about the dinosaurs, the plants and the lands, and less about how to kill them.

They'd discovered another few food sources. One was a strange colour – bright orange – and a long cylinder-like shape. But it was edible, and a lot tastier than cornup. The other was round and peeled back in layers, with a strong pungent taste that added flavour to a lot of the dishes that they made. These, added to the other fruits they'd found growing in Piloria, meant that people could see themselves living off the land here for good.

Now, Storm had hope. Hope that things might work out here. Hope that she would finally have something that resembled a family. Hope that maybe Lincoln…

She pushed that thought away. There was too much else to focus on.

There was a knock at the door. Jesa pulled it open and stepped back quickly as Silas stepped inside the house uninvited.

His very presence made them all suck in a breath.

"Ah, Storm, Lincoln, Leif – just the people I was looking for." He saw Octavius sitting at the table and hesitated for a moment – he appeared a little unnerved. It was obvious he hadn't expected to find Octavius within Jesa's

276

family home. "Octavius." He gave a nod of his head and forced a smile.

"Silas," said Octavius, in a voice that dripped with disdain. "What brings you here?"

Silas tilted his chin upwards. "Civic duty." He cast his eyes back over Storm, Lincoln and Leif. "I understand you've been taking more groups out to the surrounding area." He walked over and purposely stared down at the map. "Oh, isn't that handy? The map." His gaze narrowed towards Octavius. "We wondered where that had gone."

Octavius gave a smile. "Why would you wonder? Wouldn't property stay with its rightful owner?"

Ignoring his comment, Silas folded his hands across his chest. "The safety of our people is imperative."

Storm almost burst out laughing. Silas had finally decided safety was important?

"It looks like your escapades have encouraged other people to explore the surrounding area."

Octavius raised one eyebrow. "You mean, you actually let people leave the camp?"

Silas looked annoyed. "Not everyone does what they should," he snapped. He stepped over, as if he were trying to cast a shadow over Octavius. "I mean, surely you agree that we must ensure the safety of the camp?"

Octavius stared straight at him. It took much more than casting a shadow to intimidate him. "Oh I do, I'm just surprised that it's finally occurred to you," he shot back.

Silas stared down at the map and pointed with one finger.

"A small party went out, and one of them – a man called Fariq – appears to have got lost. This is the area they were in."

Storm's frown increased as she leaned over the top of the map to study the unfamiliar and scarcely charted area. She had no idea what kind of creatures lived around that part of Piloria.

Silas spoke again quickly. "With your superior knowledge of the land, and your tracking skills, it made sense for us to ask if you could go and find our missing man." He waved one hand. "Of course, we could send out another party, but they don't quite have your" – he paused for a second – "skill set." He smiled in a forced and awkward kind of way. "And, on Piloria, every life matters."

She looked up, almost wincing at his delivery. Octavius's face was set. He didn't seem happy about any of this.

"Does he have any supplies?" Lincoln asked.

Silas blinked, as if he had to think about his reply. "Only the regular stuff – a backpack with some water and food."

"Any weapons?" Lincoln persisted.

Silas scowled and shook his head.

Storm sighed as her stomach churned. "What do you think?" she asked the others. If someone was lost out there, they could end up in trouble. They could be injured, disorientated – anything. And if they stayed out there for any length of time, they would essentially become dinosaur bait – particularly if they had no survival experience.

Jesa waved a hand. "I'm happy to help."

Her hand came back down and lingered on Leif's arm for the briefest of seconds and he shot her a smile.

"I don't mind coming along," he said. Storm tried not to smile – not while Silas was breathing down their necks anyhow – but Leif wasn't looking at anyone else while he said those words.

Silas looked around the room at the backpack on Storm's shoulder and the one at Lincoln's feet. "Well, isn't that lucky? You look prepared already."

Leif picked up the pack at his feet and slung it over his shoulder. "If we're going, then let's go. Who knows how long this will take? We don't want to end up out there after dark," he said. "Come on." He gestured with his head towards Lincoln, Storm and Jesa, before shooting Silas a glare. It was clear he was done listening to Silas

Storm looked back to Octavius. She didn't trust Silas. But could they really say no to this request? Not when someone could potentially be in danger.

Lincoln seemed hesitant. He kept glancing between Silas and Octavius, as if he wanted to say something else.

Then he did something unexpected. He put his hand on Storm's arm the way Jesa had done to Leif. "Are you sure about this?" he asked. Lorcan's warning was obviously turning about in his head, the way it was hers.

It was like he was pretending Silas wasn't even in the room. It was like he was pretending *no one* was in the room with them. He had a protective glint in his eye, like he was worried, like he cared.

It flooded her senses and for a few seconds she didn't speak. Then she took a deep breath and put her hand over his. "I'm sure. Now let's go."

And, with a nod to Octavius, she walked out the room, praying she wasn't about to make a huge mistake.

TWENTY-FIVE

LINCOLN

It was the first time in for ever that it had been just them, the group who'd been on Piloria together before. Lincoln, Storm, Leif and Jesa.

For the last few weeks, they'd mainly been in the company of others. And that was fine, but there was something freeing about only being with each other. They'd seen each other at their best and worst.

Lincoln didn't wait. "What about Silas?"

Leif side-eyed him. "What about him? We hate him. The guy is an idiot."

Storm looked worried. "He doesn't really strike me as the civic-duty type."

"And do you think he deliberately waited until Reban wasn't around?" Jesa added.

Lincoln turned towards her. "I hadn't thought about that." It didn't seem like much of a stretch of the imagination.

Reban had set off earlier that morning in one of the transporters, with some of the other men, to head back to the ships to collect some of the supplies that there hadn't been room for. His brow wrinkled. "The guy who's lost – Fariq. I think he might be a Stipulator and Silas just left that part out. Maybe that's why he seemed…odd."

The others murmured in response and continued to trek across the uneven ground.

"Do you know they can track the transporters now?" asked Storm.

Leif frowned. "What? How on earth can they do that?"

"I saw one of the workmen fitting something to the transporters and asked him what he was doing." Storm held out her hand and pointed to her palm. "It was this size. Just a small metal disc. Apparently it sends some kind of signal, so they can see the transporters moving and whereabouts they are."

Lincoln shook his head. "Silas is watching you?" he said mockingly.

"Give them another week and they'll probably put them on all of us," said Leif. Lincoln wasn't sure that he was joking.

Storm shrugged. "They said it was for safety. At least if anything happens to the transporter that Reban is in, we'll know where it is."

They moved quickly across the grassy plains and over the nearby hills and valleys. They circled the loch with the vulcanodons and walked around the other side, heading north.

By the time the sun was high in the sky, they were all dripping with sweat. Even though they'd only walked for a number of hours, the further inland they went, the more the temperature seemed to rise.

The vegetation started to get thicker. The ground more squelchy. A forest lay ahead, dark green dotted with lots of bright-orange flowers.

Jesa bent down to touch one. "These are so pretty," she said. She inhaled. "And they smell gorgeous."

"You should pick some on the way back," said Leif. "Your mother would probably love them."

She nodded and grabbed her hair, twisting it up and pulling a tie from her pocket to keep it off her neck. They were only at the edge of the forest, but the air seemed even more humid than before. Storm kept looking from side to side, one hand positioned at her hip, next to her knives. Leif had swapped his old axe for a gun, but Jesa still had her crossbow.

"I haven't seen a single sign of anyone having been here." Storm put her hands on her hips as she looked around. "But Silas definitely pointed to this area."

"What were they doing in a forest?" asked Jesa, wrinkling her nose.

Leif shrugged. "Maybe they're searching for new food types again? Or somewhere else that grows the evergreen leaves? Who knows?" He shook his head. "Let's just get this over with. If the guy was tired, he might shelter in the forest to get out of the sun. We should check inside."

The others nodded.

Lincoln had borrowed the weapon that Reban had used before. It was a long, double-ended staff. One end had an axe, the other a thick knife. As the forest growth got thicker, he used it to swipe some of the leaves and branches out of their way.

Past experience had taught them to be quiet when moving through an unknown area, keeping all their senses on alert. "What kind of dinosaurs do you think could live in here?" whispered Storm.

Lincoln shook his head. "Here's hoping we don't meet any therizinosauruses again."

Storm shuddered. "Yeah, please no dinosaurs that we need to climb to get away from. I've had enough of swinging from the trees."

Leif gave her a sideways glance. "Maybe we won't meet anything. Maybe we'll finally find a bit of land that no dinosaur has tried to conquer. We might even find somewhere we could set another camp up later."

Lincoln was surprised. It sounded as though Leif was making plans here, imagining a future that meant they would stay here for good. It gave him a bit of reassurance. When they'd set sail on the ship, Lincoln had fully believed he'd never see Earthasia again. But he was lucky, he had his family with him. For Leif it had been different – he wasn't even sure what had happened to his mum, dad or brothers and sisters. He'd been angry and distant for those first few days on the ship. It was only Jesa's quiet persistence that had finally managed to get him involved in things again.

Lincoln had wondered if Leif would want to find a way to get back to Earthasia to search for his family, but it seemed as if he'd started to settle here. Started to realize that going home might not give him the answers he'd been looking for.

"Do you really think we'll need another camp?" asked Jesa. "Do you think there could be another ship?"

"They hid one ship from us, why not hide more?" said Storm. "You arrived a month ago now though. If another was going to appear, surely it would be here by now?"

"Could be," replied Lincoln, conscious of the thoughts that might be going through Leif's head right now. "Maybe they've just landed elsewhere. They could be further up the coast, or on the other side of the continent."

"Or there's nobody," said Leif briskly. "And we're it. We're what's left." He gave a wry smile. "Last of the human race, and Silas is among us. Hardly seems fair, does it?"

"People are still left on Earthasia," said Jesa quickly, obviously doing her best to reassure him.

Leif ran his fingers through his hair and answered first. "Yeah, but what state are they in? Starving? Fighting? Who knows if things will ever change there. Let's face it, the land won't. It's been overworked and stripped. It'll never be able to produce enough food for the people that stay there. The only way they'll stay alive is if they start fishing again – and how likely is that? People are terrified of the ocean."

Jesa shivered. "I hate to think of people fighting to survive back on Earthasia. I dread to think what that place has become."

They walked in silence for a few moments, the jungle getting denser and thicker the further they continued.

"Have you noticed something?" said Storm casually as they kept walking.

"What?" asked Leif.

"We haven't seen a single creature since we came in here. Not a bird. Not a Barney. Nothing. Doesn't that seem odd to you?"

It hadn't even occurred to Lincoln, but all of a sudden he realized how odd it was. Usually there was always a sign of some creatures. Whether it was tracks, or droppings, or... something.

Just at that moment, some of the denser foliage gave way and they found themselves in a clearing in the middle of the forest.

There was a rustle to Lincoln's left and he automatically froze. "What was that?" he hissed.

The rest of the group froze too. They'd become too relaxed. They'd been chatting instead of paying attention. That was dangerous on Piloria.

Lincoln concentrated, trying to focus on the noise he'd heard before. After a brief pause, he heard it again. He lifted his finger and wrinkled his brow.

It was an odd noise. Not feet – or claws – walking through the squelchy undergrowth. It didn't sound like footsteps.

Whoosh.

There it was again. Leif nodded. He'd heard it too. He lifted his hands to Lincoln and shook his head in confusion, not saying a word.

Jesa crouched a little lower, trying to see if the noise was coming from the jungle floor.

Whoosh.

There was a gentle breeze making its way through the lush jungle. Leaves and branches rustled again, making it harder to pick out the sound they were trying to identify.

Whoosh.

Lincoln flicked his head to the right. This time the noise was louder. And definitely coming from another direction.

Storm looked up. Her mouth opened. But before she had a chance to make a sound, something landed part on her face, part on her neck. She screamed.

It was a spider. But like no spider Lincoln had ever seen before. This spider was enormous, bigger than both his hands put together, dangling on a thick, visible line of web from the trees above. It was black and hairy with large orange stripes and bulging eyes.

In the blink of an eye another spider fell on Storm's back. She was jumping, her hands thrashing at the spider still covering her face. Jesa and Lincoln jumped forward in the same instance, trying to brush it from her face. But the spider was holding on fast.

"Look out!" shouted Leif as the whooshing sound amplified and dozens of spiders dropped from the trees at once. One landed on Lincoln's shoulders, its legs tightening quickly, anchoring itself in position. A few seconds later he felt a sharp sting.

Every instinct told him to keep thrashing to get it off but Storm dropped to her knees and his instincts changed. He sprang forward and grabbed at the spider fixed to the side of Storm's face. Her head was still flailing from side to side, underneath the spider he could hear her struggling to breathe. Choking and gurgling noises were all he could hear. "Storm! Hold on, I'll get it. I'll get it."

No matter how hard he pulled, the spider held fast. He grabbed at one of the legs and ripped it free with both hands. He didn't stop, yanking at a second, then a third. With three legs gone, he grabbed at the body of the spider again and pulled hard. This time the spider released its grip, sending him falling backwards with a thud.

There was a squelch – and it wasn't only Lincoln landing on the ground. His whole body weight had hit the spider on his shoulder. Storm was bent double, her hands over her face. As Lincoln blinked he saw another batch of spiders dropping from the trees. He dived over, covering Storm's body with his and wrenching the second spider from her back. "We need to get out of here!"

He risked a glance at Jesa and Leif. Jesa had a spider stuck to one of her arms and was smacking it against the nearest tree. Leif was waving his gun above her head to stop any of the other spiders from landing on them.

A few spiders had landed on the jungle floor and scuttled towards them. Lincoln kicked one with his boot and grabbed

Storm, keeping her under his arm. Her legs kept buckling underneath her and Lincoln had to press her close to his hip to try to take her weight.

The spider attached to Jesa's arm fell after her relentlessly smashing it into the tree. Leif kicked a few more that had landed on the ground at their feet, and knocked off another that landed on Lincoln's shoulder, before it could get a grip on him.

He kept their heads low as he ran from the jungle clearing, dragging Storm with him. Jesa and Leif were close behind them. Storm stumbled again and again. The jungle seemed never-ending.

"This way!" shouted Leif as he ran past, his hand in Jesa's as he pulled her behind him.

As they ran, a few other spiders dropped from the surrounding branches. Lincoln and Storm dodged them as best as they could, finally bursting from the jungle a few minutes later. Storm dropped to her knees again, hands over her face.

Lincoln dropped beside her, hearing the wheeze of her breathing.

"Let me see, Storm. Take your hands away."

He tried to sound calm, even though his heart was thudding in his chest. He couldn't help but keep glancing back into the jungle to make sure none of the spiders had followed them out.

Jesa and Leif kneeled beside them. Jesa took one of Storm's hands and gently lifted it from her face. "Breathe,

Storm. Just breathe. You're fine. It's gone."

Storm's whole body was shaking. As Jesa moved her hand, Lincoln's breath caught in his throat. Storm's face was swollen, puffed up, her eyes now slits, her skin bright red.

He shot a frightened look at Leif and Jesa. He had no idea how to deal with this.

Leif stood up quickly. "Where are those big leaves? The huge ones? The ones they've started using for blisters, stings and swelling?"

Lincoln had no idea what they were talking about, but Jesa leaped to her feet too. "Yes, I know the ones." She glanced at her arm. Lincoln could see the swelling starting there too, and feel it at the back of his shoulder. But Storm was the one in trouble here – they had to prioritize her.

They spread out, searching the surrounding foliage. Storm's head kind of slumped to the side. Panic spread across his chest. He grabbed hold of her shoulders and shook her harshly. "Storm! Storm! Wake up! Wake up!"

She was still breathing. He could see the rise and fall of her chest. Lincoln took a deep breath and pulled out his water canister. He had to stay calm. But he hated every second of this. He hated to see anyone he cared about sick – and this felt like his fault. If he'd been paying attention – if he'd been more mindful, he might have noticed those horrible giant spiders hiding in the trees. Why hadn't he even looked up?

The rational part of his brain told him he hadn't looked up because they'd never encountered a predator hiding in the trees before. Their experience of trees had been a place to climb and hide from the predators. A place of safety – not of attack.

Guilt was swamping him. He knew it was irrational. But he didn't care. He would always look out for his mother and sister, and he worried about Jesa and Leif, but Storm? She was different. From the moment he'd realized he'd have to betray her on that first trip, she'd gotten under his skin. When they'd sat in the darkness of the *Invincible* on the way home to Earthasia, and she'd told him about being alone, how she'd received the injuries on her back, and the overwhelming feeling she had that no one cared about her, it had felt like his heart had been ripped out of his chest. No one should feel like that. Especially not someone as special as Storm. He was noticing a change between them. Her touch felt different. The air between them seemed different. He could tell as soon he saw her – from how she held her head, or how she walked – what kind of mood she was in. And even on days when it was a very bad mood, he still wanted to see her. Still wanted to be around her. Piloria wasn't just opening up a whole new world to him. Storm was too.

He took a deep breath. "Tip your head back. I'm going to pour some water on your face – see if we can cool things down."

Storm was shaking as she tipped her head back. As soon as she did, he saw the problem. There was a sharp black barb stuck to the side of her face, just next to her ear. He gulped.

He poured the water gently over her face, hoping the

barb would dislodge, but it held fast. He looked down at his fingers. His nails were short, hardly designed for the task.

"Storm, hold still. There's something in your neck. I need to pull it free."

His fingers shook as he tried to grab the barb that was sticking from her skin. It took a few attempts before he could finally feel it at the edge of his fingertips and he yanked with all his might.

Storm gave a yelp. She collapsed back onto the grass, breathing fast.

A few moments later, Jesa and Leif reappeared, clutching a pile of leaves in their hands. Jesa gathered some of them and gently pressed them against Storm's swollen face. She put a few on her own arm, and another few on Lincoln's neck and shoulder. Her eyes met Lincoln's. He could tell she was panicking, but her voice was steady. "Storm, we're going to stay here for a bit. These leaves should help the swelling. I don't know how quickly they'll work." She changed position, crossing her legs on the ground to make herself more comfortable.

Leif frowned as he picked up the barb from the ground. "What do you think is in this?" He looked over at Storm. "It's obviously designed to do something to a creature's breathing. And do you think it tries to sedate them? To knock them out?"

Jesa looked horrified. "But that means that…" Her voice tailed off but it was clear what she was thinking.

The spiders obviously waited until their prey was either sedated or suffocated, then they inflicted their damage.

None of them wanted to even think about what that meant.

"Why didn't it affect us?" asked Jesa. She nodded to Lincoln. "You and I got stung too."

He shook his head. "I don't know. The barbs didn't stay in us, though. Maybe that's what made the difference." He put his hand up to the leaves that Jesa had pressed to the back of his neck.

Jesa stuttered. "I guess they're not used to prey as big as humans. That's probably why it didn't work completely on Storm." She looked down, her face serious. "Take a seat, guys. We're not going anywhere until Storm's face is better."

"Do you think Silas knew? Do you think there even was a lost guy?" Leif's voice cut through his thoughts.

"What?"

"He sent us here." Lincoln could feel the anger building in Leif. "He looked at the map and told us someone was lost – knowing we'd never leave someone out here alone. Do you think this is deliberate? Who else is questioning his authority in the camp, apart from us and Reban? Maybe he knew about the spiders. Maybe he planned for us all to be killed."

Jesa looked horrified and shook her head. "No. How could he?" She wrinkled her nose and looked thoughtful. "Unless my father had been here, and sent a message back with the Stipulators that it was dangerous. He was here for years. We don't know he always stayed in the same place. Maybe he explored, moved around, and mapped the treacherous places." She was thinking out loud. "But then, that message would have got back to Octavius – wouldn't it?

293

And he would have marked it on the map?"

"Octavius would never have sent Storm into danger, he couldn't possibly know," said Lincoln.

"But did Silas?" Leif was right at his shoulder.

Jesa's face was shocked. She shook her head again. "I know he hates us, but I think he hates Reban more. Isn't he really the biggest threat to Silas's leadership?"

Storm pushed herself up. Her voice was husky, obviously still affected by the swelling. "Do you think Reban's in danger? He's gone back to the ship in the transporter."

Lincoln pushed her shoulder back down. He didn't want her to panic. "He's in a transporter that has the new tracking system on it." He kept his voice steady. "Reban can look after himself, just like we can. Lie back. Relax. We need to wait a while until the swelling goes down and you feel better." He glanced at the others. "And when we get back, let's keep our suspicions of Silas to ourselves. We can't hide the attack we faced, but we don't have any proof that Silas knew about the spiders. We watch. We listen. Things will come to a head at some point and we need to make sure we're ready – whatever that means."

Leif sagged back down next to Jesa and flung his arm loosely around her shoulders. After a brief pause, she leaned her head against his shoulder.

Lincoln felt sick. They'd been happy – laughing even, exploring a new part of the continent.

They couldn't stop paying attention on Piloria – not for a single second.

TWENTY-SIX

LINCOLN

By the time they reached the camp it was pitch black. Torches were burning at each of the lookout posts with a host of guards leaning over each rail. The camp wasn't usually lit like this at night – they didn't want to advertise to any predators they were here – but it was obvious someone had given the order for a change of plans.

As they stumbled across the plain, there was a cry. "It's them!"

The gates were flung open and several guards came running out to meet them – Reban leading the charge.

"Where on earth have you been?" he spat.

He took one look at the weak-limbed Storm and swept her up into his arms. Now his words turned into a snarl.

"What did you do?"

Lincoln was instantly annoyed. He felt guilty enough. He didn't need Reban blaming him too.

Jesa moved alongside Reban as they hurried towards the medico care centre. "We were attacked. By spiders. From the trees. They stung Storm somehow. It affected her breathing, and her ability to walk. Lincoln carried her out. He saved her."

Lincoln cringed. Her words were pointed – Jesa had clearly heard the dig at Lincoln.

Reban didn't reply, he just strode swiftly into the care centre and put Storm down on a bed. "Someone take a look at my daughter. She's been stung by a spider."

One of the medics appeared quickly and started to check Storm over. Octavius appeared at the door in his dark-green cloak and hurried over. "What happened?"

Lincoln frowned. How on earth did he know they were back? Octavius must have guessed his thoughts – he gave Lincoln a quick glance. "One of the guards came and got me," he said by way of a quick explanation. He gave the briefest shake of his head. "The lost man – Fariq? Silas said he turned up a few hours ago." It was clear he wasn't convinced.

He leaned over Storm and lifted a frail wrinkled hand to her face. "What happened to her?"

Lincoln swallowed. "We were attacked by spiders. Giant spiders. They bit her with some kind of barb. Her face was swollen nearly instantly and she was having trouble breathing. Then her legs went."

Octavius and Reban shared a glance. Leif spoke from the side. "I guess it's time to mark that spot on the map as a no-go area." He gave a hollow laugh. "Strange thing was,

Storm had just mentioned how odd it was that we hadn't seen or heard any other creatures in the jungle. I guess the rest of the world knows not to go in there. We just didn't get the message soon enough."

Lincoln wondered if Octavius and Reban were picking up on the edge to Leif's words. There were other people in the care centre. They couldn't voice their suspicions out loud.

Octavius gave a solemn nod as he peered closely at Storm's face. There was still some residual swelling. Her cheeks and neck were still puffy. The medic came over with some cream. "What is that?" Reban snapped.

The medic look surprised. "It's a cream. It's made from the same leaves that they already had on her face. The cream's just a bit more concentrated than the natural source. Leave it on overnight and by morning she should be fine."

"What about the effects on her limbs?"

The medic shook his head. "If it's a kind of sedation, it will work its way out of her system naturally. Leave her here overnight. You can check on her again in the morning."

Lincoln settled down in the chair next to Storm's bed. Reban glared at him. "What do you think you're doing?"

"Staying."

"No. You're not. Get out."

Lincoln shook his head. Reban had spent his life ordering people around. It was probably inbuilt in him to expect people to do what they were told. Lincoln leaned back in the chair and put his feet up on a nearby stool. "I'm not going anywhere until I know Storm's okay."

He saw a glimmer of amusement in Octavius's eyes. The old man leaned over the bed and kissed Storm's forehead. Lincoln smiled. It was the first time he'd really seen Octavius reach out towards Storm. She was still practically sleeping, still affected by the sedation. He wished she'd seen this. He wished she'd been more awake, to witness the clear sign of affection from her great-uncle.

Something flickered in the normally impervious Reban. He shook his head a little. His words were barely audible. "She's so like Dalia."

Octavius's grey eyes turned to Reban's. "Yes." He straightened his small body. This time his words were crystal clear. "But she's not Dalia. She's better. She's more." He touched her hand. "She's so much more."

Lincoln was stunned. Not at what he said, but at the fact that Octavius had said it.

Leif and Jesa shot each other a glance and faded away. Octavius straightened his cloak and walked proudly back out of the door.

For a few moments, Reban looked momentarily stunned. His eyes were fixed on Storm. She was sleeping peacefully now, the rise and fall of her chest giving them both the reassurance that they needed.

Reban turned to face Lincoln and folded his arms across his chest. It seemed as though Lincoln was about to be the receiver of all Reban's pent-up anger.

He was ready. He was ready for this. He'd expected it.

"This has to stop."

"What has to stop?" Lincoln was determined to match Reban every step of the way.

"You. You have to stop. Every time you're near my daughter, you put her in danger."

"That's ridiculous. Are you actually listening to yourself?"

Reban stepped forward, his violet eyes seeming darker than normal. "I knew you were trouble the first moment I set eyes on you."

Lincoln stood up. He was the same size as Reban now and they were eye to eye. "That was the reason you tried not to name me as a Finalist, back on Earthasia?"

Reban snarled. "I knew you had an agenda. I knew you were up to something."

He leaned forward until they were practically nose to nose. "Really? Then why didn't you stop me?"

"I should have. Then you wouldn't be here."

Anger flared in Lincoln. "I have every right to be here. I fought for my place, and I found you the eggs. I did everything I was asked to do. And it's you who put Storm in the most danger. She stayed on Piloria with *you*!" Lincoln knew he should tell Reban about their suspicions about Silas. Of course he should. But right now the animosity that had been simmering in him since Storm had made her choice – deciding to stay on Piloria with her father instead of going back to Earthasia with Lincoln – was bubbling to the surface.

"Stay away from my daughter!" Reban hissed.

"Oh, she's your daughter now, is she?" Lincoln stepped

back and laughed. "How long did it take you to acknowledge her existence? You denied her for as long as you could." He leaned forward and poked his finger into Reban's chest. "What kind of a father are you anyway?"

Reban grabbed his hand and twisted Lincoln's arm up his back, shoving him into the nearest wall. "I'm the kind who knows when a guy's getting ideas about my daughter."

Lincoln elbowed Reban sharply with his other arm, sending him barrelling backwards. "That's what this is about?" he said incredulously.

Reban coughed for a moment, clearly winded, his eyes streaming. "Of course that's what this is about. You get into danger all the time. I want her to be safe – and that means staying away from you."

Lincoln shook his head. This is what Octavius had been hinting at the other day. It wasn't such a surprise, in a way. He and Storm had been spending more time together and getting closer.

He held out both hands. "What do you want, Reban? There are four hundred people here. And that could be it. We all have to try to get along. Storm doesn't belong to you – and she doesn't belong to me. You don't get to save her all the time." He gave a smile as he looked at her sleeping. "Maybe you haven't noticed, but most of the time she saves herself." He stepped a little closer to the bed. He wanted to reach out and touch her, but after Reban's reaction that was likely to anger him all the more.

He held his hand just above hers and met the angry violet gaze. "Storm gets to choose. She gets to choose the life she leads, how she lives it, and who she lives it with." He took another breath. "And just so you know, I plan on being by her side every step of the way, if she'll have me." His gaze didn't waver for a second. "If Storm doesn't want me around, fine. But you? You don't get a say in this, Reban. Just know that I will never knowingly put her in harm's way. She's too important to me for that." He felt some of the anger dissipate from his body. What if Storm had been on a scouting party with others and came back like this? Would he have been angry? Probably. That was the truth. Would he have looked for someone to blame? Highly likely.

He turned to face Reban. "Why don't we just agree to let Storm live her best life? If you're in it, and if I'm in it, then we'll just have to learn to get along." He lowered his voice, glanced at the medico staff nearby, then back at Reban. "And at some point, when we're away from other ears, there's something we all need to discuss."

Storm made a little murmur and turned onto one side, curling up her legs. She might not be awake, but it was obvious she was aware of them around.

Lincoln took a step and settled back into the chair at her side. "It's going to be a long night," he said, and waved his hand at the chair on Storm's other side. "Why don't you grab a seat."

Reban's jaw clenched, then slowly relaxed. It felt like they'd reached an understanding. An uneasy truce.

After the longest pause, he gave a brief nod of his head and walked around to sit at the other side, putting his feet up on the edge of the bed.

Lincoln tried not to smile as he mimicked Reban and put his feet up too.

One thing he was sure about.

He wasn't going anywhere.

TWENTY-SEVEN

STORMCHASER

She looked out into the centre of camp. Things were quiet. Too quiet.

The last few days had been odd. She felt back to full health, but Reban and Lincoln had been pacing around each other in the strangest way. It was clear they'd had some sort of fight when she'd been sick, but neither of them would fill her in on the details. Octavius was no help either. He just kept chuckling away to himself, leaving her wondering what on earth she had missed.

The day after she'd got out of the medico care centre, all of them had sat down together to discuss their suspicions about Silas. Octavius was the one who was most upset. He'd never made the journey to Piloria before – he'd relied on the Stipulators who met with Blaine each year to tell him everything they'd learned, and to bring back Blaine's sketches. It hadn't occurred to him that some of the information might not have made it back to him.

Reban had been surprisingly composed.

"We watch him," he'd said. "We watch him like a hawk. We can't prove anything about the spiders, but we can make sure he doesn't deliberately put any of us in harm's way in future."

And so they had.

A few days later, Storm woke early. The camp seemed eerily quiet.

A quick glance told her all the lookout posts were double-manned, which was unusual. She wandered over to the nearest one.

"What's going on?" she shouted up.

Aron, one of the guards, looked down. "Silas and a hunting party left at first light."

Every hair on her back stood on end. What was Silas up to now? "Silas went out with a hunting party? He doesn't usually do that."

Aron shook his head. "What do I know? I just got the pleasure of closing the gate behind them all. They took one of the transporters this time though. Silas was inside."

"Do you know where they went? What they wanted to hunt?"

Aron shook his head again. "They all just look like dinosaurs to me."

There was a horrible feeling in the pit of her stomach.

She ran back to the houses, rattling her own door to wake Reban, and Lincoln's and Jesa's too. It only took a few minutes for them all to appear, bleary eyed.

"What's wrong?" Leif asked. He was still only half dressed.

"Silas has taken a hunting party out. This time, they went in one of the transporters."

"What?" Reban ran his hand through his short dark hair. "Why on earth is he doing that?"

"Silas has plans of his own." Octavius's voice cut through all their confused thoughts. She'd no idea where he'd come from, but the last few days he'd taken to wearing his heavy dark-green cloak again. She was hot just looking at him. "He thinks he's some kind of bounty hunter. Silas sees the dinosaurs as trophies. He's trying to be the leader around here. If Silas comes back with some kind of dangerous dinosaur that he's killed, some of the people might see him as a conqueror." His voice went quiet. "More of a leader than I am."

"No." Storm shook her head. "He's crazy. And he's devious. He's been getting worse ever since we arrived here. He'll put us all in danger."

Reban seemed the most awake. "If he took a transporter, then he's headed somewhere he thought it was too far to walk to. It could be the T-rex nest or the raptors."

Her skin prickled as she saw the horrified expression on Leif's face. "We aren't even sure if any T-rexes are still alive. The virus could have wiped them out. But if there are... A T-rex tracked us for days the first time we were here.

If he doesn't kill it, he could bring it directly to our door."

Leif gulped and looked over at the distant wall made of thick trees bound together. "I'm not sure that our wall will hold out an angry T-rex."

"How could he be so stupid?" said Lincoln angrily. "He's put us all at risk. This can't go on. We can't live like this!"

Storm's stomach clenched. He was looking over to where his mother and sister were standing, woken by the commotion – obviously worried about how this could affect them. But then Lincoln turned his head and his green eyes locked on hers. It made her catch her breath, because the look in his eyes told her that he was every bit as worried about her as he was about his mother and sister.

"We should gather everyone together," Octavius said. "We have to prepare the camp for what might happen. How long until they're back?"

Reban shook his head. "Who knows? We don't know for sure where they've gone."

Octavius gave a slow nod. "Let's plan for a worst-case scenario. Let's imagine it's the raptors or the T-rexes. Reban, you check the weapon store. See if we have anything that will be of any use against the T-rexes. I'm going to speak to the work crew."

"What for?" asked Storm.

Octavius sighed. "To see if there's any chance the plan might work for electrifying the outer wall. The work's far from finished, but it might be the only way we can keep them out."

The rest of them disappeared quickly back inside to get dressed and to start to prepare for what might lie ahead.

Storm stood with her arms wrapped around herself. "Silas, what have you done?" she said as she stared out across the compound.

Nothing good could come of this. Nothing.

PART SEVEN

THE ATTACK

TWENTY-EIGHT

LINCOLN

The lookout post to the west gave the first cry. It had been two long days and nights of living on their nerves and constantly scanning the horizon. Storm and Lincoln were ready. It only took them both a few moments to scale the lookout post to get a clear view of what was happening.

Lincoln's heart sank. Men were running with looks of terror on their faces from the woods to the right. The rumble of the transporter could be heard. The engine sounded strange – laboured. Probably because whoever was driving was trying to make it go at top speed.

"Open the gates," yelled one of the guys.

The guards at the gate looked hesitant. Octavius's old legs found a burst of energy and he headed quickly towards them. He shook his head. "Only open the gate far enough to let the men and women in. If you open it for the transporter, we'll not get it closed again in time. You only run like that when something is chasing you." He turned to some men further along the outer wall. "Turn the power on. Sound the alarm."

The alarm went on almost instantaneously. It was a loud, piercing sound that made Lincoln want to put his hands over his ears. The alarm had only been devised in the last day – a warning to the whole compound to stand clear of the outer wall prior to the electricity being turned on. Jesa and Leif scrambled up to the lookout post, pulling their weapons from their shoulders. Lincoln put his rifle on his shoulder, training it to face the wood, waiting for whatever creature might emerge.

They all held their breath.

The transporter came out from the woods, one side of it crumpled. It was moving oddly, as if the damage had made it unbalanced. Part of the side door had been ripped raggedly from the metal machine.

Up till now, the new transporters had always travelled smoothly and slowly across the land. This time it was different – the driver apparently paying no care or attention to the rugged ground outside the camp. At times it seemed to launch in the air, flying awkwardly then thumping back down with a hideous crunching sound.

The men who were racing ahead were red-faced and sweating, terror clearly powering them on. There were others running alongside the transporter but continually stumbling as they kept glancing behind.

"Keep your eyes on the woods," said Storm quietly.

Lincoln nodded, as Jesa put her arrows at her feet and loaded the first one into her crossbow.

Octavius was beneath them, Reban at his side. They were arguing over something. Storm's head flicked between the woods and the scene below her, obviously trying to work out what was going on.

The first attack was over in the blink of an eye. One minute there was a woman running near the back of the pack, next second there was a flash of something dark brown and she disappeared without even a scream.

Before Lincoln had a chance to process what had happened, there was a flurry at the edge of the woods and the creatures came streaming out.

"Raptors," he breathed, shooting anxious glances at his friends.

For a moment no one spoke – everyone's eyes were on the raptors. Storm had warned them all about the changes, but now they could see them for themselves. This was real.

There were five of them. They were bigger and stronger than they'd been before. The biggest one stood haughtily on its thick hind legs – as if it were contemplating its new hunting ground. It cawed loudly and the other raptors moved, as if they were choreographed, spreading out around the transporter and the people running wildly by its side.

"There's no way they can outrun the raptors." Storm's voice was barely a murmur. "And the raptors aren't close enough for us to shoot yet."

There was a squawk, and another person disappeared from the back, swept away by the killing claw on one of the raptors' feet. This time they heard a sickening crunch.

Storm's hands were trembling as she held a knife near her ear. The creatures were too far away for her knives to be any use. Lincoln took aim with his rifle, but he barely managed to line up a shot before the raptors moved. Their pace was quicker than he'd seen before, their red crests high on their heads as they cawed and squawked at each other. One of the other guards at the lookout post turned around wide-eyed. "They're talking to each other," he said in horrified wonder.

Lincoln nodded. There was no time for a conversation like this. He fired, again and again, but none of his shots were meeting the targets. Shots were coming from the east lookout post too. But they were even further away, and it seemed their aim was as bad as his.

The first man reached the gate and squeezed through the gap, collapsing on the other side at Reban's and Octavius's feet.

Reban didn't hesitate, he pushed himself out through the gate, a gun in each hand and started firing wildly. "Come on!" he yelled at the running people.

"What are you doing?" yelled Storm, her hands gripping the guard rail, knuckles turning white.

Another brown flicker – and another person disappeared. The caws continued. This was almost like a game to the raptors. Two more men reached the gap and dived through.

The leader of the raptors tipped its brown head back and let out a squawk that more than matched the alarm still sounding. It must have triggered something in Storm's brain because she leaned down and called to Octavius. "The fence, is it working?"

There had been no noise. No gentle hum of the electricity coming through. In the chaos of the events, Lincoln hadn't even noticed. Octavius shook his head and shouted down the line at some of the workmen.

The biggest raptor bent its hind legs and leaped high in the air, landing on the roof of the transporter, which crunched down like a metal can and ground to a stuttering halt. Two seconds later, Silas ran screaming from inside it.

The nearest raptor was too busy slicing another of its prey with its sickled claw to chase him. The dinosaurs were closer now and Jesa started firing arrows wildly as Lincoln tried to reload his rifle. But nothing was having any effect.

Another woman and then another man were taken out cleanly by the raptors; dispensed with loathsome ease. The creatures weren't feeding on them – they seemed to be killing for fun. They made it seem like a game.

Storm leaned over the wooden rail again. "Octavius. What about the wall? Will the electricity work?"

Octavius was further away, talking furiously to the work crew, where one man was throwing up his hands and gesturing to the junction box outside.

Panic started to overtake Lincoln. In another few moments the raptors would be on them. From the size, speed and intelligence of these creatures, he didn't think it would take them long to figure out a way over the camp walls. If they didn't get the electricity switched on soon, they could all die.

Storm looked scared. Her eyes darted from Reban outside the gate to Octavius and the frantic look on his face. No matter what they'd faced before, he'd never seen her look quite so terrified. But before, it had only been about them.

Now, it was about four hundred other people – or however many were left – his mother and sister amongst them. His stomach clenched. He'd told his mother and sister to hide back at the house. To pile things on top of them and smear themselves with the evergreen ointment. But one look at these raptors told Lincoln it would never be enough. These creatures were here to hunt. Maybe not for food – but certainly for sport. They wouldn't be happy until they'd felled all their prey. Silas had led them to their ultimate playground.

Silas. There was a swoop of a tail and his cloak was snagged, pulling against the momentum of him running forward, choking him and bringing him to his knees. Storm's reaction was instant. One knife after another flew from her hands. They whistled through the air, most hitting the hard, brown skin of the raptor with no impact at all. But one caught the raptor's face, making it halt for a second to shake off the annoying object, and giving Silas a chance to scramble to his feet, leaving his cloak behind and streaking towards the gate. Reban was in front of the gate, his guns firing directly at the raptor too, as one of the other men squeezed in the gate behind him.

Silas was the last man standing. And he still had a long way to run.

TWENTY-NINE

STORMCHASER

She didn't think before she scrambled down the side of the lookout post. Storm didn't care about Silas. She didn't care if she never, ever had to set eyes on him again. But she cared that her father was out there trying to save the life of a man who'd virtually condemned him to death. She cared that other people had already died as the pawns in Silas's game. She cared that Silas had led the killer raptors directly to their camp – their home.

And because of that – because she defended what she believed in – she pushed past the black cloaks at the gate into the exposed area outside. Standing side by side with Reban as Silas still raced towards them.

"Stormchaser!"

She heard Octavius's anguished cry but she didn't have time to listen.

Storm grabbed at the rest of the knives on her belt and

started throwing them, taking only a second to aim each one. It was hard to aim at a moving target – particularly when that target moved at speed and was heading straight towards you.

One of the other raptors mimicked the head raptor's earlier actions and leaped onto the transporter, crushing the roof even more.

Please tell me no one was left inside. The thought flew through her head. Any chance of checking the transporter was virtually gone now. She didn't even know how many people had gone in the initial hunting party. She didn't know how many people she was trying to save.

There was a flicker to her left. She could see a woman hiding behind a tree, peeking out in terror, obviously trying to get back to the camp gates.

"Reban," Storm hissed at him, flicking her eyes towards the woman.

Reban caught sight of the woman, wincing as he realized exactly how slim her chances of survival were. They'd thought Silas was the last man out here. They'd thought they would only have to last a minute or so until he reached the gate. They'd been wrong.

Reban didn't hesitate. He moved directly to the right, pulling the attention of the raptors away from the trees on the left. Storm signalled for the woman to move. "Give her some cover," she yelled over her shoulder, hoping someone would hear.

"Got it!" The shout came from Jesa, who had swapped her

crossbow for a gun and started firing rapidly. Her brother and Leif appeared at her side in an instant and started firing too.

The woman was running frantically, fear laced across her face. It took a few moments for the raptors to notice her. The smallest one moved instantly, as it was closest.

Reban reached behind his back, for his staff.

He moved forward, hacking at the raptor with the sword end, as soon as it was in reach. Although it was the smallest in the pack, it was still slightly bigger than Reban. Its eyes were so fixed on its potential prey – the woman – that it didn't notice the attack by Reban until it was too late. Reban's sword pierced the thick hide of the raptor, making it turn its head in surprise. It let out a yelp of shock as the woman streaked past Storm.

Reban didn't stop with the attack. The raptor swung its thick muscular tail around in Reban's direction, but Reban seemed to anticipate it and leaped in the air. His weapon came down again, this time the axe end in a chopping motion, catching one of the beast's clawed feet.

Storm turned her head just in time to see the woman squeeze through the gap in the gate.

Silas was still coming towards them, heading straight for the gate. Twenty seconds, that's all he would need. The small raptor let out another high-pitched caw and she saw Reban quickly scanning the horizon, realizing the only hunter left was Silas.

He moved away from the raptor quickly. There was no

point in continuing an attack that wasn't necessary. But the caw from the injured raptor had sent its counterparts into high alert.

Storm could swear she could almost see the calculations going on in the biggest raptor's head. It let out a ferocious caw to the others and leaped through the air, landing only a few millisectars from Silas's feet. But Silas wasn't looking back – sweat streamed from him as he ran straight towards the gate.

Reban appeared at her side. "Move, Storm!" he yelled.

For an instant she was frozen. Then everything was a blur of brown. The raptors seemed to move as one, advancing from all sides. And all of a sudden she seemed to be the focus of their attention. Her breath caught in her throat.

"Storm!" yelled Lincoln. There was a yank at her back. It was Lincoln, he'd come for her and he was pulling her back towards the gate. She didn't think – there was no time. She just started running the thirty steps back to safety. The ground reverberated beneath her feet. The raptors were coming.

She could sense Lincoln practically on her shoulder, running just behind her. He'd come out here too. He'd come out here because of her. She knew that instantly – even though she had no time to process it. No time to think about the fact he'd just chosen to save her, while leaving his mother and sister behind in the camp.

Her brain was such a mess. She'd come out here because of her father – and Lincoln had come out here for her.

It was like a thunderbolt going off in her head. Adrenaline coursed through her system. She would fight for them, just like they would fight for her.

The muscles in her legs ached. The gap at the gate seemed even smaller than before. Reban was right there – waiting for her in front of it, firing his guns as quickly as he could. There was a click just as she held her breath and tried to squeeze through the gap. Her brain made a sickening realization. His gun was empty.

"Go!" It was Lincoln. She fell through the gap on the other side, her heart slamming against her chest. The few Stipulators who still wore their black cloaks were nearby. They shot each other a glance and she could read their minds in an instant. That glance said it all. They wanted to close the gates.

"Don't you dare!" she shouted.

"Go! Go! Go!" a voice screamed above and to her side. Leif shouted from the lookout post, leaning forward alongside Jesa, both of them firing as many weapons as they could, trying to give Reban and Lincoln some cover.

There was a scuffle. An arm appeared then disappeared. Reban seemed to fly through the gap as there was a resounding thud, and a huge impact on the gate. It rocked. The gap widened, then Lincoln pushed through, his right arm covered in blood and hanging limply at his side.

He didn't even stop for a second. "HELP!" he screamed at the top of his voice, as he turned and put all his body weight on the gate.

It took the others a few seconds for their brains to click into gear. There was another thud, this one so strong it sent some of those holding the gate flying backwards. Storm scrambled to her feet. People were realizing what was happening. More people ran to put weight behind the gate. Anything to close it securely.

Leif's voice yelled from the lookout post. "Brace yourselves. They're coming again."

The next thud was the heaviest. The gate creaked under the strain. Reban started shouting instructions. Several of the labourers who'd been working on the cables ran over to lend their strength. Large logs were anchored across the gates and lashed into place.

Reban turned, pushing his back to the gate until it was secured. Storm tried to catch her breath. Lincoln's legs seemed to crumple beneath him, next to her. "Get some help!" she shouted to a person nearby. She placed her hands over the large gaping wound on his arm – obviously caused by a raptor's claw – to attempt to still the blood flow.

Reban caught her gaze.

"What are they doing? Throwing themselves at the gate?"

He nodded, his face a picture of fury. "They can smell us now. They know that we're here. Four hundred pieces of prey, just waiting to be eaten." He glared at Silas, who was lying, shaking, on the ground. "You led them straight to us." He leaned forward and hissed in Silas's face. "Who are the hunters now?"

"Enough!" The shout came from Octavius. "We have no time for squabbles. We have to fix the fence."

Leif gave a shout from the lookout post. "Get up here someone, we have trouble."

Storm glanced at Lincoln. His whole body was quivering – most likely from the effects of the terrible wound on his arm – a wound he'd got while protecting her. A man appeared at her side with some strips of cloth in his hand which he helped her bind around Lincoln's wound to stem the flow of blood. Lincoln's face was tight.

"Hurry. We need to see what we can do."

Reban had already started climbing up to the lookout post, with Octavius close behind him. Storm waited until Lincoln was ready, then let him climb up first. He only used one arm – much like the way she'd been on the cliff face when doing the Trials. It brought back a flash of memory and she put her hand at his backside to help push him up. He glanced over his shoulder and gave her a smile of recognition. "Payback?" he said hoarsely, as he hauled himself up the last few steps.

"Of course," she replied, smiling as she pulled herself up alongside the rest of them.

The raptors had stopped trying to ram the gate open and were now collected in the middle of the clearing in front of the camp. All five of them threw their heads back and cawed loudly, at a pitch Storm had never heard before.

"What are they doing?" she whispered.

Her friends all shook their heads. The raptors spread out.

Jesa shouted down for some more ammunition, preparing for whatever lay ahead. Storm loaded a gun for Lincoln, passing it to his left hand.

Leif was leaning over the front of the lookout post. "What on earth are they— Aaargh!"

It happened so fast they barely saw it. There was a raptor underneath them, close to the wall. It had shot up so quickly and at a height they were completely unprepared for, missing Leif's face by only a few millisectars. A stunned Leif landed on his backside in the middle of the lookout post.

He gave his head a shake and brushed his face with his hand – as if checking it was all still in one piece. "Since when can they jump so high?" he asked.

"Since the virus," Reban answered, with a glance at Storm. "This was us. We did this."

There was a yelp from the lookout post on the east side. They watched in horror as one of the guards – who was leaning out too far – was yanked from the post to the ground beneath. There was a gut-wrenching crunch and Storm knew not to try to look any further.

"The attack hasn't finished. It's only just begun," said Octavius gravely.

Jesa had perched on the edge of the guard rail to get a better aim at the raptor below, but she jumped back down. "I can't fire at them from here," she said with frustration. "This is useless. How can we fight them off?"

Storm watched in horror. The raptors were relentless and didn't seem to tire easily. They jumped time and time again, the largest of them frequently looking clearly at them all in the lookout post. There were scratching noises too, and when Leif dared to take a quick look down again he was shaking when he turned around. "They're damaging the wood. They're trying to find a way to get a hold of the wall. If they do that – then they're inside."

"Keep firing," shouted Reban. "We have to keep them out!"

But the bullets were useless. The design of the lookout posts meant that they just overhung the wall underneath. This created just enough protection for the predators below to make their damage unchallenged. The group fired every time a raptor leaped, but the bullets rarely hit their mark. Octavius muttered to Reban. "We need the fence. We need the electrified fence. It's the only way to keep them out."

"The power supply is down," said Reban as he kept firing. "We've no way of getting it going."

There was another bunch of loud caws and Storm's stomach sank to her feet. Her mouth was so dry she could barely speak as more and more raptors emerged from the trees.

The firing stopped for a few seconds and those on the crowded lookout posts looked at the scene. "Oh no," she whispered.

The raptors stopped jumping for a second and gathered together. This time it wasn't five. This time it was more than twenty. Twenty raptors with the sole intention of getting into the camp. All of them were bigger than the first lot of raptors they'd met on Piloria.

"How did they get here?" Jesa shook her head in horror.

"Their friends called them," Reban answered shortly. "The virus didn't just enhance their strength, it enhanced their intelligence, their senses and their speed."

They watched in horror. "It's almost like a conversation," whispered Leif as they watched.

"B-but they're dinosaurs."

They all turned at the voice. A ragged and pale Silas had climbed the lookout ladder. He was watching in shock.

Reban's voice was steady. "We tried to tell you this. We tried to tell you that the virus might have worked for some creatures, but for others...there were unintended consequences. We weren't meant to mess with these creatures, Silas. This is a situation we've created. You've created."

Behind the walls of the camp, people were starting to panic. Storm could feel her chest tightening. She'd already seen Lincoln injured. Tamb, Arta and Kayna were all hiding back at their homes. What chance would they have if these raptors breached the walls? What chance would any of them have against such fearsome and adept predators?

She tried to breathe and think straight, but it was impossible in this situation. The raptors were stalking forward to the camp walls again now, their behaviour slow and deliberate.

Storm's skin chilled. They'd made plans. These creatures wouldn't stop until they *were* stopped.

Storm held her breath as the tight feeling spread across

her chest. Her gaze fell on her friends. Leif. Jesa. Reban. Octavius. And Lincoln.

This was it. It was time to fight. It was time to fight or die.

THIRTY

STORMCHASER

It happened so quickly. A planned attack.

They'd moved down to ground level as the gate was being rammed again and again by some of the other raptors continuing to target it with their combined strength.

One smaller raptor leaped onto the back of another and used it as a stepping stone into camp, flying over the gate to a hail of bullets and knives. The place erupted into chaos.

People screeched, fleeing in all directions. The stampede was so frantic that several people fell; others pushed and shoved each other around doorways, clamouring to get inside. But most were not as fast as the raptor.

The small raptor made short work of the people closest to it, taking out one with its killing claw and one with its tail. Several others ran screaming. One guy stood his ground, shooting round after round. If the bullets penetrated the raptor's skin, they had no effect. In the blink of an eye, the man was sliced almost clean in two.

"Take cover," Reban urged quickly. "Get out of sight."

The group scrambled immediately, hiding around various buildings in the camp. Octavius was next to Storm as they crouched behind the wall of the school.

He was oddly calm. She didn't like that.

They could hear the noise of other raptors trying to repeat the actions of the first – but, thankfully, failing. What would happen if more raptors got inside the camp?

Her hand went automatically to her waist. But her belt was empty. Her knives gone. She reloaded her gun and took aim, watching the ground in front of them carefully. As soon as the raptor appeared she'd fire. She was trembling, her arms shaking a little.

"We need the fence," said Octavius quietly. "If they all get in here, everyone dies."

She flicked a glance at him. He had a strange look on his face. Then she glanced back in front – afraid to look away in case the raptor appeared.

He pressed a frail hand on her arm. Its grip had surprising strength. The thuds at the gate had stopped.

"They must be regrouping. Replanning," she said quickly.

His grey eyes met hers. "Then it's time for us to do the same," he said swiftly.

There was something in his tone, something in his gaze that made her stop focusing in front of her. A scream sounded to their right and she jumped, spinning around with her gun in front of her but still keeping low.

Octavius gave her a smile. He had the oddest expression on his face. One of complete calmness in the face of chaos. "I'm glad to have met you, Stormchaser Knux," he said. "I'm proud to have you in my family." His hand went to his throat and he unclipped his green velvet cloak, letting it puddle to the ground at his feet.

She was stunned. And her stomach plummeted. "NO!" she shouted.

But it was too late. He turned and ran directly towards the gate. His speed and strength was surprising. He'd unlashed the first log before she'd even made after him. Unlashed the second as she reached him. He pushed the gate, creating a tiny gap. Too small for anyone of a normal size to fit through.

But Octavius was not a normal size. She grabbed at his arm. "Are you crazy?" she shouted. The raptor inside could be anywhere, not to mention the ones waiting out there. The small one was prowling in the camp now, looking for prey, and she'd probably just alerted it to their presence.

Octavius blinked. His grey eyes sparkled. "The needs of the many outweigh the needs of the one. You're more special than you'll ever know, Stormchaser Knux." His arm slid from her grasp as he slid through the gap in the gate.

"Octavius!" she yelled. It was madness. It was utter madness. Who knew what the raptors were doing out there. He wouldn't manage five steps before they were on him.

Someone gave a shout from the east lookout post. "Give him some cover!"

Leif barrelled into the gate, slamming it closed again. She wasn't sure how she managed to cross the ground so quickly and scramble up the wooden ladder, but she did.

Maybe it was genetics, because she would never have expected Octavius to show that much speed either – not at his age. His small frame covered the ground easily, and he dropped to his knees as he reached the junction box outside. For an instant, it looked like he'd fumbled. By now the raptors had noticed him and were advancing quickly on their prey.

Storm couldn't breathe. She couldn't move. Tears brimmed in her eyes. This was suicide. No one could survive this. But Octavius had known that before he'd set foot outside. Those words. *The needs of the many outweigh the needs of the one.*

He'd told her he was proud of her. The way that he'd looked at her. It hadn't been the look of a Captain Regent. It had been the look of an elderly uncle. Someone protecting his people and his family to the end. Someone who knew and accepted that this was their only chance of survival right now.

Her whole body started to shake. She'd just found her family. She wasn't ready to lose them. There were so many conversations that she still needed to have with Octavius. So many things she needed to ask him.

As she watched, Octavius reached into the box and grasped something. Connected something. His head turned for the briefest of seconds, his gaze connecting once again with Storm's. There was a glimmer of a smile.

And then there was nothing. A blur of brown.

His body was tossed in the air as if it weighed no more than a feather – caught by one of the killing claws of the biggest raptor. Even from far away Storm heard the sickening crunch of bones as he hit the ground.

And then the raptors were on him. She turned her head. Her brain had just ground to a halt. She moved to the ladder, stumbling back down onto the ground. She didn't need to see this. She couldn't bear it.

There was a second of nothingness. Then something buzzed next to her. A hum. A surge. Then a spark.

There was the start of a thud at the now weakened gate, followed by a queer kind of yelp. She moved quickly, reaching out with her foot to push the gate completely closed again.

"Don't!" One strong arm yanked her back.

The hum grew louder. There was a thud over to the right. Then something that sounded like a sizzle, or a hiss.

She was shaking. She couldn't help it. She couldn't get that picture of Octavius flying through the air out of her mind, or the sound of his frail bones crunching as he hit the ground.

"Storm. Don't touch it. It's worked. He's got the power on. He's electrified the fence."

It was Lincoln's arm that was over her shoulder and across her chest. Hearing his voice was a relief. She turned around immediately and buried her head into his shoulder. "It was just like Kronar," she whispered. The memories of Kronar flying through the air after being hit by the mighty T-rex tail and the way his lungs had gurgled for the few seconds after she reached him were alive in her brain right now.

Her voice trembled as she lifted her head. "May-maybe… Kronar was still alive. Maybe Octavius will still be alive?"

Lincoln looked up to his left and mouthed something to Leif, who bowed his head and shook it, not even meeting Storm's gaze. Her legs buckled and Lincoln slid his good arm around her waist.

His uninjured arm hugged her tightly, the other still hanging at his side.

Leif moved off, back to the lookout post, his face pale but determined.

"We have to move," Lincoln whispered. "The other raptor is still here."

But as soon as he said the words, there was a loud bang to their right. Moments later, Dell and his father came around the corner, both of them covered in dark blood. The large gun in Dell's hand was still smoking.

"We got the raptor," he said bluntly.

Both of them looked shell-shocked. Dell wiped his sleeve across his face, which was speckled with blood. "I better never see one of them again."

There was another yelp directly in front of them. Leif shouted down. "It's working. They're confused. They definitely don't like the electricity."

Storm and Lincoln clambered back up the tower. They watched as the raptors seemed to confer with each other. If it were at all possible they looked frustrated. Angry. A few were scraping their killing claws on the ground. One came back over and seemed to hesitate before touching the outer wall again, leaping back when it came into contact with the electricity. It scurried back to the group. The largest raptor walked nearer, then slowly but surely paced around the circumference of the camp, as if looking for an alternative way in.

It seemed such careful behaviour. And the circumference of the camp took a long time for the raptor to cover. The rest of its pack just scraped around the ground and trees – obviously losing interest in the apparently impenetrable camp.

By the time the largest raptor came back around to the main gates it had obviously decided the search was futile. It cawed to its companions and they disappeared into the trees. There was almost a collective sigh of relief within the walls of the camp.

Reban appeared beneath the tower, gesturing for Storm to come down. He was breathless, blood dripping from one elbow and some smeared across his brow. She didn't even want to ask what he'd been doing. He took one look at Storm and snapped at Lincoln. "What have you done?"

Lincoln shook his head. "It's Octavius. He went outside. He turned on the power."

She could swear that her father swayed on his feet. "He did what? No. No..." Reban ran to the gate, then slapped his hand on his thigh in frustration as he realized it was electrified and he couldn't get through.

He ran over to the west lookout post, climbing quickly and leaning out from the top. This time there were no leaping raptors. She saw him wince as his eyes landed on something in the distance and he bent his head and spoke to Leif and Jesa for a few moments.

Tears started to flow down Storm's cheeks. Octavius was gone. His words haunted her. He'd accepted what he needed to do to save their people.

Reban bent over the rail that looked out across their camp. He leaned his arms on it and put his head in his hands. It took her a moment to realize what he was doing.

He was crying. Reban, her father, was crying.

Her heart twisted inside her chest. She'd always wondered about the strange relationship between Reban and Octavius. There definitely had been some aspects of mutual respect, but for a time she'd wondered if Octavius had only helped Reban in parliament because of her. Now she knew that he'd done it for both of them. Maybe he wouldn't have approved of Reban's relationship with his niece, Dalia. But now she could see exactly what Octavius's sacrifice had done to Reban.

Lincoln's arm stayed around her, giving her the warmth and comfort that she needed. Leaning on someone helped more than she'd ever really imagined.

Slowly, people started to appear from the buildings around them. Faces were unsure and worried, constantly looking over their shoulders to ensure that the raptors were indeed not inside the camp. Storm heard a few yelps from those who were obviously walking past the body of the slain raptor. Hopefully most people would never see a raptor up this close again.

Something sparked in her brain.

Just then, Leif and Jesa appeared at her back. "I'm so sorry," said Leif quickly. She could see the sincerity in his pale-blue eyes.

Storm pressed her lips together and gave a stiff nod. "Can…can you find Lorcan? Ask him to look at the raptor? Maybe he can work out why the virus had such a different effect. Why it made them stronger, faster, more intelligent."

Leif squeezed his eyes closed for a second. Almost as if he still couldn't accept that it had been their actions of planting the virus which had resulted in this.

He leaned against Jesa and she, in turn, put her head on his shoulder. She looked tired. Weary. "Do you think they'll come back?" Jesa asked in a quiet voice.

Lincoln cleared his throat. Storm winced as she looked at the blood spotting through his bandages. He was clearly in pain, but he hadn't complained. She felt him take a deep breath. "Who knows? Thanks to Octavius, we can use the electricity on the outer wall whenever they come near. The idea clearly works. Will they remember it? They might. They seem to have some kind of intellect. But, more importantly, will they remember us – that we're here? Because that's the thing we should fear most. If they remember that we are here, they could literally set up a nest outside, and just wait for us to leave the camp. We can't stay in here for ever."

"Who can't?" said Leif quickly. "We have everything we need in here. There are still dried food supplies that came from Earthasia. We have fresh water. We have electricity and power. We could stay behind the camp walls quite happily." He frowned. "And if we did need to go out for something, we could use a transporter."

As soon as he said the words, the scene outside must have come into his mind. Jesa gave a sigh and said the words out loud. "After seeing that transporter outside like a crumpled can, I'm not sure I'd feel safe inside one any more. First the triceratops, then the raptors. Imagine what a T-rex or a titanosaurus could do? The transporter could be completely flattened by one step."

Leif gave a shudder. "Okay, we'll go and speak to Lorcan. He can examine the body of the raptor, just like he did the quetzalcoatlus."

"Thank you," said Storm. She stared back up at the lookout post.

Reban had lifted his head and was looking out over the scene outside. He signalled to a few of the labourers beneath him. "We'll wait a bit longer, then a few of us need to go beyond the fence." It wasn't a request. It was an order. Then he turned. "Storm, what do you want to do?"

The words jolted her and brought back a completely unexpected thought. Tears started to fall down Storm's cheeks. Stormchaser. Octavius had been the only person to use her full name. And now it was likely that no one would again.

It was crazy. She didn't know why that mattered so much now. But it did. It just did.

A sob bubbled its way up to the surface as Lincoln's arm tightened around her waist. It was like he knew. He knew when she needed someone to take her weight. To let her lean.

His mother and sister appeared in a flurry, running towards them.

"Lincoln! What happened? Oh my, your arm. Did you get hurt? Storm, are you okay? Let me look at you."

She felt frantic hands pat her down, looking for any injury where of course there was none. None that could be seen at least.

Storm tried to make sense of her thoughts. She could see the stress on the faces of both Lincoln's mother and sister, and he was holding his other arm awkwardly. She took a deep breath. "Come on, Lincoln. Let's get you to the medico care centre. Someone needs to take a look at that arm for you."

Lincoln gave a tight-lipped nod. "Okay, then. Let's go."

Storm looked up once more at Reban. Pain was etched across his face. It made her stomach twist in horrible ways.

But the thing that worried her most was the trace of underlying anger she could spot beneath the surface.

Things were going to get even uglier than they were now.

PART EIGHT

THE FAREWELL

THIRTY-ONE

LINCOLN

He winced with every stitch that the assistant put in his arm a few hours later. It was unlikely he'd be able to use his arm properly for the next few weeks. And that bothered him. On a continent like Piloria, that could be dangerous.

The atmosphere in camp was weird. In some ways it was subdued, all voices quiet or whispered. There was the backdrop of the constant electric hum. No one had decided to turn the electricity off yet. People were still wary that the raptors might come back – particularly under cover of darkness.

Storm stayed by Lincoln's side the whole time he was in the care centre. It was busy here. A number of people had been injured. His mother fussed around and ended up assisting with a few others. Storm was particularly quiet. She seemed numb, and he couldn't blame her. She'd just watched her great-uncle die at the claws of the raptors.

No words he could say would help, and he was fully aware of that.

They all knew the only reason they were still here was because of Octavius's actions.

So, he didn't try to fill the silence between them. Instead he just slipped his hand into hers and intertwined their fingers, giving them a gentle squeeze.

By the time the shout came from outside, Lincoln was so tired he was ready to fall asleep. The adrenaline from the day had finally left his system and taken every part of his energy with it.

Storm was resting her head on his shoulder and straightened up when the guy came running inside the care centre.

"Everyone, come now. You're needed. There's going to be a vote."

Storm screwed up her face. "A vote on what?"

Lincoln shook his head. "I have no idea. I guess we better go see." The painkillers were starting to kick in, his arm now held in a sling. He pushed himself up and walked outside with those who were able.

There were some lights in the camp but what was different this time was the use of torches. They flickered orange against the night sky and were placed strategically around the central point of the camp. It made the place look different. More ominous.

The pair walked to the centre of camp and found Reban standing on a makeshift stage. Lincoln had no idea where he'd been these past few hours. He knew that Reban had intended to retrieve Octavius's body – but he wasn't sure what else he'd been doing.

Leif, Jesa, her brother and mother were standing close to Reban. All of them had their chins tilted upwards. Whatever he was about to do, it was clear he had their full support.

Just about everyone who hadn't been seriously injured had amassed in the centre of the camp. Storm and Lincoln were amongst the last to get there. There were a few Stipulators off to the side – dressed in their black cloaks.

Reban waited a few moments, then started talking.

"It's time to make a choice," he began.

Lincoln felt his skin chill. The unsettling feeling in camp had been obvious for the last few weeks. There were those who wanted to embrace living on Piloria, and those who wanted to take it for themselves. One side had to win out eventually.

But part of him was apprehensive. Today had been terrifying. Reban had lost the man who would probably have been standing on his right-hand side – or indeed been addressing the crowd himself. But Octavius wasn't here. And the gap he'd left was enormous.

"Today, we lost a number of members of our camp. We also lost a friend of us all. Our Captain Regent. A man who guided our parliament for many years. Octavius Arange sacrificed himself for us. He sacrificed himself for us all." Reban stopped for a second then drew himself up and pointed over to a figure in the crowd. "Silas brought this on us.

His actions were deliberate. He must pay the price."

The crowd started to murmur. People's heads were turning as they shot worried looks at each other.

It seemed that Silas had regained his earlier confidence. His trademark sneer appeared on his face. He strutted up next to Reban on the stage and looked him up and down. "Pay what price? This planet is ours. After today, it is clear we have to find ways to kill the dinosaurs – kill all the dinosaurs. We can take them out one by one until this whole continent is ours." He held out his arms. "We can conquer this place." A few people nodded their heads in agreement.

"I can't listen to this. I can't. I'm going to do something about this." Before he could do anything to stop her, Storm pushed her way through the crowd and stepped up beside Reban. She didn't waste any time. She walked straight up to Silas, her voice loud and clear. "The only decisions you make are bad ones. *You* decided on the viruses. *You* convinced the parliament. Look what you've created – raptors that are stronger, faster and more intelligent than before."

"They're just beasts." Silas waved his hand dismissively.

"Beasts that tracked you for days. Followed your scent across a continent. Beasts that could run faster than you thought possible. Could jump further than anyone expected. Beasts who seemed to be able to communicate with each other and plan an attack. Yes, Silas, they're beasts. But they're your beasts – your creation. And you led them to us." She poked a finger in Silas's chest. "The only reason we're all still alive is because Octavius connected the power supply.

If he hadn't" – her voice wobbled a little and she held out her hand – "every single person here today would probably have been killed by the raptors."

Lincoln watched as the people around him visibly shuddered. Storm's clear voice was captivating.

"This is ridiculous," mocked Silas. "It's time to make plans. We have to make more viruses. We have to find a way to conquer the dinosaurs." He was so dismissive. It was almost like he thought the people here weren't worthy of his time, or of any kind of explanation.

Reban strode across the platform and grabbed Silas by one shoulder. "You're a fool, Silas. You've always been a self-centred fool. And I for one have had enough of you." Reban thudded one foot on the platform as he turned back to the people. "This isn't Earthasia. This is Piloria. And in Piloria there is a whole new set of rules. The first one is this" – he pointed to the people in the crowd – "you get to decide what happens next. We can't continue like this. We have to find a way to survive in this world. It's time to put this to a vote."

"A vote?" Silas's voice dripped with disbelief. "A vote is for parliament."

Reban smiled. It was like Silas had just played into his hands. "This is your parliament now. Four hundred of your peers. Does that sound familiar, Silas?"

Silas moved closer. "You? You and your offspring aren't even entitled to a vote. You were banished here for your crimes. You aren't good citizens. You shouldn't even have a right to speak. There's no vote here."

It was the way he said it – in his usual dismissive manner – that made people straighten a little in the crowd. Storm could sense it, the change in atmosphere. Reban had just called this a parliament of peers – and Silas had immediately made the people feel unworthy. It wasn't his wisest move, but he was too arrogant to see it.

Storm decided to act on the momentum, and took up her father's appeal. "We can't keep living like this. I won't live in a camp where the number-one priority is to destroy the living creatures in this land. Yes, some are dangerous. Yes, some are deadly." She pointed to the wall. "But we've already found a way to keep the dangerous ones out, and ourselves safe. We can learn how to live here. We can learn how to make a life for ourselves. If you don't understand that – or you don't want that – then please know that I won't be by your side. We haven't come here to rule this land. We've come here to try to live side by side." She put her hand on her heart. "I believe" – she glanced at Reban, then out at Lincoln – "*we* believe, that we can find a way to do that. So let's do it together."

A smile flickered across Reban's face. Lincoln recognized it as one he frequently saw on his mother's face – one of pride.

But Silas wasn't to be outdone. He stepped forward, his dark cloak billowing in the wind behind him. He must have found a way to retrieve it after the raptor attack. But his cloak wasn't what it used to be. Parts were tattered and torn. It didn't have the same prominence here. It didn't have the same wonder. Now, he just looked like some kid playing dress-up.

"This is ridiculous. I'm your Chief Stipulator. You all know that I'm in charge here – particularly now our Captain Regent is gone." He didn't even bother to sound upset about that. "Don't listen to a word they say. They're fools – already cast out from our way of life – a pair of vagabonds. They were lucky that we ever let them in here in the first place, and we could easily just throw them back out – back out there, to survive in amongst the dinosaurs. After all, that's what they want, isn't it?"

There was laughter in his tone. Along with a whole host of underlying threats, he was mocking them.

"You weren't so brave when you were running for the gate, Silas." Lincoln's voice cut through the dark. This man had annoyed him enough. "You looked terrified. And you were saved. Because, let's face it, you couldn't save yourself. You weren't smart enough to realize that you'd led the raptors straight to us. You're still living on Earthasia, Silas. You have no place here. What use are you to us? What skills can you offer? None that I see or recognize. Octavius had a low opinion of you. He said you needed other men around you to make yourself seem bigger."

Lincoln had stepped forward, and now he was standing right in front of Silas. He turned back to face the crowd.

"Well, here we are, your peers. And it's for us to decide the way forward. We won't be told by you, Silas. We'll choose, for ourselves." He started walking in front of the platform, making eye contact with every man, woman and child he could see, nodding at them in the flickering lights. "For the first time, we'll decide our own way of life. Do we try to kill the dinosaurs, or learn to live with them? Every person will have a vote."

Lincoln nodded to a man by the side of the platform. A man he recognized from the parliament building. "Let's make a count of every man, woman and child in the camp."

There were murmurs, people breaking off into groups and talking amongst themselves. One of the former Stipulators, who'd managed to dispense with his cloak, shouted people over. "Everyone, we have a register of names. Come forward and we'll mark you off. Quickly."

Silas folded his arms and started muttering. People began forming a queue.

Storm jumped down from the platform beside Lincoln. "Impressive." She smiled. "I almost think you want to stay."

"You don't get rid of me that easily," he replied promptly.

Although she had a smile pasted across her face, he could see the tension in her eyes. "What do you think will happen?" she whispered.

He shook his head. "I know how I'll vote." He reached down and squeezed her hand. "People have started to see themselves really living here. The days you've shown them around have helped. They've started to understand that not all dinosaurs are deadly. And some of them are just as curious as we are." He nodded to the wall. "Yes, we have a first line of defence, and it needs to be our priority. But there's so much more we can do here. There's so much more for us all to learn. This could be the start of something wonderful – if we'll just let it be."

As he said the words, he finally understood how much he wanted to be here. How much his whole outlook on life had changed since he'd got here. Yes, he understood the dangers. Yes, he would always worry. But the worries on Piloria were different from the worries on Earthasia. He wasn't worried about starving to death. He wasn't worried about Arta dying from the effects of the blistering plague – her skin had never looked better. He wasn't worried about living in a damp, dark cave that he had to share with another family.

As the sense of awareness spread through him, Lincoln looked out over all the faces. They were watching, waiting to see what came next. Silas opened his mouth to speak again, but Lincoln got in there first.

Reban had already spoken. Storm had just worn her heart on her sleeve. It was time for him to stand and be counted with his friends.

He looked over to where the former Stipulator had been gathering names. "How many do we have in our camp?"

The man looked up and gave a serious nod. "Three hundred and eighty-six."

"Then we have three hundred and eighty-six votes to decide how we want to live our lives."

Some people still looked a bit confused by it all. No one had ever had a vote before, back on Earthasia. The Stipulators and government in turn had made every single decision about what happened in the zones. No other person was ever consulted or asked to vote for what they wanted. This was all new, with no real time for people to process it.

Lincoln put his hand up to his heart. "Listen, we have to decide now. It's our job to decide what happens next. You can vote for Silas's way of life, or for Reban's. Do you want to conquer the dinosaurs, or live alongside them? Think about it, and decide now. We can't have a divided camp. However the vote goes, we all have to live that way or leave."

Silence fell over the crowd. The only noise was the wind rustling through the bushes and trees around them.

Storm spoke next. "Let's do this the easiest way possible." She gestured to Reban. "You go to one side of the platform" – she glanced at Silas – "and you go to the other." She turned back to the people. "Make your decision. If you agree with Silas, move to the right. If you agree with Reban, move to the left."

Lincoln could tell she was nervous. Her hands were clutched into fists at her sides. For the first few seconds no one moved.

Then his mother walked over and stood in front of the platform, directly beneath Reban. She gave him the slightest nod of her head. Arta followed quickly, as did Leif, Jesa, Kayna and Caleb.

Leif, the person who had more reason than most to want to kill the dinosaurs. The person who'd just made his choice to try to live in harmony with the creatures he'd originally despised.

Lincoln felt his heart swell in his chest. He was proud of his family and friends. Proud that they were willing to make a choice and take a stand.

People started to move. Slowly, but surely, in the flickering lights, the crowd started to divide.

Several of the labourers collected in front of Silas. Who knew what promises he'd kept making them about Piloria? Some of the Stipulators still wearing their black cloaks moved in front of Silas too.

But the man who'd collected the names pushed himself up and walked across to Reban. He was the first former Stipulator to make that move.

A few moments later, another Stipulator removed his black cloak and let it fall at his feet. He walked over, folded his arms and stood in front of Reban with a half-smile on his face. "You and I need to talk," he murmured.

Gradually, everyone moved. One figure weaved his way through the crowd and stood in front of Storm. Dell. Lincoln could see all the emotions she was trying to button up on her face. Her eyes were windows to her soul. She wanted Dell to stay so badly it was a wonder she wasn't screaming it to the world. She wanted so much for him to stay and that made Lincoln's gut twist in a way he didn't like.

Dell and Storm locked eyes. Lincoln couldn't help but stare. After the longest time, Dell tore his eyes away from Storm and, with the slightest sigh, moved over in front of Silas.

There was a tiny guttural sound from Storm as she pressed

her lips together and stared straight ahead. She blinked. Her eyes were instantly glistening with unshed tears.

Lincoln held his breath. More and more people were moving. It was clear that a few were struggling with their decision, looking first one way, then another.

But within a matter of minutes, it was clear.

Silas started shouting, panic gripping him. "Think about this. These are beasts – ferocious animals. They'll kill us in our beds at night! We have to wipe them out. We have to take this place as our own." There were a few worried glances – a few who changed their mind at his words. But it wasn't enough. It was nowhere near enough to change the result.

Lincoln tried not to smile with relief. The crowd in front of Reban was much bigger than the crowd in front of Silas.

As the last person made their decision, Reban turned to the ex-Stipulator. "Why don't you take a count? Make this first voting process of the camp official?"

Everyone stayed silent as the man moved amongst the crowd, nodding his head as he counted. When he was finished he came back to the front. "For Reban, three hundred and forty-one. For Silas, forty-five."

Silas let out a cry of frustration, even though it had been clear which way the vote had fallen. It was as if the final numbers just tipped him over the edge. "You fools! You'll all be dead in a few months. Not one of you will survive here if you don't do something about these dinosaurs."

Reban kept his voice steady. "Pack up your things, Silas. This continent isn't big enough for the both of us." He turned to the forty-five standing in front of the stage. "You can make up your own minds. You can either return to Earthasia or agree to try to live in harmony with the creatures of Piloria. The choice is yours."

Lincoln held his breath, waiting to see what they would do. Only two people moved over to the other side. The rest remained near Silas.

Reban gave a nod. "Forty-three people is a big enough crew to man a ship. Take the *Invincible*. She's yours. Go back to Earthasia. Find out what you left behind."

A few of the men who'd chosen Silas's side glanced at each other. They seemed surprised. It was like they hadn't expected it. Did they expect Reban to throw them out into the forest and the path of the raptors? Maybe that's what they would have done to the others if they had won the vote.

One man stomped off angrily to his home. Another muttered under his breath, eyeing Reban as if he wanted to start a fight. Lincoln moved quickly, pulling the man's gun from his grasp.

"Be ready to leave in an hour," shouted Reban. "You'll be escorted to the ship then."

Arta ran over and flung her hands around Lincoln's neck. "It's over," she said breathlessly. "We can finally be at peace here" – she gave him a quick glance – "as long as we can keep away from the raptors."

Someone cleared their throat near him. Lorcan. Like most of the people today, he looked exhausted. "I might have an idea about that," he said.

"What do you mean?" asked Reban.

Lorcan ran his fingers through his shock of white hair. "You know we managed to find a way to put a tracking device on the transporters?"

Reban nodded.

"Well, I think we might be able to adapt that to something smaller – something we could fit on a raptor, so that we always know where they are. Know if it's safe for us to be outside the gates."

Reban stepped closer. "You think we can track a living creature?"

Lorcan nodded. "I think it's a possibility."

"But how will we fit a tracker to a raptor?"

"I was hoping you might help me with that. We'll need to design something."

Reban flung his arm around Lorcan's shoulders. "Let's talk."

Lincoln was still watching Storm. She had wrapped her arms around herself and was rubbing them up and down. In the midst of a crowd of people, she'd never looked so alone.

He pulled back from Arta. "We have an hour left. There's something else we need to do before the rest leave." She frowned and he added. "Before we can start anew, we need to finish some things with the respect they deserve."

CHAPTER THIRTY-TWO

STORMCHASER

She was sitting in the dark in her home. The space was echoing around her, half reminding her that she was lucky to have so much space, and half mocking her because she was all alone. Octavius's heavy book was in her hands, and she spent her time running her hands over the thick dark cover. This was likely the last thing he'd touched before he went outside.

Reban had insisted on supervising a few of the more angry people who were packing up to leave. She knew he was right. But being alone gave her time to think. And that was the one thing she didn't need right now.

The victory felt so hollow. More people lost today. The reality was that all of the people Storm was closest to had been at risk today. Whether it was Jesa and Leif in the lookout post, Lincoln and her father out in front of the camp, or Octavius.

A lump formed in her throat. Numbness was better.

Numbness meant you really didn't feel anything. It was a simpler place to be.

The knock at the door jolted her. Before she had a chance to stand up, Lincoln pushed it open. "Storm? Are you there?"

He'd changed. His dirty, bedraggled clothes from earlier were gone and he was wearing a fresh, dark tunic and a new sling for his arm. He had something else folded under his other arm.

She wiped at her face and stood up. "What are you doing? Is it time already?"

He shook his head. "Not yet. But we have something else to do. Something more important."

He led her outside to the back of the camp, far away from any of the houses or new buildings. "Where are we going?" she asked in confusion. "There isn't anything down here."

He nodded. "I know. But there will be."

They turned the corner and Storm stopped walking. There was a large pyre in front of her, topped with something wrapped tightly in white. Reban and the others were standing with their heads bowed. Her voice wobbled. "Wh-what are we doing?"

Lincoln turned to face her, blocking out the view behind. All she could see was his blond hair and green eyes. "We're going to say goodbye. It's the right thing to do."

Her body started shaking. "But, a fire…?"

He nodded. "We can't have graves. We did that last time and it attracted scavengers. The bodies were dug up. We don't want that. This is the best way."

She looked over Lincoln's shoulder. As they'd been talking, other members of the camp had appeared from the shadows. They'd obviously been told about this too. People had respected Octavius, admired him. It wasn't only her who wanted to say goodbye.

She didn't even want to think about what was inside that tightly wrapped bundle. She knew exactly what a raptor could do. She squeezed her eyes closed for a few seconds, then took a deep breath and opened them again.

Reban was standing with one of the flickering torches in his hand. He gave her a nod. "You should do this," he said. "You're Octavius's family."

Her legs were shaking as she stepped closer to the high pile of sticks. She reached out her hand to take the flaming torch from Reban. This was her job. Octavius was her family. But he was more than that.

She turned around to face the others. It didn't matter how strong she was trying to be. Storm couldn't stop the tears streaming down her face.

She tried to keep her voice steady as she spoke.

"When I first met Octavius, I was astounded," she said. "He was such a tiny man with such a booming voice." A few people in the crowd laughed. "It took Octavius some time before he let me know that we were family. His niece Dalia was my mother. But when I was with him, Octavius spent much of that time encouraging me to learn, encouraging me to ask questions."

She lifted one hand.

"He was mesmerized by this place. He wanted to learn more. Some of you will know that Octavius had a book. It is called *The Continent of Monsters*. He valued it, he had pride in it, but above anything he wanted it to be accurate. He wanted it updated. Since he reached Piloria, he updated nearly every page – and created a few more. But I think the time has come to rename that book. This isn't a continent of monsters, and it shouldn't be called that. It should be called *The Book of Dinosaurs*. And from now on that's what it will be called."

Storm held the heavy bound book up and turned it around so the others could see it.

"Octavius spent the last few months updating some of the information in this book. From now on, that will be my job. It's important we understand the dinosaurs as best we can." She hugged the book close to her chest for a moment then handed it over to Lincoln. Her hand shook as she held the flaming torch.

Reban stepped back to give her space. She stood next to the pyre.

"Farewell, Captain Regent Octavius Arange." She gave a weak smile to the crowd, but it was Lincoln who caught her eye. He gave her a nod. The smallest of movements to let her know that he supported her. She lifted her chin. "Lots of people knew Octavius. Some feared him. Most respected him. Octavius sacrificed himself in more ways than one. I didn't always understand him. But I understood that he always did what he thought was best for me – his family –

and for us all, his people. Octavius wasn't just my family – he was yours too. Today's actions weren't unexpected. They were" – she gave a sad smile – "very Octavius. They showed the kind of man that he was. And in his honour, I'll explore this new world and live the best life that I can. That's what we should all do."

There was a murmur of agreement in the crowd and she bent and dug the torch deep into the packed branches. It only took a few moments for the fire to take hold. The flames climbed rapidly through the puzzle of tangled twigs, with crackles and spits. The flare of heat was rapid and Storm stepped back as orange and yellow flames licked high into the sky, encompassing the body of Octavius swiftly.

The wind caught the flames and smoke quickly, thankfully taking it up and away from the eyes of the people around. Several people were still standing with their heads bowed in reverence to Octavius and his memory.

The emotions that Storm had been choking back bubbled to the surface and tears flooded down her cheeks again. Lincoln appeared at one side and slid his hand into hers. Reban appeared on the other side and did the same, and Tamb, Jesa, Leif, Kayna and Caleb joined hands until they were all in the circle with their heads bowed.

Reban looked out across the people still standing. "Octavius had one other wish. That we should find a new name for our camp. I think we should. This is a fresh start for us all."

People in the crowd started nodding in agreement.

He continued. "I have a suggestion. It's from an ancient language from Earthasia. Civitas. It means community. What do you think?"

The word echoed around, as people tried it. There were murmurs of agreement. "Civitas." The word became a chant around them.

"Civitas," said Reban softly.

"Civitas," repeated Jesa.

"Civitas," said Leif, his voice louder and more determined.

"Civitas," repeated Tamb and Kayna, glancing at each other and smiling.

Storm could feel the energy around her. The buzz.

The feeling of being part of something.

For the first time ever. Belonging.

THIRTY-THREE

STORMCHASER

Those leaving were packed up. Reban had arranged for two transporters and a number of guards to accompany the people to the *Invincible*.

Storm was standing on the sidelines watching as Dell and his father lugged their gear inside one of the transporters.

Her heart was twisting in her chest. She didn't know why she was surprised. Dell had never had any love for dinosaurs – he'd always hated them, and being injured by one hadn't helped.

But seeing him here had lifted her spirits. She'd wanted to show him the beauty of Piloria that she'd experienced, in the hope that he would learn to love it too. But it was never going to happen. He was too close-minded. He'd ended up here because he'd thought there was no hope on Earthasia. The first chance he got, of course he'd head back.

His father walked over and touched the side of her face.

"Be safe, Storm," he said, before turning and heading back into the first transporter.

Reban appeared in front of her, a gun slung across his body. "Want to come along?"

She bit her lip. Part of her did. But another part of her didn't want to see the people leave. It was like they were turning their back on the potential of Piloria.

Silas appeared, gripped on either side by a guard, still wearing his tattered black cloak. "Just you wait, Reban Don. I'll be back. I'll be back with an army to take you down. You and your silly little followers."

"Just pray you get across the ocean in one piece," said Reban smartly. He raised one eyebrow and smirked. "I've heard there are megalodons out there. Let's hope they're not hungry."

Silas continued to glower as he was thrown in the back of one of the transporters and the engine started up.

Reban looked up at the dark night sky. "Wouldn't normally travel at night, but we should be safer in the transporters, and with these guys, I think it's better to get this done."

Storm nodded. She knew he was right.

Lincoln walked up and joined her. "Need any help?"

Reban shook his head. "Everything's under control. It'll take us about five hours to get there, and another five to get back. I'll see you tomorrow."

He paused in front of Storm. She was confused, wondering what he was doing, but then he bent and dropped a kiss on the top of her head. "Keep my girl safe," he muttered to

Lincoln with a nod, before turning and heading back to the transporters.

Reban waved his hand in the air. "Right, folks. Let's move out. Let's get these people off Piloria."

Storm watched as the transporters moved through the gates and out of the compound. Lincoln slung his arm around her shoulder. "Come on, there's someplace else we need to be."

PART NINE

THE BEGINNING

THIRTY-FOUR

LINCOLN

He moved his arm from her shoulders and let his fingers intertwine with hers. It seemed completely natural. It felt right. She walked easily beside him, letting him lead her down to the beach. Their beach. Barney snuffled around their feet.

They sat on one of the ridges overlooking the sand, with the dark ocean outstretched in front of them. The sky was littered with stars and the moon was clear and high above them.

He waited until they'd been there for a while. He was exhausted and he knew she was too. She laid her head on his shoulder and closed her eyes.

"I'm so sorry about Octavius," he said hoarsely. "I know how much you loved him."

Her head came back up. "Did I? I never told him that. I never got a chance." He could hear the anger and frustration in her voice.

Lincoln knew Storm. He knew her better than most. She needed someone to lash out at. And he could take that.

Lincoln picked up some sand and let it run through his fingers. "You might not have told him – and he might not have told you – but it was clear to everyone who saw you both." He took a slow swallow, trying to remove the huge lump in his throat and lifted his gaze to meet hers. "Sometimes you don't need to say those words out loud."

Her mouth was open – as if she was about to say something but she stopped herself. She stared at him. He could almost see things flickering in her brain – starting to hear what he wasn't quite saying.

Lincoln took a deep breath and licked his lips. "Last time we were here… You know I had to go back, don't you?"

She gave a nod.

"But I hated it. I hated not knowing how you were. I hated not being able to see you. To talk to you."

It was the most honest he'd been with her. The relief that had swamped him when he'd finally set eyes on her again had been overwhelming. He'd always known that, but these last few months, things had changed again between them. He hated it when she was hurt. He hated that she'd been treated poorly in the past. He wasn't here to protect her, or to tell her what to do, but Lincoln's feelings towards Storm had definitely grown, like some kind of fireball streaking across the sky. She was watching him carefully. He could sense her trying to find the right words.

She gulped, her eyes getting a little wider in the dim light.

"You came out," she breathed. "Even though it wasn't safe, you came out the gates when we were being attacked by the raptors." Her words landed in the air like a question.

"Yes." He nodded. "I did."

Her voice trembled. "Why?"

There was no one else here. Only the two of them.

It was now or never. Time to speak the truth or forget about it for ever.

"I let you down once, Stormchaser" – he shook his head – "I won't do it again." He'd never meant anything more in his life.

She started. "Why did you call me that?"

He gave a little smile. "Because Octavius used to. And you acted like it annoyed you, but I think you secretly liked it. So I thought I might call you that too."

He pulled something out from his side. She seemed not to have noticed he was carrying it. "I thought you should have this."

She recognized it instantly and her hand flew to her mouth. "Oh my." She gathered up the thick, green-velvet cloak in her arms and hugged it to her chest. Some of the gold adornments caught the light and glinted in the dark. "Where did you find it?" Her voice was shaking now and a tear trickled down her cheek.

"Octavius must have dropped it just before he left. I think it got bundled up in all the confusion. I thought it only right that it went back to his only living relative."

He tugged it gently from her hands and shook it out.

It rippled in the breeze coming off the ocean, a remnant rich and lush from a land they'd left far behind. He let the wind fan it out as he swept it around and settled it on her shoulders, clicking the gold clasp at her neck.

"I thought it might need a few adjustments, but you know what?" He kneeled down in front of her. "It looks just perfect."

He reached up and brushed away the tear on her cheek the gentlest way that he could. His words were only a whisper.

"You don't have to do everything alone, Stormchaser. You don't have to think it's you against the world." His heart was beating so quickly now. It was time to put it out there. It was time to tell her how he really felt.

Her bottom lip was trembling.

Lincoln put his hand on his chest. "I came out to face the raptors because there was no way I was leaving you out there alone. I came out because I can't think about being here on Piloria without you being by my side. I came out because somewhere in this whole crappy mess, I've sort of fallen in love with you, Stormchaser Knux. And I think" – he raised his eyebrows – "you might have fallen in love with me too."

There was silence. He held his breath, waiting to see what would come next.

Storm stood up, shaking her head and putting her hands on her hips. Then she did something totally unexpected. She threw back her head and laughed. "You love me? Are you crazy? Do you know what that means? I play dinosaur bait for fun! I'm an explorer. And I've only just got started. I've got a whole dinosaur book to update and add new pages to.

Who knows how many volumes I'll end up with?" She threw out her hands. "And have you met my father?" There was a glimmer of a smile beneath all her words.

He stood up too, moving forward, sweeping his good arm behind her and pulling her close to him. Lincoln held her there, wondering if she would object.

But she didn't. Instead she wound her hands around his neck and pulled him down towards her, silencing anything else he might say with a kiss.

By the time they broke apart, they were both breathless. Storm had both hands on his shoulders. "Hey," he said. "I was going to do that."

When she looked up at him there was a twinkle in her eye. "Yeah, but you were too slow. You might not have noticed, but I don't like to hang around."

He laughed. "Really?"

"Nope." She laughed too as she shook her head. The sun was starting to rise in the sky behind them, sending streaks of lavender and purple across the dark ocean. A head flickered above the waves for a second, then disappeared again, a large body and long tail breaking the surface before it disappeared.

"Watch out," she said. "Milo's keeping an eye on you." Storm tilted her head up towards him. "How about we give him a replay?"

Lincoln leaned closer. "Well, if you insist."

And she did.

ACKNOWLEDGEMENTS

A book is a journey and I've been on this journey for quite a while now.

A few years ago I sent my first YA manuscript to an agent's office (which I like to think looks a bit like Hogwarts) and had the joy and pleasure of becoming Sarah Hornsley's first sale. She sent my book out with such enthusiasm that I didn't have a single doubt she would find it a fabulous home – and she did, with the wonderful team at Usborne.

That's when I was privileged enough to meet Sarah Stewart, who loved my characters – and my dinosaurs – just as much as I did. *The Extinction Trials* was finished, *Exile* was half-formed, and *Rebel* was not even a figment of my imagination. Thanks to these two ladies, *Rebel* was brainstormed into existence and the series became complete.

Working on these books has been such fun and the lonely life of a writer has been made so much more full by having my two wonderful Sarahs, who shout out about my books and tell the world how much they enjoy them. Thank you both for believing in *The Extinction Trials*.

There's always a team of people involved in books. A huge thanks to Will Steele for capturing the magic of *The Extinction Trials* in the three covers he created for the series. Every time I see them they send a little tingle down my spine. Also thanks to Stevie Hopwood and Jacob Dow for their great publicity plans and enthusiasm in getting my books into the hands of readers – the most important people!

A bow of thanks also goes to Matilda Johnson, copy editor extraordinaire, who I'm sure I made go and lie down in a darkened room. Thanks for all your hard work and patience. And to the rest of the Usborne team, Rebecca Hill, Stephanie King, Anne Finnis and Becky Walker, thank you so much for shouting out about my books.

Social media can be such a scary place but I've met so many lovely book bloggers and vloggers on Twitter and Youtube during the life of *The Extinction Trials*. Zoe at nosaferplace, Steph (now a fabulous teacher!) at alittlebutalot, Kelly at kellysrambles, Nicola at fantasticbookdragon, Rebecca Stobart, and Basically Britt. All your reviews are truly appreciated.

No writer is complete without a cheerleading squad and mine is a truly international gang: from the UK and Ireland, Fiona Harper, Heidi Rice, Daisy Cummins and Iona Garrett; from Australia, Rachael Blair and Janette Radevski; and from the US, Maisey Yates, Caitlin Crews, Nicole Helm and Rusty Keller are my squad. I like to surround myself with people who share in my inappropriate comments, sarcasm and random shenanigans. My workie, Kathleen Winter, is also in this squad. I won't forget you're holding out for the part of Lincoln's mother in the movie!

Thank you to all the people who've read and enjoyed *The Extinction Trials* series. The reviews, random comments on Twitter and Facebook, and emails always brighten up my day. It gives me so much joy that there is a group of readers out there who love the thought of a continent of dinosaurs and a continent of humans, and that it makes perfect sense. Love you all.

Finally, as always, I never, ever forget that for some children, young people and adults, reading can be their safe place.

HAVE YOU
EXPERIENCED
ALL OF

THE

EXTINCTION

TRIALS?

ONLY THE STRONGEST WILL BE CHOSEN
ONLY THE RECKLESS WILL SURVIVE

THE

"The Hunger Games meets Jurassic Park."
The Bookseller

EXTINCTION

TRIALS

S. M. WILSON

In Stormchaser and Lincoln's ruined world,
the only way to survive is to risk everything. To face
a contest more dangerous than anyone can imagine.
And they will do anything to win.

But in a land full of monsters – human and
reptilian – they can't afford to trust anyone.
Perhaps not even each other...

*"A fast-paced, high-stakes adventure
that I couldn't put down."*
Amy Alward, author of *The Potion Diaries*

A PARADISE FILLED WITH PREDATORS
A DESTINY LACED WITH DEATH

THE

"The
Hunger Games
meets
Jurassic Park."
The Bookseller on
The Extinction Trials

EXTINCTION

TRIALS

EXILE

S. M. WILSON

To ensure the survival of the human race,
three killer species must be destroyed. It's a deadly
mission – one that Storm and Lincoln are not
allowed to refuse.

But in the jaws of danger, would you obey orders
– or fight for the secret that might save
those you love?

*"This is sincerely the most jaw-dropping and
phenomenal sequel I've read in a long time...totally
beats* The Hunger Games *in my book."*
Never Judge a Book by its Cover

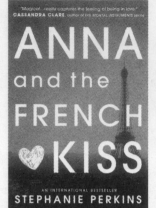

Love this book? Love Usborne YA

Follow us online and sign up to the Usborne YA
newsletter for the latest YA books,
news and competitions:

usborne.com/yanewsletter

 @UsborneYA